The UNSEEN

Written as Lee Driver

Chase Dagger Mysteries

The Good Die Twice

Full Moon-Bloody Moon

Short Stories

Sara Morningsky, *Mystery in Mind Anthology*

The Thirteenth Hole, *Mystery in Mind Anthology*

Written as S.D. Tooley

Sam Casey Mysteries

When the Dead Speak

Nothing Else Matters

Restless Spirit

The UNSEEN

LEE DRIVER

Full Moon Publishing LLC

Library of Congress Catalog Number: 2003115121

ISBN 0-9666021-7-X

Published March 2004

Printed in the United States of America
10 9 8 7 6 5 4 3 2 1

Full Moon Publishing
P.O. Box 408
Schererville, IN 46375

www.fullmoonpub.com

ACKNOWLEDGMENTS

A special thanks to:

Dr. D.P. Lyle, for his forensic expertise; **Pamela Jean Owens,** Ph.D., Professor of Native American Studies and Religion at the University of Nebraska at Omaha; **Patrick Redig,** DVM, Ph.D., Director of the Raptor Center at the University of Minnesota College of Veterinary Medicine; **Shirley Robinson** for her keen eye; my editor, **Chris Roerden; Garnett Watson,** Chief of Police/Gary, Indiana, for answering all my nuisance E-mails; and **Luci Zahray** (the "poison lady").

The UNSEEN

1

Wheels squeaked and whined, keeping slow tempo with Seymour's footsteps. The suitcase trailed behind him like an obedient puppy.

"You have what I want," the caller had said. At first Seymour thought it was a wrong number. What could he possibly have that anyone would want?

He looked up and squinted at the street sign. Half the letters were weathered and chipped making it difficult to tell if he had found the right street corner. The man had said to wait on the park bench at Kennedy Avenue under the bridge at midnight. There weren't any street lights under the bridge. How convenient.

"You have what I want." The words played in his head as he nudged his hat down lower and turned up the collar of his down-filled parka. He hated this coat. It was too bulky, especially when he tried getting behind the wheel of his car. But Ruth insisted he needed something warmer.

Grasping the handle tightly, Seymour continued along the sidewalk toward the bridge listening to the steady rhythm of the squeaking wheels. His breath billowed out in frosty puffs and he could feel his eyes tearing from the cold.

This was one of the oldest sections of town. Some buildings were boarded up with realtor signs pasted across the doors. Very few people walked the streets in the daylight. Tonight, Seymour's shadow was the only one cast on this desolate sidewalk. He located the park bench and sat down. His joints creaked and moaned from the effort, none too happy with the icy feel of the wooden slats.

"You have what I want."

"What do you mean?" Seymour had asked.

"In your lab."

Few people knew what was in his lab. "I don't know what you're talking about." He had stalled for time. Then the caller told him just enough detail to convince Seymour. Still, he denied any knowledge of a so-called project. The caller repeated his demand, this time with a little something added.

"You have what I want. And I have what you want."

Ruth had gone to her monthly bridge club meeting. She should have been home by ten o'clock. Seymour's catnap started sometime after the nine o'clock news, but something jarred him awake at eleven. Maybe it was the chill in the room. The roaring fire he had built earlier was reduced to cold embers. Or maybe it was the stillness, eerie and unsettling. Ruth usually chatted from the moment she walked in the door, darting from room to room, all full of the latest gossip from the bridge club members. But tonight there wasn't the excited rhythm of Ruth's voice.

"You have what I want. And I have what you want."

His cell phone rang. Seymour fumbled in his pocket, almost dropping the cold chunk of plastic.

"Yes."

"Cross the street to the other side of the bridge. There's a parked car with the trunk open. Set the suitcase in the trunk and return to your car."

"Not without knowing Ruth is okay."

"She's in your car now, waiting."

"How do I know she's…?"

"You'll just have to trust me, the way I have to trust you that what I want is in that suitcase."

So Seymour did as he was told, walked across the street and placed the suitcase in the trunk of a car whose license plate number he memorized. He expected to hear the sound of gunfire or see a partner of the caller waiting for him in the shadows. As he hurried back to his car, Seymour listened for the sound of quick footsteps or a weapon being engaged. The man had kept his word. Ruth was sitting on the passenger side of the car, eyes staring ahead, seat tilted back slightly. As he climbed into the front seat, he knew he should have paid more attention to the approaching footsteps, the rustling of fabric as someone hurried toward him. He should have slammed the door shut and locked the doors. But Seymour was too shocked at the realization that his wife wasn't alive.

One hundred miles up the shore on the Michigan side, a gray wolf charged through darkened forest preserves, leaping over fallen tree limbs and dodging fence posts. It broke through the underbrush and headed for the shoreline. The wolf paused on the shore and gazed at blinking lights across Lake Michigan. Beyond the smokestacks of the steel mills and glitter of the various casinos was home—Cedar Point, Indiana. The desire to get back was strong, but the fatigue was stronger.

A rustling in the underbrush prompted the wolf to jerk its head around. Unfamiliar territory was not a good place to rest. The wolf, gathering speed as it turned from the shore, bolted for the cover of the woods, then stopped abruptly to listen for human sounds. When certain there were no witnesses, the wolf picked up speed again, then leaped toward a sturdy tree limb twelve feet above the ground. In the dark, no one would see the change. It had been swift. One moment the wolf's paws had reached for the branch, the next moment they were the sturdy talons of a gray hawk. The hawk's vision would detect more in the dark than the wolf's. Pushing off the limb, the hawk's powerful wing beats propelled it higher. Wind currents caught its underwing coverts and the hawk gracefully glided in a circular motion as it searched for a place to spend the night.

A row of pricey homes dotted the shoreline ahead. From this altitude the hawk's visual acuity could enable it to count the legs on a spider. It detected blinking lights through the windows of the homes. It knew these homes had alarm systems. It didn't smell smoke from the chimneys or sense heat. The homes were closed up for the winter.

Several of the homes had boat houses. One boat house was larger than the rest. Through the windows the hawk could see living quarters, a fireplace with wood stacked next to it, and blankets folded and laying on a bed. The hawk circled slowly looking for an alarm system or any type of surveillance cameras. There weren't any. It swooped down and shifted swiftly back into the wolf who splashed into the icy waters and paddled to the boat house. The wolf dipped under the double doors, then leaped onto the concrete floor, shaking the chilly waters from its fur. Two jet skis were stored on a trailer to the left. A boat covered with a tarp was on a trailer to the right.

Paw prints dotted the walkway between the inlet and the dry-docked jet skies. The wolf halted again to shake the water from its fur. As the door to the living quarters drew closer, there was an abrupt change to the paw prints. They were unmistakably human.

2

Dagger set the newspaper on the table and hung up his leather coat. Heartburn was digging a small crater in his stomach, and he cursed himself for eating at a truck stop. After filling a cup with cold coffee from the coffee maker, he placed the cup in the microwave and pushed the reheat button. Outside the window the snow clung stubbornly to trees and bushes. It had been a brief dusting of snow last night that had quickly melted from the streets and side-walks.

He wrestled the tie from his ponytail, wincing at the hairs pulled from his scalp. He already regretted the job Simon had talked him into. A friend of a friend, Simon had said. A very rich friend of a friend who lived in Indianapolis, Indiana. For the past eight weeks Dagger had turned down every request, no matter how desperate it sounded, claiming he was too busy. He certainly didn't need the money. Truth was, Dagger hadn't felt like doing any-thing, choosing instead to wallow in guilt. It was his fault Sara had left.

With cup in hand, he moved through the house with the nagging sense that something had changed. After gulping down half of the stale brew, which only served to irritate the crater, he set the cup on his desk and checked on Einstein. The macaw was perched by the door inside the aviary, his eyes following Dagger's moves. Einstein shoved his beak between the grated bars and Dagger stroked the top of the bird's head.

"Hey, bud, what's wrong?"

Einstein blinked slowly and shuffled his claws on the perch. Dagger retrieved a Brazil nut from his desk drawer and held it up. Einstein looked away and buried his head under his wing.

Dagger sensed that change again, as though the very air in the house had shifted. And there was something else. The scent of sunflowers, subtle yet familiar. Einstein finally emerged from the safety of his wing and trained one yellow-ringed eye on a spot over Dagger's right shoulder. Even before Dagger turned, he had identified the change. He knew the scent. He felt her presence.

"I'm home, Dagger." Sara descended the stairs slowly, left hand gliding along the steel railing.

Dagger had thought about this moment for weeks, how he would react if Sara ever returned. Would she look the same? Could anyone change that much in two months? Sara's dark hair hung loose to her waist, the raven color streaked in a myriad of shades. The turquoise in her eyes had not dulled. She hadn't gained or lost weight, didn't look as if she had lost sleep. It may as well have been yesterday that she'd left, and all Dagger felt right now was hurt and anger.

"It's about time." He stalked to his desk and tossed the Brazil nut back in the drawer. "I was just about ready to hire your replacement. I am running a business here, you know."

Sara giggled. It was that shy, carefree giggle Dagger had grown to love. "You've always worked alone, Dagger. You'd never hire another assistant."

He sifted through mail, tossing junk advertising in the garbage, suddenly aware that most of the mail was two months old. Out of the corner of his eye he saw Sara approaching. She was rubbing her hand across red marks on her forearm.

"Einstein is a little upset with me."

"He bit you?"

"Just nipped. It didn't hurt. I promised him I'd never leave again."

Dagger glared at her and let the words spill out. "I guess that's something you'll have to prove to both of us." He returned to the stack of mail and continued dropping most of it into the garbage.

"You're angry."

She said it as though Dagger didn't have a right to be angry, which angered him even more. He pulled a briefcase from the top of the filing cabinet and slammed it on the desk. Papers scattered and drifted to the floor. Einstein remained silent, bobbing his head and cautiously eyeing Sara.

"I have to go out of town."

"Want my help?"

"I've done without it for two months." He shoved files into the briefcase, slammed it shut, and walked to his bedroom. Several minutes later he emerged carrying a gym bag. Dagger expected Sara to trail him to the back door, but she remained rooted by the aviary.

"Will you call?" Sara asked.

"Maybe I will, maybe I won't. What's a phone call between partners?" He shrugged into his leather trench coat, picked up his briefcase and gym bag, and rushed out of the house.

Sara turned to Einstein, her hand rubbing the marks on her arm. "I guess you could say he's still angry."

"AWWWKK." Einstein thrust his beak between the grating and emitted a hissing noise from deep in his throat.

"Oh don't you start. I'm not in the mood." She slid the aviary door open just wide enough to slip through, then closed it immediately. The macaw was quick and could easily fly out. Sara made a quick assessment of Einstein's home. The food in the food dishes looked fresh, as did the water in the water dishes. On the far side of the room, a fifteen-foot climbing tree, sprouting palm-like fronds, reached up to the vaulted ceiling. Splotches of excrement were visible on the leaves and branches. Under the tree, Sara noticed scraps of food littering the Astroturf as well as more excrement.

"What's been happening the past two months, Einstein?" The macaw padded across the perch and dipped his head. "What is this?" Sara made a sweeping motion toward the tree. Then she noticed the area under the perch by the window and the one by the shower. Picking her way around the blotches was like maneuvering a mine field.

"I don't believe this. So, you are no longer trained, is that it?" They had trained Einstein to use one alcove of the aviary as his bathroom. Now she wasn't sure if even the tree could be salvaged.

"That's it!" Her outburst startled the bird. He flew to the safety of the perch by the window. She stormed out of the room and rushed upstairs to change. Ten minutes later, dressed in cut-offs, a tee shirt permanently stained with paint, and a pair of summer flip flops, Sara retrieved a garden hose from the greenhouse next to the kitchen and cleaning supplies from the laundry room. After pulling back her hair in a long braid, she filled a sprayer with disinfectant cleaner and attached it to the hose nozzle. Einstein observed her from a safe distance as she removed all of the food, water dishes, and hanging toys. After sweeping up food scraps, Sara sprayed the cleaning solution onto the most heavily soiled areas.

"Hope you are watching, buster, because this is the last time I expect to see your room in this condition."

Einstein remained silent.

Sara turned off the hose and plodded through the puddles on the tiled floor to the Astroturf under the tree. She sprayed the cleaner full strength onto the heaviest of the stains. While she let the mixture sit for several minutes, she continued to hose down the tree, walls, and tiled floor under the shower area.

Turning toward the macaw, Sara rapped the hose nozzle against the perch in the alcove. "Einstein." She waited until the macaw turned his attention toward her. "This is your bathroom. If you go any place other than this area, I will turn the hose on you."

Einstein responded by letting loose with a stream of excrement.

Sara screamed, "NO," and turned the hose full force on him while repeating, "No, bad boy." A flash of scarlet red and royal blue charged toward the tree. Einstein took refuge on the top branch, spreading his wings and shaking the water from his feathers. Sara turned her back on him, a tactic used to make him understand he had done something wrong.

Once his most recent mess was cleaned up, Sara disconnected the hose, rolled it up, and removed the cleaning supplies, continuing to avoid eye contact with Einstein.

Slamming the aviary door shut, Sara chose not to fill Einstein's food dishes just yet. "Men," she mumbled. Thoughts of the condition of the aviary made her examine the living room more closely. Dagger had purchased a large flat screen television set which was framed inside the wall of bookshelves by Dagger's bedroom. The bookshelves looked new and expanded. The tiled floor on one half of the room was dusty but void of droppings. The area rug on the remaining half of the room was worn but not soiled. She was sure she didn't see any droppings upstairs by her bedroom or on the catwalk which dissected the living room. Thankfully, Einstein had destroyed only the bird room. She plopped down on the living room couch and dragged her feet onto the coffee table. This was not how she had anticipated her return.

The landscape beyond the wall of windows did little to improve her mood. Flowerbeds were dried stalks, some too weak to hold up their flower heads now lay flat. Trees, whose branches during the spring held bouquets in a variety of aromas, now were skeletal remains. The snow from last night had melted, exposing yellow and brown patches of grass that had once been lush green.

Gradually Sara became aware of her surroundings.

While she'd been silently surveying the view through the wall of windows, her fingers had played with tufts of white stuffing from a fresh rip in the arm of the couch. Moving her foot, she noticed gnaw marks on the coffee table. Her eyes immediately were drawn to the railing cordoning off Dagger's desk. More gnaw marks. Although Einstein had not soiled the living room, he had destroyed it in another fashion. Her house looked ravaged by a band of hatchet-wielding thieves. Anger soon gave way to disappointment. No wreath on the door nor luminaries lining the driveway nor even a tree. There were hundreds of evergreens on the property to choose from. That's all right, she thought. If no one else was in the holiday spirit, at least she would be. She ran upstairs to change again—this time into lumberjack clothes.

3

At ten o'clock the next morning Dagger found himself standing between two marble pillars on a mansion that could have been uprooted from Georgia. According to Simon, the Van Pelletiers raised horses, a few of which had won the Kentucky Derby and Preakness. But there weren't any horse barns Dagger could see.

The woman standing in the doorway had been tsk-tsk-ing for thirty seconds. "You don't look like a detective." She squinted behind her sequined glasses as she sized up Dagger. "Are you packing? All authentic detectives pack heat."

Dagger pulled open his coat to reveal the Kimber .45 attached to his belt holster on the right and a knife sheathed on the left. Unimpressed, one penciled eyebrow lifted slightly. Dagger pulled up his pants leg where a compact pistol that looked more like a toy gun nestled in an ankle holster.

"Hrmpph, you look more like a terrorist." She hugged what looked like the business end of a dust mop to her chest. Two beady eyes like black pearls stared intently from the dust mop. As if to punctuate its mistress' attitude, the dust mop squeaked out a yip. "Don't you ever shave?"

Dagger rubbed a hand across his chin. Truth was, he had shaved but his face had a permanent five o'clock shadow. "Mrs. Van Pelletier, I can certainly refer you to another detective if you don't feel comfortable. However, that is a decision you could have made before I drove all this way only to stand on your doorstep freezing my ass off for the past three minutes. Not to mention I spent the night in *Motel Hell* where the walls were so thin I could hear the couple next door..."

"Please, spare me the details. Come in." Mrs. Van Pelletier stepped aside. The fluffy mop let out another yip and kept its eyes on Dagger as he followed through the marbled foyer.

Dagger wondered exactly how far a size eleven shoe could kick a dog that size. He made a mental note to pummel Simon for talking him into this case.

"We'll have coffee, Tanita," Mrs. Van Pelletier instructed a young woman who was dressed more like a nurse than a maid. She pointed a well-manicured finger toward a loveseat. "Please have a seat, Mr. Dagger."

"Just call me Dagger." He scanned the artwork on the walls, then let his eyes roam over the Oriental pottery, gleaming wood tables, and thick Persian rugs. There were even gold monogrammed cocktail napkins sitting on the coffee table next to several bottles of pills and a glass of water.

"Mrs. Van Pelletier," he began.

"Josephine, please. I know my full name is a mouthful." There was a crinkling of crinoline as she took a seat on the couch across from him. The Queen of Hearts came to mind as Dagger glanced at the high collar on her dress, balloon sleeves, and scooped neck. A string of pearls was draped just low enough to entice the dust mop who had shifted its attention from Dagger. It licked and slobbered at the pearls.

"I'm curious why you didn't call the police." For some reason Simon had been unwilling to explain, or hadn't known, Mrs. Van Pelletier preferred to keep the disappearance of her husband from the police. His gaze dropped to the prescription bottles on the table.

Tanita returned with a tray and set it on the coffee table. The dust mop yipped again prompting a "Quiet, Cedar," from Josephine.

Cedar Dust Mop, Dagger thought with a chuckle. "Did your husband name the dog?"

Josephine's eyes brightened. "How did you know?"

"Lucky guess." He took a sip of coffee weak enough that he could see the bottom of the cup. Cedar went back to licking the pearls and Dagger settled into his seat. "When did you discover your husband missing?"

She looked toward the door to make sure Tanita had closed it. "Night before last," she replied. "He's always with me when I go to bed. But when I got up yesterday morning, he was gone. It was so disturbing I couldn't bring myself to tell the children. They would think I was hallucinating."

Dagger's attention drifted to the wealth oozing from the woman's pores. The dog's nails were painted the same color as Josephine's. The old woman's make-up had been applied with care and expertise. It made him think of another elderly woman, one who had cared little for her appearance, never made extravagant purchases, grew most of her own food, yet in his eyes her wealth was wisdom. Ada Kills Bull had turned her milky-filmed eyes to him and patted his hand with veined and shaky fingers. "You will take care of my granddaughter," her eyes had said, as though she had been waiting for him to come along so she could finally die. And then she did, leaving him with her black cord necklace, which held a sterling silver pendant in the shape of a wolf's head, and a granddaughter who had rarely left the confines of their property. Little had he known then how special her granddaughter was.

Josephine rattled the fine china cup on the saucer and eyed him suspiciously. "You aren't taking any notes."

Dagger tapped the side of his head. "It's all up here."

"Hrmpff. This is a serious matter, young man. I am completely traumatized by the whole ordeal." Cedar punctuated her concern with a couple of yips, then went back to licking the pearls.

"I take my work very seriously, Ma'am. I usually don't do missing persons but a friend said you were looking for someone who was quick and secretive."

"I'm sure the money wasn't a factor. Fifty thousand dollars plus expenses should buy me the best, especially when the detective promises results in twenty-four hours." She rubbed her gnarled fingers through the dog's fur.

"That's what I promised." He finished his coffee, which wasn't saying much. The demitasse cups in a Chinese restaurant hold more liquid. He nodded toward a photo framed in silver sitting at the end of the coffee table. "Is that your husband?"

"This was taken the year Chuck's Pride won the Derby," she said. She handed the picture to Dagger. "He was Charles' favorite horse."

Dagger studied the picture of what could have been a duke decked out in a crested blazer and ascot standing next to a horse the color of chestnut. Two younger versions of Charles, who Dagger guessed to be in their thirties, stood opposite to Charles. What they said was true, Dagger thought—owners and their pets start to look alike. Charles' hair was the same color, although his had threads of silver. The old man appeared in good shape, sleek and firm, with a long nose and flared nostrils. Dagger couldn't help noticing that Josephine and Cedar both had nests of salt-and-pepper curls and small, beady eyes peering from under a fluff of bangs.

"Did your husband have any enemies?" Dagger asked, placing the picture back on the coffee table.

"Everyone loved Charles. Very personable. We are a philanthropic family."

"Was he having money problems?"

"What?" Josephine found this amusing. She fanned one arm in a gesture that said *look around you.* "Does it look like I'm hurting for money?"

"What about blackmail or extortion?"

"Oh, no, nothing like that." She dismissed him with a wave of her hand.

Dagger's radar was sending off mixed signals. Josephine wasn't worried enough to call the police yet was suspicious or desperate enough to call in a P.I. He thought that with all of her money and influence, she would have little problem getting the police department to put all other cases on hold to find her husband. And she hadn't called her sons. That was puzzling. His gaze returned to the bottles of pills. Was she getting senile and imagining things and didn't want her sons to worry? Is that why she was on medication? Maybe he was asking the wrong questions.

"Josephine, you said you discovered your husband missing night before last."

"Correct."

"So that is the last time you actually saw him."

Her penciled brows scrunched in thought. "Well, no. The last time I saw him was three years ago, when he died."

Huh?

4

The Gingerbread House was located in a strip mall near the Cedar Creek Shopping Center. What should have been a ten-minute drive stretched to thirty because of all the traffic. Sara had to drive past several stores before she found a parking place.

Miniature lights outlined the doors and windows of the two-story shop. The Gingerbread House stocked the latest in home décor, wall hangings, yard ornaments, and unique floral arrangements. It was especially known to have the most elaborate Christmas decorations and drew many out-of-town shoppers to Cedar Point, Indiana.

Sara paused in front of a display window of decorated trees. Glittery pine cones, bird nests, berries, and a garland of raffia decorated one while an adjacent tree was trimmed in traditional globe ornaments of mauve, pink, and cream color.

Sara pushed through the door and made her way quickly through the aisles. Garland and lights decorated every square inch of the ceiling. Sara was so enamored with the displays that she failed to notice the mass of shoppers until it was too late. Panic—a reaction she hadn't felt in two

months. Those months had been like a sabbatical with
rarely another human being in sight.

Taking slow, deep breaths, she tried to block out all the
chatter, but the urge to flee became compelling. Her fingers
grappled for a table edge as she slowly made her way back
to the entrance, pushing her way between shoppers and gaping kids. Once back at the entrance, she grabbed the door as
it was being opened and fought her way into the fresh air.

She huddled in front of the window and pulled the collar of her jacket up around her neck. Anxiety was quickly
replaced by anger and disappointment. How silly to think
she could shop during the busiest time of the year. How
ignorant to think a store in a strip mall would have fewer
holiday shoppers. Her fingers clenched as she stared
through the display window at the shoppers who strolled the
aisles, oblivious to the swarms, accepting crowds as a part
of the shopping season. She was near tears as she wondered
if the store had a catalog or took orders over the phone.

"Sara, child, is that you?"

Sara turned to see a dark-skinned woman, eyes wide in
surprise. Ringlets of salt-and-pepper hair snaked out from
under a fur-brimmed cap.

"Eunie?" Sara let the woman gather her in a bear hug.

Eunie's wool coat splayed open, revealing a chest so
massive that even the buttons resisted any attempt at being
fastened. "When did you get back, child? Simon didn't
mention anything."

"Yesterday. Simon doesn't know yet."

"My lordy. You mean I know something before Simon
does?" Her eyes twinkled and she let out a boisterous laugh.
She cast a glance at the display window. "Something catch

your eye?"

"Everything," Sara said with a sigh.

"Then let's go in." Eunie tugged at Sara's sleeve.

Sara pulled back. "That's okay. I've already been in." She looked away quickly and fought back tears. "Everything's beautiful," she stammered.

Eunie's fingers swept Sara's hair back from her face. Then she placed a beefy arm across Sara's shoulders. "I see," she whispered. "Tell you what. You tell Eunie what you need, and I'll go in there and get it for you."

Tears hovered on her bottom lids and her lips quivered. "I tried," Sara whispered back.

"I know you did, child. It's okay. You just need to get your sea legs back. Got yourself a tree?"

Sara nodded.

"So you probably need a tree stand, skirt, lights, and ornaments."

Sara nodded again and pulled a wallet from her pocket. She had brought several hundred dollars with her and shoved the wallet into Eunie's hands.

"I like both." Sara pointed at the two display trees.

"Ahhh, yes. Those are beautiful. I think we can find a way to combine traditional with nature." She gave Sara's shoulder a final squeeze. "How about you stay right here and, if I see something else you might like, I'll hold it up in front of the window."

Eunie spent twenty minutes in the store, returning like a woman on a mission, weighed down with several shopping bags.

"Thank you so much. I'm sorry if I cut into your shopping," Sara said as she helped carry packages to the truck.

"I've got all afternoon. I'm going to go back in and do some of my own shopping now, unless you'd like to go for lunch."

Sara thought of how crowded the restaurants would be at this time and thought better of it. "That's okay. I want to get started on the tree."

"I understand." Eunie leaned in close. "Don't pay it no mind, child. As my mama used to say, 'Everybody's got a cross to bear.'"

Sara watched Eunie hurry back to the store and wondered how Simon's wife would react if she knew exactly how many crosses Sara had to bear.

Dagger set his gym bag and briefcase on a kitchen chair and shrugged out of his coat. The odors running through the house were a mixture of spice, probably chili, a hint of baked goodies, and an underlying scent of cleaning solutions. He inhaled long and deep. They were odors sorely missed for two months.

During the drive home from Indianapolis, he debated what he would say to Sara. He dreaded a face-to-face encounter. It would only end up in arguing and tears. Right now he was just too damn tired to talk.

He picked up his bag and briefcase and walked into the darkened living room. Both the grated and Plexi-glas doors to the aviary were slid shut, lights off. Macaws were light sleepers so it wouldn't take much to jar Einstein awake.

Dagger turned and set his briefcase down next to the filing cabinet—except there wasn't a filing cabinet. Nor was there a desk. He did a slow survey of the room. Light filtered in through the wooden slats in the pass-through by the bar, revealing a room stripped bare of all furniture except for the bar and barstools. A sinking feeling settled in his stomach. Sara must have packed up everything while he was gone and moved. But the furniture was his, not hers. The sinking feeling intensified. She had packed him up to move out. It was a wonder she didn't have Einstein in a cage sitting by the door.

Multi-colored lights and a rustling of paper drew his attention to the Florida room. There wasn't a Christmas tree in the house yesterday. Shapely legs were folded under a torso clad in gym shorts and a sweatshirt. Sara was sitting on the floor wrapping a present, fingers folding corners and applying tape. Three presents nestled under the tree.

"I could swear when I left yesterday there was furniture in the living room."

"There was."

Dagger inhaled the odor of fresh evergreen and studied the various ornaments, garland, and tree skirt, all just a few shades of pink and mauve too much for him. "You went shopping?" He knew shopping malls were crowded this time of year and Sara had panic attacks around crowds.

"Eunie went shopping for me."

He cocked his head toward the living room. "And you, what? Burned the furniture?"

"Einstein chewed up just about every piece of furniture, including your desk. I called a removal service and they carted everything away."

"I liked my old desk."

"Too bad." Sara tucked the wrapped package under the tree, grabbed her cup of tea, and scooted onto the couch. "And you can clean the aviary the next three times by yourself. The condition of Einstein's room was appalling."

That accounted for the strong cleaning odors. "Do I get to pick out my own desk?"

"No." Sara nursed her tea, avoiding Dagger's eyes. "Everything that was in your desk and filing cabinet are in boxes in your room."

Cocking his head, he studied the name tags on the presents. They were all for Einstein. He circled the tree slowly, examining the unusual vine that snaked through the branches and the lights the size of larvae tucked in close to the trunk. He glanced down at the tree stand. "You do know you have to make sure there's always water in the stand."

She flashed a look that said, *I'm not stupid.*

Dagger winced inwardly. This was not going well. He was still on unfamiliar ground when it came to knowing exactly how much of the outside world Sara understood. Friction settled in the air in as little time as it took for her to ball her hands into fists. Dagger took this as his cue. He picked up the gym bag, walked to his bedroom, and shut the door.

6

The next morning Sara sent Dagger to Wickes furniture store with a sale flyer in hand. She had circled what she wanted in the way of an area rug, furniture, and accents, but had conceded and let him pick out his own desk, filing cabinet, and chair.

She was just putting away the mop and bucket when the alarm from the front gate sounded. The monitor in the living room showed Simon's cherub face grinning back at her. She pressed the button to open the gate for their mailman, then waited by the kitchen door. He was soon stomping his shoes on the porch.

"Lordy, lordy." Simon's face lit up at the sight of her. He placed a large box on the kitchen table. "You are a sight for sore eyes." Simon wrapped her in a bear hug identical to the one Eunie had given her yesterday. He nudged the box on the table with one finger. "Eunie says you are to open this right away."

The name of The Gingerbread House was stamped across the top of the box. Sara lifted the lid and gasped. "They are beautiful." Eunie had purchased two wreaths for the doors in the same color scheme as the tree. "I'll call later

26

and thank her."

Simon eased his body onto a chair, his barrel chest overhanging in much the same way as Eunie's.

"Coffee, Simon?"

"Sure. Dagger knows you're home, I take it?"

Sara frowned as she measured coffee into the filter. "He had a case to work so he packed up and left within minutes after I arrived. He returned last night."

Simon rubbed a beefy hand across his face and shoved his chair back a few inches. The first thing Sara noticed was that Simon wasn't surprised to learn of Dagger's reaction.

"He seemed angry that I came back."

Simon clasped his hands on his stomach and stared out of the kitchen window at the dried wildflowers and leafless trees. "We all were pretty worried when you left, but Dagger especially. You never called, never wrote. He had no idea if you were even alive."

But Sara had communicated with Dagger in her own way. She had told him she needed time. The coffee machine started dripping.

"You know," Simon said, "there was even a report on the news about a body found in a ditch in Wisconsin. Dagger was..." Simon paused and let out a deep breath. "Well, it tore him up. He was ready to drive up there to identify the body when Padre found out the victim was believed to be around forty-five years old."

Sara sank onto a chair across from Simon. It hadn't crossed her mind that something like that could happen.

"We were all worried, Sara. Even Einstein." When he mentioned Einstein, Simon smiled.

Sara showed him the bruises on her arm. "Einstein has

a strange way of showing it. He's angry with me, too. Whenever Dagger is gone, Einstein won't eat for me."

"They both need time. I'll see if I can coax Einstein to eat if you want."

The coffee maker hissed and dripped and spouted steam from the filter cup. There was so much Sara couldn't explain to Simon and so much she couldn't undo. If only she could have predicted Dagger's reaction. She stared across the table at his cherub face and smiling eyes. He and Dagger made strange friends.

"What was he like, Simon, when you first met him?"

Simon hobbled over to the coffee maker on spindly legs that appeared too thin to hold up his large frame. He took his time pulling out cups and saucers from the cabinet and setting cream and sugar on the table. After doctoring his coffee and fixing a cup for Sara, he set the cup in front of her and settled back into the chair.

"Quiet, secretive, only went out at night. It was like he was hiding from something or someone or just waiting for his hair to grow." The memories brought a smile to his face. It was five years ago that their paths had crossed. "I knew someone was renting out the apartment above the bar, but Casey, the bar owner, didn't know much about him other than he was willing to pay him six months rent in advance and said his name was *Occupant*. Casey didn't have no formal lease so there weren't no papers to fill out. And getting six months' rent in advance was good enough for him." Simon took a sip of coffee and shook his head. "He was a character. I'd go up there and knock on the door. Wouldn't answer, but I knew full well he was in there. I'd ask him if he had any mail, that I'd take it to the post office for him.

He'd tell me 'no' and say he won't ever have any. He was rude, angry. Most days he wouldn't even talk. But one day I took a bunch of mail up there. It was all addressed to *Occupant*. He didn't even crack a smile. And me," Simon chuckled, "I just walked on in and asked if he had any coffee. 'Nope,' he said and out I went. But the next day I showed up with more mail for *Occupant* and two cups of coffee. I just made myself at home."

"What did he do?"

"Didn't kick me out, for one thing. I started making it a daily thing, bringing coffee, mail, and, every now and then, a newspaper. Finally got around to asking him his name. That was when he told me it was Chase Dagger."

Sara's eyebrows lifted, as if to ask, *so?*

"Thing is," Simon continued, "I had just handed him a *Reader's Digest* that the previous renter had subscribed to. One story advertised on the cover was titled, *Chasing the Elusive Dagger.* It was a story about an ancient dagger believed used by Henry the Eighth."

The words swirled in Sara's head and she remembered Dagger had once told her there were things about his past she didn't know.

"You mean that isn't his real name?"

Simon shrugged. "I've learned several lessons in life. One is to know when not to ask questions. But Dagger seemed safe enough. I didn't get the feeling he was some escapee from prison or had just murdered his family. I got pretty good instincts when it comes to that."

Sara tried to picture a clean-cut, short-haired Dagger hiding out in an apartment above a bar. Sullen, moody, angry. Exactly what she had witnessed when she came home.

"He never left the apartment except at night. Got curious enough to watch from my parked car, not that I was watching him all day long. Still had to work. But it was at night I would see him go to the store." Simon chuckled, his heavy chest moving like something was struggling to get out. "One night I'm sitting in my car across the street and I feel this piece of metal pressed to the back of my head. Then someone whispers, 'I've killed men for less than spying.'"

Sara's eyes widened at the word *killed* and she remembered the day she had witnessed Dagger kill a man. What she also remembered was the look of untamed pleasure in Dagger's eyes.

"Anyway," Simon continued, "I says, 'Hope you used something other than the end of a pipe.'" He chuckled again, his eyes twinkling. "Oh yeah, 'gotta get up early to fool me,' I told him. He obviously didn't have a car, so I told him 'Get in.' I says, 'You're obviously a man in need of a few things.' That's when I introduced him to Skizzy. Skizzy may seem a few dimes short of a roll but he knows the crooks from the good guys. He knows who to sell a gun to and who to kick from here to Detroit. Every single weapon Skizzy brought out from his secret stockpile, Dagger knew how to assemble and load. Skizzy knows a government guy from a merc."

"Merc?" Sara asked. She had sat silent, fascinated by the story.

Simon finished his coffee and pushed the cup aside. He leaned forward and whispered across the table, "Mercenary."

Sara had heard of mercenaries. They were guns for hire and most times didn't care if they killed the good guys or the bad, as long as the price was right. She remembered Joey Keller. Dagger had pressed a knee to the man's back, then placed his hands on Joey's head and twisted. She shuddered at the memory of the sound of a neck snapping. It had been clean, quick, and professional. Not that she blamed Dagger. It was a previous case they worked on several months ago when Joey was seconds away from raping Sara.

"Skizzy doesn't let anyone into his basement, let alone his back room. But after talking with Dagger for five minutes, he put the closed sign on the door and led Dagger down the steps. Within thirty minutes he had a set of identification and enough weapons and ammo to fill a large gym bag. Dagger obviously wasn't hurting for money but he couldn't hold out in his apartment forever. Not good."

"That's when he became a P.I.?"

Simon nodded. "One day I told him about a little girl who was kidnapped and her parents had an award of twenty-five thousand dollars. He looked smart enough to figure out the puzzle. All I did was leave the newspaper on the table, fill him in on a few details I picked up off the street, and within twenty-four hours Dagger had the little girl and the police had the man. Course he wanted no publicity, no picture in the paper. That was his agreement with the parents."

"So that was the start of Dagger Investigations."

"Yep. And the rest is history."

A loud SQUAWK erupted from the aviary.

"Maybe he'll eat now." Sara grabbed a bowl of fresh vegetables off the counter and carried it to the aviary. Einstein was sitting on one of the top branches of the tree. Sara held up a celery stick. "Look what I have, Einstein." The macaw slowly edged toward the trunk, then turned around and faced the wall like a kid in time out. "Don't be like that, Einstein."

"Here, let me try." Simon grabbed the bowl of vegetables and rattled it. "Feeding time, Einstein." The macaw didn't budge.

Sara retrieved one of the presents from under the tree and unwrapped it.

"Whatcha got there?" Simon asked. Einstein cocked his head toward the doorway. "It's like a huge wooden Rubik's Cube."

She set the toy on the floor of the aviary. "This should make him curious enough to leave his branch."

Simon did a quick survey of the aviary. "Dang, this place is sure sparkling clean."

"I couldn't believe Dagger let Einstein run wild." She motioned Simon toward the aviary's doorway, then closed the grated door. "I feel so guilty. I squirted Einstein full force with the hose. Now he's probably so traumatized he won't ever take a bath in his shower again."

"Hey, what happened to all the furniture?" Simon gaped at the empty living room.

"What Einstein didn't gnaw on he pulled the stuffing out of. I threw everything out and ordered new furniture. Dagger's picking it up now."

"Oh, no. All in Dagger's favorite colors—black and gray?"

"No. I picked out everything. Dagger went to the store to make sure they have what I want in stock. He gets to pick out his office furniture."

A loud clatter erupted from the aviary. They looked over to see Einstein tossing the wooden cube around.

A shrill chirp from the phone cut through the air. "Great, now what did I do with the phone?" She located it on the bar. "Hello?" She listened for several seconds but all she heard was a dial tone. "I wonder if that was Dagger."

Simon said, "He'll call back."

Thirty seconds later, the phone rang a second time. "Hello?" Again, all she heard was a dial tone. "What is going on?"

"Maybe Dagger's in a bad cell and he can't hear you."

Sara stepped closer to the window, made sure the antenna was up and then pushed the auto dial to call Dagger, but the phone started to ring again. "How can that be? I'm in the middle of dialing." She jerked her head toward the aviary. Einstein was on the floor with his back to her, facing a wall, his head slightly turned with one eye trained on her. He quickly turned away.

"Why, you little sneak."

Simon chuckled. "That was Einstein imitating the sound of a telephone? What a hoot."

"You are so smart." Sara retrieved a can of cheese curls from the kitchen and slid open the grated door. "Who taught you that, Einstein?" She leaned down and held out a cheese curl. Cheese curls were another one of his favorite treats. Sara kept praising him as he inched his way forward and snatched the cheese curl from her fingers.

"I think he's going to be just fine, little lady. You got your two men back to normal again."

7

"Any problems?" Sara asked when Dagger walked through the kitchen door.

"No. Deliverymen should be here sometime this afternoon." Dagger gave a nod to Simon.

"Today? What the hell did you do? Wave your forty-five at them?" Simon asked.

"Money talks. You of all people should know that, Simon."

"They had everything in the ad?" Sara asked. "Even the leather loveseat?"

"I'm going to feel like I woke up in a powder puff factory."

Sara stifled a laugh. "Thanks for going. I'm sure you had more important things to do."

"Oh, yeah," Simon piped up. "He's been a real go-getter the past two months."

Dagger looked sharply at his friend. "Speaking of which, remind me, Simon, to kick your ass for dumping that case in my lap."

"You want the well-paying ones and I gotcha one." Simon turned to Sara. "Mrs. Pratts on my route has a close friend, a big contributor to the Museum of Natural History, who had a huge personal problem, so she said, and needed help. She didn't know the details and I didn't ask."

"Well, you should have found out if she was looney tunes first."

"I'm sure you didn't mind the load of money she paid."

Dagger shook his head. "I didn't take it."

"You didn't help her?"

Dagger couldn't help but smile. "Oh, I helped her." Then he told Simon and Sara about the mansion, Josephine Van Pelletier, and Cedar the mutt. Josephine had corrected him upon leaving that Cedar was a she and she was a pure-bred Lhasa Apso.

"Her husband was where?" Sara asked, her coffee cup halted inches from her mouth.

"Charles died three years ago. Rather than have him buried in a vault, she had him made into a diamond."

"A what?" Simon stared incredulously until he realized Dagger was serious. Then he burst into raucous laughter.

"They can do that?" Sara asked.

"Latest thing, supposedly, according to Mrs. Van Pelletier. She showed me a brochure on the subject. It's a matter of controlling the oxygen levels during the cremation process to prevent carbon in the body from converting to carbon dioxide. They collect the body's carbon and ship it to another facility where the powder is heated in a vacuum at extreme temperatures to produce graphite. Then it's shipped to another facility to simulate the pressure and temperatures required to create the diamonds. One body could yield up to fifty stones."

"So," Simon asked, "Mrs. Van Pelletier had what? A tennis bracelet made of her husband?"

"Tennis bracelet, earrings, and a three-carat, teardrop

diamond pendant. It's the diamond pendant that had broken off of the gold chain." Dagger started to chuckle again as he told them about Cedar and how the dog would nestle on Mrs. Van Pelletier's chest and lick her pearls. "I figured the dog nibbled just a little too much on the pendant. The dog slept with its mistress and that would have been the perfect time for the dog to bite the damn thing off."

Simon and Sara were silent for a few beats, then exchanged glances. Sara's face contorted. "Eyuuuu! The dog ate it?"

Simon said, "There are some things even I wouldn't do for fifty thousand dollars. And picking through doggy doo-doo on a palatial estate is one of them."

"Not me. I just called over the groundskeeper and asked where the pooch does its duty."

"So why was she afraid to mention to her sons that she had lost the diamond?" Sara asked.

"They wanted his ashes spread over Churchill Downs. That was the request in his will. But Mrs. Van Pelletier had heard about this latest trend and thought it was a wonderful idea. To admit to her sons that she lost a part of their father would have been too embarrassing."

"And you didn't even take gas money?" Sara asked.

Dagger shook his head. "She was embarrassed and I was embarrassed for her. I told her just to make a donation to her favorite charity for whatever she felt my services were worth."

"Better watch it, Dagger," Simon cautioned, "or people will start to say you are turning nice."

Sara unfolded herself from the chair. "I have another ad to show you."

Simon crooked his head as his eyes followed her out of

the room. "Ummm ummmm," he whispered and swiveled his head back to Dagger. "So, how are things? Where has she been for two months?"

"She's not saying."

"Hrmppf. She's not sayin' or you're not askin'?"

Dagger glared at his friend.

"Don't give me one of them looks."

Sara returned and handed Dagger a magazine. "I tossed out both of the perches with the furniture because they had been chewed through. I thought these perching towers would be nice." The towers contained several perches and places to hang ropes and other toys. "I thought we could buy one floor model for behind the couch and one table model for the top of your file cabinet."

Dagger took a quick look at the pictures and handed back the magazine. "Sure. Any other rooms you plan to redo before you leave again?" He held her gaze and watched as her face flushed. He hated himself for being such a cold bastard but it was too late to rein in the words. They had already done their damage.

"I take back my comment about you turning nice," Simon said. An uneasy silence crept through the room. Simon flicked his gaze from Dagger to Sara and back to Dagger. "Uh, listen, I'm going to head out. Looks like you two have some talkin' to do."

"You're pretty unforgiving, you know," Dagger said after he heard the kitchen door close behind Simon.

"Me?" She backed away, dropped the magazine onto the kitchen table and walked out of the room.

Dagger followed. "I told you I had made things right, after the nurse took your blood. I told you I destroyed the vial. But you still left. You still refused to contact me."

"That's not true." She walked to the aviary door to see if Einstein had been disturbed by their conversation. He was napping on one of the branches.

"Pardon me. It was one telepathic message. My god, Sara. I saw the wounds. You were in no condition to leave the hospital." He moved toward her. She turned away, wrapped her fingers around the grating on the door. The phone shrilled. He located it on the bar and answered on the third ring.

"Yeah?" It was Mrs. Van Pelletier thanking him again for his services. He listened politely, trying to gently cut her off and end the call, but she rambled on about taking Cedar to the vet to make sure the diamond hadn't torn up the mutt's digestive track. The call finally ended and he turned to find that Sara had left, taking the magazine from the kitchen table with her. Seconds later he heard the truck ambling down the drive.

"Were the stores crowded?" Dagger asked when Sara returned two hours later.

"Not this one." She set the boxes on the floor by the bar.

Dagger wanted to continue their conversation, but Sara no sooner hung up her jacket than the alarm for the gate rang. On the monitor he saw the delivery truck.

"AWK, WHO'S THERE?" Einstein clamped his beak onto the grating and pulled the door open. Dagger had forgotten to slide the bolt lock in place. Einstein flew up to the catwalk and landed on the railing outside of Sara's bedroom.

Dagger kept a cautious eye on Einstein, not sure if the macaw was going to try to christen the new furniture or start nipping the deliverymen. The two burly men were linebacker-sized with thick necks and thighs like tree trunks.

"You are Miss Morningsky?" one Popeye twin asked, a smile widening across his broad face.

A hacking noise erupted from the railing and the two men looked up in unison. Einstein had one foot raised in an attack mode. Dagger cleared his throat. He moved his arms to reveal the Kimber .45 holstered on his belt. Sara rolled her eyes.

"You under house arrest?" Popeye Number One asked her.

"Just deliver the furniture," Dagger said.

As soon as the two linebackers skulked out of the house, Sara jammed her fists at her waist and turned on Dagger. "Did you have to do that?"

Dagger unfolded his arms and shrugged. "Do what?"

She opened her mouth to speak, then glared up at the railing where Einstein perched. "You, too," she barked. The macaw ruffled its feathers and readjusted its claws on the railing. She raised her arms and pushed at the air. "Forget it. Just forget it." Sara stomped to the door and propped it open for the deliverymen.

They brought in the area rug first. It was a deep wine color bordered with broad stripes of pink and mauve. The men adjusted it several times before she had it exactly where she wanted it. Before they went out for their next load, Sara pressed a one-hundred-dollar bill into each of their hands.

"Why did you do that?" Dagger demanded after the men left for the next load.

"Simon said I should tip them if I want them to…"

"The store got enough of a tip from me. Besides, it's their job."

"It's my money. If I want to tip them…"

"That's what they get paid for."

"Just go." She pointed a finger at his bedroom. "Go clean your guns or something."

He stood firm. It was another thirty minutes until the sections of the desk were brought in and the two hulks started to assemble it.

"Would you like to take a break? I have coffee and brownies in the kitchen," Sara offered.

Dagger opened his mouth to protest but Sara shut him down with an icy glare. He stared at the black granite sections strewn on the tiled floor while chatter and laughter erupted from the kitchen. He vaguely heard one guy ask Sara if Dagger was a "cop or something." Sara responded, "Something."

Studying the curved couch, Dagger had to admit it was a far cry from his black leather furniture. The fabric was a pinwale corduroy with bright splashes of yellow, pink, and mauve flowers against a wine-colored background a shade darker than the rug. Each end of the couch had a built-in recliner. Popeye Number Two had been more than happy to demonstrate it for Sara. The only leather she had purchased was the loveseat, a deep navy blue that matched the shade of blue outlining the flowers.

Dagger looked up at Einstein and gave a soft whistle. The macaw flew down and clamped its claws on Dagger's arm. Curiosity got the best of him, not to mention the smell of coffee, so Dagger charged into the kitchen with Einstein in tow.

The two men stopped talking when he entered. Dagger placed Einstein on his shoulder and poured a cup of coffee. Sara introduced him to Sid and Charlie. Dagger wasn't sure who was who and could care less. He gave an attempt at a nod and said, "You know, the sun is going to be setting soon."

Sid and Charlie exchanged glances. One of them said, "Well, Pops, Edison made a great invention years ago called electricity." The two linebackers laughed. Sara smiled.

Dagger scowled and walked out, set his plate and coffee on the bar, and placed Einstein in the aviary. He checked his reflection in the mirror on the wall by the aviary door. No gray in his hair nor that many lines on his face, although the last two months had mentally aged him. His fingers brushed the wolf head pendant. Two bright turquoise stones served as eyes. The color matched Sara's eyes perfectly. Ada's note had told him to never remove the necklace. Some days he wondered what would happen if he did. He studied his face again, the dark deep-set eyes, olive complexion. Maybe the five o-clock shadow made him look older than his thirty years, but he would match his energy against the two bruisers in the kitchen any day. After closing the grated door to the aviary, Dagger settled on the couch with his coffee.

When Sid and Charlie finished assembling the desk and filing cabinet, Sara gave each of the men another tip, ignoring the verbal protest from Dagger. While Sara fluffed and re-fluffed couch pillows, Dagger carried the boxes from his bedroom, which contained all the contents of his desk and filing cabinet. He spent the rest of the night finding a place for everything. They worked in silence, ordered Chinese takeout, and ate in silence.

Einstein was afraid to open his beak.

* * *

The ATM on Stover stood on the outer edge of the parking lot of Sheffield Trust and Savings Bank. At nine-forty-five in the evening, a man in a dark warm-up suit jogged through the empty lot and slowed as he approached the cash station. He dug around in his pocket, pulled out a card, inserted it in the machine, and pushed buttons. A soft breeze whipped up dried leaves clinging to the slatted fence separating the bank from a vacant lot. Across the street was a row of single family homes. Holiday lights twinkled in the windows, on trees, and the bushes dotting the homes.

The man blew on his hands as he waited for the machine to spit out money. Across the street, a garage door rolled open and a white mini-van pulled in. He watched for a few seconds as a woman exited the van. A boy in what looked like a Cub Scout uniform slid out of the passenger side door and slammed it shut. The man turned back to the machine. After several seconds he looked sharply over his shoulder, eyes scanning the dark parking lot.

Mom and son made their way down the driveway to the curb where a brick pillar housed a mailbox. The woman sifted through mail and made inaudible responses to her son's constant chatter. As they started their trek to the house, a loud pop shattered the quiet street. Mother and son both jerked their heads up. The boy uttered, "firecracker."

"I think it's a backfire," the mother said. She looked across the street as the man in the jogging suit slowly slumped to the ground in front of the ATM. She quickly ushered her son into the house and dialed nine-one-one.

8

"Brent Langley, age twenty-four, jogs to the ATM just before ten o'clock last night and gets popped from behind." Sergeant Padre Martinez dropped the file folder on Chief Wozniak's desk. "Two eyewitnesses. One, a seven-year-old boy who thought he heard a firecracker, and the mother, who saw Langley and heard the shot but didn't see where it came from. She hustled her son into the house and called the station. The victim is a Cedar Point firefighter, single, was jogging back to the fire station. According to bank records, the man withdrew two hundred dollars which was not on him nor in the machine tray."

"Is he going to make it?"

"Still unconscious in ICU so we'll know more later. Took one shot to the right shoulder, some lung damage, but doctors are hopeful."

"Ballistics?"

"Nine millimeter. Crime techs dug the bullet out of the brick. Fired possibly from a Sig Sauer." Padre walked over to the monitor on the side credenza and popped in a videotape. "This is the tape from the camera at the ATM." He ran a hand through his receding hairline and dropped into a chair in front of the chief's desk.

They watched in silence for several minutes. On screen a man came into view, stocking cap on his head, jacket zipped. He jammed a finger between his teeth and yanked the glove from his right hand. While his left hand took the glove from his mouth, his right pulled a card from his pocket and jammed it into the machine. His eyes were tearing and puffs of frosty air billowed around his face as he exhaled. The monitor showed the victim from the chest up. Langley bounced up and down as though keeping warm while waiting for the machine to respond.

Padre pointed toward the screen. "Here is where it looks like he hears something." On the screen Langley turns sharply, then slowly turns back. Soon after, his body jerks and is propelled forward, pounding into the monitor before slumping from view.

"Play it back." Wozniak leaned forward, elbows on his knees. A lock of flaming red hair streaked with silver drifted over his forehead. Between cheeks just as red jutted a bulbous nose that was a Wozniak trademark. "Did the mother hear a car screech away? Maybe footsteps running?"

"No. My guess is the car might have waited several minutes and slowly pulled away so as not to draw attention. Had to be a pretty good shot to nail Langley with one bullet."

They reran the videotape several times, stopping the tape to look for shadows, parked cars at the curb, flashes of light from a weapon. Even when Langley had turned away from the camera as if he had heard something, the tape showed he was alone.

"Has he had any altercations with fellow workers? Maybe sleeping with someone's wife?"

"Nothing I've uncovered so far. He's a hard worker, gets along with everyone, and he's engaged to his college sweetheart."

"Makes no sense," Wozniak mumbled, "unless we got some sniper shooting from several hundred yards away." The chief rubbed his face with his hands. "Dear god, don't let there be a sniper."

A lanky man in a close-cropped Afro appeared in the doorway. "I can confuse things even more."

"Seeing you is a sign of bad news, Luther," Wozniak said. "We only get a visit from our esteemed medical examiner after our vics have died."

"It's slow in the office and one of the crime techs asked me to take a look at something from the ATM shooting." Luther took a seat next to Padre and handed copies of a report to each of them. "This, ladies and gentlemen, is burn residue."

"Burn?" Padre scanned the report quickly. "How can that be?" He took his time examining the report and photos of Langley's jacket, shirt, and the wound itself.

From behind the desk, Chief Wozniak leaned over the photo with a ruler in his hand, measuring the flame marks. He could easily tell by the burn mark and lack of soot on the clothing that this was more than a close shot.

Padre said, "The assailant was standing close enough to kiss him. Was he crouching?"

"Crouching gunman, hidden perp. We can make our own movie," Luther quipped. "Bullet went straight through. A nine millimeter, right?" He looked at Padre, who nodded. "I spoke with the surgeon. We've got ourselves a star-burst, gentlemen," referring to the condition of the skin around the wound. "Our assailant pressed the gun against the victim's back and fired, through and through, straight in, no passing go, no angles, no short people need apply."

Loud voices carried from the outer office where a woman with fire engine red hair towered over the desk of one of the detectives. She was as wide as she was tall. Her finger waggled with the fervor of someone who might have been a school teacher at one time.

"Hate to be on the receiving end of her venom," Luther said.

"Second time that woman has been in here. Says her neighbor was supposed to take her to The Lighthouse outlet mall last Wednesday but never showed up. Doesn't answer her phone. The husband is missing, too." Wozniak pulled a report from his In box. "A Mr. and Mrs. Seymour Cohen are the neighbors. Detective Baylor has located a daughter-in-law in New Jersey who says the son is in Israel on business. Denise Cohen says she spoke to her mother-in-law last Monday and everything was fine. She said her in-laws were planning a trip to Michigan to a bed and breakfast but Denise wasn't sure exactly when. So far, no other leads."

Padre exited the elevators on the third floor of Cedar Point Hospital. Medicinal odors blended with cleaning fluids and food from the steel carts lining the walls.

Padre passed through a set of doors to the Intensive Care Unit and stopped at the nurses station. Two men in green scrubs were on the phones while nurses dressed in pastel uniforms were studying a wall of monitors. Gone were the stark white uniforms of the past in an attempt to put a less clinical feel to a patient's stay.

Padre tapped his shield against a flower vase, eliciting an immediate response from one of the men in scrubs.

"You must be Detective Martinez." He moved to the doorway and shook Padre's hand. "Doctor Connors."

Padre nodded. The doctor's handshake had the firmness of someone used to consoling relatives...strong and steady. "How is Langley doing?"

"Considering the blood loss and damage to his right lung, remarkably well. Not sure he can remain a firefighter though." The surgeon led Padre to the last room down the corridor.

"He is able to talk, right?"

Doctor Connors' voice lowered to a whisper as they paused outside Langley's room. He had the voice of a commercial pilot, soft and seasoned, deep and authoritative. Someone you would readily trust with a plane or a scalpel. "I'm limiting you to ten minutes. I don't want him getting agitated or fatigued," Connors instructed. He gave Padre's back a quick pat and walked away.

The figure in the bed was tethered to several monitors that blinked and hummed. It was a windowless room, void of flower vases and plants. The covers rose and fell in a slow rhythm. The sounds and smells of the hospital brought back unpleasant memories. It wasn't too long ago that Padre had been a tenant of Cedar Point Hospital.

Padre pulled a chair close to the bed. It made a scraping noise that echoed off the empty walls. Langley's eyelids fluttered. He slowly turned toward his visitor.

"Sorry. Thought I would be quieter." Padre tossed his trench coat over the back of the chair and sat down. "Actually, I wanted to make a lot of noise because the doc is only giving me ten minutes."

Brent Langley forced a smile. "Cop."

"Sergeant Jerry Martinez, and right now, I'm your best friend." Padre smiled warmly. "And you are my best eye-witness."

Langley winced, his right hand gingerly touching the bandage. "Wish I could tell you I saw my attacker, but I didn't."

Padre leaned forward, tapped his pen to his notepad. "Let's back up a little to the point where you were jogging to the ATM. Do you remember seeing anyone following, either on foot or in a car?"

"No." Langley's voice was hoarse and speech measured. "No. Roads empty."

"At one point on the tape from the surveillance camera, you turned around. What had you heard?"

The fireman stared up at the ceiling, thick brows hunched in thought. "Not sure. Leaves, I guess. Can't ...remember."

"When you turned, did you notice any cars pull up, maybe hear an engine idle or see headlights snapping off?"

Langley shook his head slowly, wincing from that small of a movement. "Just the woman...a mother and son."

"Take your time." Padre checked his notes. Nothing made sense. The videotape had confirmed what Langley was saying, but ballistics told a different story. He studied the young man who had been with the fire department bare-ly two years. Fresh-faced and green as every recruit he had ever seen walk through the doors of the precinct.

Padre asked, "Did you feel anything before you were shot?"

"Feel?" Langley turned to face him. "What do you mean?"

"Could you sense how close the shooter was to you?"

Langley blinked slowly, digesting the question and looking for answers on the ceiling. "I still don't get what you mean."

"I saw the bullet hole in your jacket. I saw pictures of the wound. There were burn marks on your jacket."

A puzzled expression formed on the fireman's face.

"Do you know what a star-burst is, Brent?" When the young man shook his head no, Padre replied, "That's what happens when the heat from the bullet erupts under the skin. This only happens from close contact. Very close." He could tell by the slight draining of color from Langley's face that the kid was beginning to get it. "The shooter pressed the gun against your back and fired."

The young man went back to studying the paint brush strokes on the ceiling. A shudder rattled through his body as if he were walking his mind through the entire event. "I really can't remember beyond the pain of the gun shot. I don't know if I felt the gun first and then he fired or I just didn't feel the gun at all."

Padre slipped the notepad back into his suit jacket and checked his watch. "Do you know anyone who would want to kill you?"

Langley flinched at the word *kill*. "No." He covered his eyes with one hand, his thumb and forefinger pinching at the corners.

Padre got up to leave, pulling his coat from the chair back. He placed a business card on the nightstand. "I would appreciate it if you wouldn't discuss our conversation with anyone, Brent. There is certain information we aren't disclosing to the public."

"You're the priest aren't you?" Langley asked as he took a swipe at the tears seeping from the corners of his eyes. "The one they call Padre?"

"I didn't quite graduate." Padre wished he didn't have the nickname. People sometimes had the compulsion to bare their souls.

"Why do things like this happen?" Langley asked. "My brother was a firefighter and my father and his father before him. But now with this lung injury, I know I'll be forced to quit. What will I do? This was my life."

Padre sighed heavily. He hated questions to which there were no answers. Force of habit prompted him to clasp a hand over Langley's forearm. "It's not the end of the world, kid. The department can always use arson investigators, instructors. If that doesn't appeal to you, come on over to our side. Crime scene investigation is always understaffed." He gave a final pat and smiled. "You may miss the food at your fire house, but we always have a box or two of Krispy Kreme donuts."

9

"Surprise, surprise." Padre scooted onto the barstool. "What brought you out of your cave?"

Dagger slid his eyes toward the cop and shrugged. "I was out of beer."

"Since when?" Padre nodded his thanks to the bartender and took a healthy swig from the chilled glass. He gazed around the hotel bar, sparsely seasoned with casually dressed out-of-towners and businessmen in stripped-down suits.

Dagger studied the rings of condensation on the bar. The festive lights strung around the mirror were reflected in the polished wood. It made Dagger realize he hadn't been aware of the pending holidays until the Christmas tree sprouted in the Florida room. He sighed heavily and lifted the glass to his lips, aware of Padre's reflection in the mirror behind the bar.

He emptied the glass and pushed it toward the edge of the bar. Turning to Padre, he said, "Did you know you can have the ashes of your beloved made into a one-carat diamond for a mere twenty-two thousand dollars?"

"That's bullshit."

"Actually, that's dog shit." Dagger told him about Josephine Van Pelletier and her dog.

When Padre realized Dagger was on the level, he started chuckling. It started as a high-pitched giggle, then a pause, then the giggle exploded into an all-out belly laugh.

"You two are having way too much fun."

The voice sounded all too familiar. Dagger stared at the reflection in the mirror of a statuesque woman with platinum hair.

"Well, if it isn't Sheila Monroe, Cedar Point's favorite nosy reporter," Padre said.

"Nice to see you, too, Sergeant Martinez."

Padre gave a nod and a quick glance at the plunging neckline and tight leather pants. "Looking good, as usual."

"Of course." She turned her gaze to Dagger and ran her hand across his shoulder. "Nice to see you getting out and about."

Dagger shrugged in response. "Even a groundhog comes out of his hole once a year."

"Yes, but why now?" Sheila slowly dragged a nail against his five o-clock shadow. Dagger pulled away.

Like radar, the bartender appeared in front of Sheila. He fidgeted with his bow tie and smoothed back his hair. "Can I get you something?"

"Vodka and tonic, and throw in a couple of olives."

Padre pushed several bills across the bar. "Take it out of here."

"Why thank you, Padre. At least there's one gentleman at the bar." Sheila accepted the drink from the bartender and asked Padre, "What's the latest on the ATM shooter?" She set her glass down and pushed her way between the two stools.

"No comment."

"Come now, Martinez. Haven't I always been good to you?" She swirled the olive around in her glass and held it up by the plastic toothpick before popping it in her mouth.

"You know as much as I do, sweetheart, probably more. Tell me what you've heard on the street."

Sheila said, "Mrs. Reeder and her son didn't see much. They both heard the shot, he thought it was a firecracker, and the mother only saw the victim. The public has a right to know if there is a sniper out there with a high-powered weapon taking pot shots at our police and firemen."

"There you go." Padre smiled broadly. "You know as much as me."

"What did Brent Langley have to say? You visited him in the hospital, right?"

"Yep."

"Didn't learn anything?"

"Nope."

Dagger leaned his elbows on the bar, one fist propped under his chin, half listening to Sheila's weak attempt at dragging information out of Padre. The Ritz Hotel wasn't on Sheila's list of stomping grounds so it wouldn't surprise him if she had been tailing Padre. Anything for a story.

Sheila offered one of her olives to Dagger. He shook his head. "Pity," she said. "You have a habit of passing up the best things in life."

Padre raised a finger toward the bartender who quickly poured another draft. "What do you actually want, Miss Monroe?" He paused, looked at Dagger, then back to Sheila. "Hey, I'm not the best damn cop in Cedar Point for nothing. I can take a hint when to get lost." As he pushed away from the bar he said, "I'm going to make a phone call." He leaned in close to her. "Word to the wise…it won't do any good."

Sheila watched Padre walk out to the lobby, then slid onto his barstool. Dagger kept his eyes trained on the ring of condensation.

"We have a lot of catching up to do, Dagger."

"Regarding what?"

She placed her hand on top of his and drew lazy circles on his skin with the tip of her nail. Dagger picked up his glass to take a drink. Sheila's hand fell away with a deep sigh of resignation.

"You're still angry. I've never lied to you, Dagger. I told you I didn't sleep with Spagnola, no matter what his alpha male ego said."

"I really don't care what you do, Sheila. We're history."

"If you believed that, you wouldn't have stayed away the last two months."

"Oh really?" He said it with a chuckle in his throat. His eyes were drawn to the large diamond on Sheila's finger. Even after their breakup, even after he told her he never paid for the ring, that it had been a payment from a client, she insisted on wearing it.

"Don't tell me you are still angry because you think I tried to frame Sara for that murder." She pulled a strand of hair behind her ear, flashing her engagement ring for him to see, like a flag that said, "I'm not giving up."

"I don't feel much of anything, Sheila, so just keep Sara's name out of it."

"Ahhhh, Sara," Padre said. "Seems every time we run into you, Sheila, that young woman's name pops right out of your mouth." Padre nudged Sheila off his stool.

Sheila's phone chirped and half the people in the bar started patting their jacket pockets. She flipped hers open and snapped, "Yes?" Grimacing, she pressed a finger to the opposite ear. "But it's only...okay...all right, Daddy." She snapped the phone closed and shoved it in her purse. "It's been a slice guys, but I have to go. Besides," she gave one last lingering look at Dagger, "I try not to hang around with *CABs* anymore."

"Say hello to Spagnola for me," Padre said, wriggling his fingers at Sheila's reflection in the mirror. She gave a back-handed wave over her shoulder as she left.

Laughter erupted in the corner of the bar where six men in business suits were clustered around a table. Dagger was becoming fond of the hotel bars. With the number of conventioneers and vacation travelers, it was easy to get lost in a crowd, his face just another in a blur of faces passing through town.

Dagger looked up from his glass to see Padre drilling him with a glare. "What?"

"What the hell is a *CAB*?" Padre asked.

"Cold, arrogant bastard."

"Oh." Padre smiled and nodded as if in agreement.

Dagger ignored the implication. With Sheila, cold was the only way to go.

"She's back, isn't she?" asked Padre.

Dagger looked away, his fingers clasped firmly around his glass. "What makes you say that?"

"As I said, I'm not the best cop in town for nothing. You hibernate for two months to be alone or for god knows why. Now you come here. Must be because you aren't alone at home any more. So..." Padre let the word hang. "Where has she been?"

Dagger pushed his glass away and waved off the bartender. Even the beer wasn't tasting good. "She didn't say."

Padre's head swiveled slowly from side to side, like a teacher disappointed in a student's homework. "She didn't say, or you didn't ask?"

"Shit." Dagger let it out in a long breath. "Have you been talking to Simon?"

"Guess we know you too well." Padre waved the bartender away from his empty glass as well and swiveled his stool toward Dagger. "I trust you were patient and understanding and didn't light into her the moment you saw her." When Dagger flinched at his words, Padre moaned, "Aww, jeez. She needs to talk to someone about what happened, Dagger. I had trouble sleeping after the Addison case. If it wasn't for all the late night calls to Marty in Indianapolis so we could both talk it out, I don't know what I would have done. I couldn't talk to the missus, or the guys at the precinct, except Wozniak. I have no idea how you handled it. But Sara? That's a lot for a young woman to shoulder on her own. She may need some counseling."

Dagger hadn't thought about that. The Addison case had been one of the more bizarre cases dumped on his doorstep by Sergeant Marty Flynn from Indianapolis and the now-deceased Professor Bill Sherlock. Paul Addison had been more than evil. He had been something out of a horror movie—a man who shifted into a wolf-type creature when a full moon and a Friday the thirteenth coincided. Sara had lured the beast to a remote warehouse in the woods where he could be destroyed. Addison had been obsessed with

Sara and she had paid the price.

Padre clamped a hand on his shoulder. "I don't know if you have unloaded on anyone. Maybe Skizzy, although in the *World of Skizzy*, Addison probably seemed pretty normal. You've practically secluded yourself for two months, haven't answered my calls but…" he held his hands out in surrender fashion, "hey, that's okay. Everyone handles stress in his own way, Dagger. But it has to be handled. Don't bottle it up. And don't let Sara bottle it up."

"All right, already. Don't nag."

"Speaking of Skizzy, would you ask that government conspiracy fanatic of yours if he's sold any high-powered rifles from that weapons stockpile he isn't supposed to have to anyone lately?"

Dagger turned to the cop and furrowed his brow. "So you do think it was a sniper."

"Just covering bases. If the mother who was less than sixty yards away didn't see anyone…"

"Then the mother was wrong and the guy was crouching to get out of camera range. Pretty easy to do."

"That's the logical explanation, but I think the mother is a pretty reliable witness."

"Everyone is and all five, six, ten reliable witnesses come up with five, six, ten different accounts. Was there another camera on the bank building?"

"Even the camera at the nearest intersection was useless. Just run it by Skizzy." He stood and shrugged into his coat. "Say hi to Sara for me."

Dagger watched the cop's retreat through the reflection in the mirror, and after several minutes tossed a five on the bar and left. Padre was right, in one sense. He had missed the company of the few friends he did have. Other than popping in on crazy Skizzy a few times, Dagger had very little contact with Padre and Simon in two months. It was hard to tell where reality started and ended with Skizzy, so if the Addison case bothered his crazy friend, he'd buried it under all his other phobias.

During the drive home he thought about Sara after Addison had died, how he'd carried her bleeding body to the truck, how pale and fragile and close to death she had been. But he'd made one crucial mistake that caused her not to trust him. He had let the nurse take her blood. Big mistake. He had forgotten her blood wasn't entirely human.

Dagger left the lit city streets behind and threaded the Navigator through forest preserve on blacktop roads. His attention was drawn to the moon suspended over Lake Michigan. A misshapen ball of light obscured by city haze. How many more days until it was full, he thought. Not too many. Prior to the Addison case he had paid little attention to when the moon was full.

Dagger listened for sounds as he entered through the kitchen door. One low-watt bulb above the sink cast the only light in the room. He didn't hear music or sounds from the television. After hanging up his coat he walked to the aviary door to make sure it was locked, then did the same with the front door. His gaze ran up the flight of stairs to Sara's room. The door was open.

Dagger climbed the stairs slowly as he tried to sort in his mind all the questions: Why did Sara leave? Where did she go? Who did she stay with? What did she do for money?

Ribbons of moonlight sliced through the tall windows and fell on Sara's bed. She was lying on her side, back to him, hair fanned out across the pillows. For several minutes he stood and watched the gentle rise and fall of her body. If she had been awake, he would have chosen this time to talk. But she wasn't and a part of him was relieved.

10

The next morning Sara maneuvered Dagger into assembling the perching towers. Dagger felt the towers weren't sturdy enough so he took off for the lumberyard where he could usually get lost for hours.

"You like them, Einstein?" Sara held up parts to one of the perching towers. Einstein was safely behind the grated door, unable to play with the wooden toys dangling from the top perch of the tower.

He climbed beak over claw until he was eye level with her. "WHAT IS IT, WHAT IS IT? AWK."

"It's a new perch. You'll love it, I promise." She poked her fingers between the grating and stroked the top of his head. "Not biting today. That's a good sign." She returned the perching tower to the floor behind the couch. The second one would fit fine on Dagger's file cabinet.

She and Dagger had done a good job of avoiding conversation, silently working around each other, responding only in one- or two-word phrases. He was pleased with the new desk and actually gave some semblance of organization.

Sara searched the floor around the desk. She was sure

she had purchased an organizer for the desktop to keep notepads and pens handy. "Must still be in the bedroom." She crossed the room to Dagger's doorway and peered in. A flat box was leaning against the exercise bike. As she bent down to pick it up, Sara noticed the door to his vault ajar. The wall was paneled with mirrors concealing any indication of a hidden room.

She crooked her finger and pulled the door to the vault wide open. Small cone-shaped lights flicked on. Weapons of various shapes and sizes were displayed on the far wall. A filing cabinet, printer, and shelves were lined up on one side of the room, a worktable on the wall to her right. She picked up one of the robot spiders Dagger used for audio and visual surveillance. The spiders were the brainchild of Skizzy and Dagger. Its metal legs and body were made of a dull, black metal. Two red eyes sprouted from the top of its head. A box on the worktable held identical robots.

She returned the spider to the box and turned to leave. That was when she saw the world map mounted in a depressed section of the wall above the worktable. Sara lightly touched the map. It felt like the plasma television screen in the living room. After the number of times she had been in the vault, she didn't recall ever seeing it before. Maybe it was just another one of the changes that occurred while she was gone. Countries were identified as well as longitude and latitude. The United States was not divided into states, but she was sure the blue light near the tip of Lake Michigan was Cedar Point. There were stationary white lights on the map in spots that made no logical sense. One was in the Midwest, west of the Mississippi. A couple in Europe and more in Asia.

Two red lights pulsed on the screen. One moved across the upper hemisphere, blinking every second. An identical blinking light followed several seconds later, crawling across the lower hemisphere. The light at the top disappeared from the left side of the screen only to reappear at the right.

This was puzzling. Airplanes? No, there would certainly be more than two. The sky would be filled with them. Certain types of airplanes? Surveillance? Maybe Skizzy was right—Big Brother was watching.

Sara's attention was drawn to a name on the bottom right-hand side of the screen—BettaTec. The name appeared over a design of what looked like a butterfly with closed wings. The wings displayed a rainbow of colors. Had BettaTec manufactured the screen? Did the markers denote their company locations? They must have divisions all over the world. But why would Dagger be interested in them?

An arm reached over, startling Sara. She jumped back as Dagger pressed a button. A wall slowly slid in front of the map. Now Sara knew why she hadn't seen it before. It had been hidden in the wall.

"What is the map for, Dagger?" Sara studied his face. His stare was stony, eyes dark, mouth set in a straight line. He didn't respond, just glanced quickly to make sure the wall had concealed the entire map. "What were the two blinking lights? Why were certain...?"

Dagger raised a hand as though stopping traffic. He clasped his hands prayer style and pressed the tips of his fingers to his chin. The glare hardened as Dagger appeared to weigh his response. When he spoke there was something about the tone of his voice that did more to halt her rapid-fire questions than his raised hand.

"It's not like you to snoop through the vault when I'm not here, Sara."

"I found the desk organizer on the floor in your bedroom. The vault was open and I just thought I would see if you had any new toys. I wasn't snooping."

He flicked his eyes to the wall again, then back to her face. "Forget what you saw." Dagger turned and walked out.

"What is BettaTec? Why do you have the map?"

Dagger stopped suddenly and turned. Sara almost ran into him. He grabbed her shoulders and gently squeezed. Each word was enunciated slowly. "Not...another...word. It's for your own good." He released his grip and pushed the buttons on the keypad to close the mirrored wall.

Sara picked up the box containing the desk organizer and reluctantly followed, her mind still reeling over the map and the blinking lights. But she knew that stare. Dagger wasn't going to open up, and that meant she would have to dig on her own.

While Dagger finished assembling the perching towers, Sara went Christmas shopping, selecting an exclusive men's store in the older, downtown section of Cedar Point. She took a deep breath and pushed open the door to Beckman's. After her last disastrous shopping trip, she was hoping fewer people would be shopping downtown.

"This I can handle," she whispered. Racks of clothing lined the walls in the one-story shop. Glass counters were arranged in a geometric pattern in the middle of the store. There were tables of sweaters, scarves, and gloves intersected by racks of shirts and ties. Mannequins were dressed in suggested ensembles.

Sara wasn't sure what to buy Dagger other than to make sure it was gray or black. He had returned Sheila's gifts in the past because she had always purchased pastel shirts and ties. Dagger was also very particular about his watch. It had more dials and buttons than Sara had ever seen. And she was sure Skizzy had tinkered with it.

A customer stood in front of a full-length mirror outside of a dressing room while a salesman with a measuring tape snaking around his neck adjusted one of the pants cuffs. A young woman, probably a wife or girlfriend, ran her eyes down his entire frame before shaking her head no.

Other than a few clusters of shoppers, the remaining people milling around appeared to be salespersons.

"May I help you?"

Sara turned to find a woman in a tailored suit with a blouse as stiff as cardboard. A pencil had been jammed into the cluster of blonde hair at the nape of her neck. Her I.D. said *Sophia*.

"I'm just browsing, thank you."

Sara wandered through the tables until she found a black crew neck sweater with gray suede patches on the sleeves. She knew Dagger's sweater and shirt size because she had sometimes worn his castoff shirts. He had a closet full of cargo pants so she scratched that idea off her list. Besides, she wasn't sure of his pants size.

She browsed past glass cases containing gold necklaces, bracelets, and tie tacks. She could feel Sophia's eyes following her around the store. Sara stopped at a case that contained diamond rings. One ring in particular had a card labeled *Raphael - $10,000*. The price tag alone probably made Sophia nervous whenever anyone was within five feet of the showcase.

"Like what you see?"

The voice was smooth and low, and something in the way he spoke told Sara he was smiling. She turned to find a man of average height, smooth face with soft brown eyes, heavy-lidded. His lips were turned up slightly at the corners, but it was his eyes that did the smiling in a strange sort of way. There was something unnatural in the way he blinked slowly, like a python before it swallowed you whole.

"Actually," Sara replied, "it's rather ugly."

He laughed this time, a loud burst that drew stares. "You don't mince words. I like that."

"Would you wear something that big?" Sara stared down at the bauble through the glass counter top.

"No." He turned and stared at the rings, his left arm brushing against hers. "I'd rather have the ten thousand. You can do a lot more with it."

Sara studied the remaining jewelry in the case. Dagger wasn't much for jewelry except a watch and one earring. "I have someone very conservative to buy for. He prefers to wear gray and black, no flashy colors." She looked at his brown herringbone sportscoat and brown shirt. "Have any suggestions?"

"Oh." He looked down to inspect his clothing. "Guess I am a little one-dimensional." He leaned one elbow on the counter and turned to glance around the store. "This for your father?"

"No."

"Brother?"

"No."

He turned his head to check her left hand. "No wedding ring, so can't be for your husband. Your boyfriend then?"

Sara shook her head. "Business associate."

His eyes smiled again and did that reptile blink. "What kind of business?"

She thought for a moment. "Research."

"Let's see." He slid his gaze to a nearby case. "Not personal, more business-like." He made his way to another counter. Sara followed. "How about a wallet?"

Sara studied the different types. Tri-fold, bi-fold, charge card. Eelskin, snakeskin, cowhide.

"What kind does he use?"

Sara knew Dagger kept his wallet in the inside pocket of his jacket and she knew it folded lengthwise. But if he wasn't wearing a jacket, he used a different wallet, one that fit in his back pocket.

"What color?" the stranger asked.

"Gray."

"The jacket wallet is a wonderful choice." Sophia had returned and was sliding open the display case door. "It's made of soft eelskin. Feel." She pressed a black wallet into Sara's hands.

Sara liked the feel of the eelskin but preferred the gun metal gray color. "Do you have this one in gray?"

"Not right now but we are expecting a shipment Monday."

"How much is it?"

"One hundred and twenty-five dollars," Sophia replied.

"That's a pretty close business associate," the man commented.

Sara avoided the stranger's eyes while she reached for

her wallet.

"No need to pay now," Sophia said. She brought out a receipt pad and shoved it and a pen across the counter. "Just fill out the top portion and I'll call you the minute it comes in."

"I also like the black sweater with the gray leather patches," Sara said as she pointed at a table several yards away.

"Ahhh, wonderful choice." Sophia smiled enthusiastically as commission dollars seemed to flash in her eyes. "That's one hundred and seventy-five dollars."

Sara finished filling out her name and phone number and set the pen down. "Can I pick it up when I pick up the wallet? I didn't bring enough money."

"No problem." She scooted around the counter and flitted to the sweater display. "What size?"

"Large-tall, if you have it."

The man smiled, did another reptile blink. "Business associate. Right," he slid his gaze to the pad of paper. "Sara."

11

"Well, well, if it isn't girlie." Skizzy crooked his bony neck around the door and peered up and down the sidewalk. "You alone?"

"Yes." Sara struggled with the grocery bag as she forced her way in through the meager opening.

He didn't move from the doorway, just stood, one hand gripping the doorknob as his eyes slid up and down her frame. "You sure you're the real thing, not a clone?"

"Skizzy!" Sara laughed at Dagger's friend but he wasn't smiling. His brows were hunched, wiry hair pulled back in a ponytail, with stray hairs sticking out as if he had walked across a static-charged rug.

One free hand scratched a stained tee shirt while his head bobbed back and forth as though listening to silent voices.

"It's me, Skizzy." She held up the bag of goodies. "See? I brought you homemade bread, jellies, and cupcakes."

Cautiously he peered in the bag, eyes bulging. Inhaling the aromas, Skizzy smiled, exposing a mouth of mismatched teeth. He jerked his head up quickly, his face distorting into a mask of doubt and confusion.

Skizzy barked, "What's the capital of North Dakota?"

"Bismarck."

"Indiana?"

"Indianapolis."

"Illinois?"

"Springfield."

"Ah ha!" Skizzy pointed a scrawny finger at her. "It's Chicago."

"No, it isn't. It's Springfield."

Skizzy scratched the gray stubble on his chin, then slowly smiled. "Welcome home."

"Thank you." Sara followed him past the display cases of watches and jewelry. She noticed bars had replaced the boards in front of the windows, the result of a break-in months earlier. Shelves lining the walls were stocked with appliances, collector license plates, bar fixtures, and other items people pawn for cash. They weaved through the drapery which served as a door to the shop's back room where Skizzy lived. She set the bag on the counter and pulled out the contents. "Do you want the jelly downstairs or in your cabinet?"

"Cabinet is fine."

Sara opened the cabinet and paused. It was strange seeing aluminum cans with permanent markers identifying the contents. Skizzy removed labels from his canned goods because he believed the barcode allowed the government to know what foods you ate.

"So, where have you been?" Skizzy asked as he turned one of the kitchen chairs around and straddled it.

"All over," Sara replied. She searched for language Skizzy might understand. "Have you heard of a vision quest?"

"Sure, sure. You go and commune with Nature out in the woods, get answers to questions. Indians do it, right?"

"That's close enough." She folded the paper bag and shoved it under the sink with the rest of the bags.

"So, what did you learn?"

Sara pulled a bottle of water from the refrigerator and thought back to all of her nights crying for a vision, an answer, a way out of the confusion. "Only that we have to live with our decisions and get on with life," she said as she unscrewed the bottle cap.

"Kinda like, 'don't cry over spilt milk.'"

"Something like that."

"Well, shee-it. I could have told you that. You don't have to go away for two months for that." Skizzy filled the conversation with talk about the growth hormones given to cows which, he felt, accounted for the unusual growth spurt in kids, with twelve-year-old girls having the bodies of twenty-year-olds. When he rambled on about companies falsifying audits and receiving tax breaks from the government, Sara took the opportunity to segue into computer searches.

"It should be easy for you to find out about certain companies. You can hack into any company's system, right?"

Skizzy smiled an all-tooth smile. "Child's play."

Confident he would take the bait, Sara brought up the subject of BettaTec.

Abel Beckman checked the clock on the wall, comparing the time with the one on his Rolex. He darted from table to table, pressing down shirt collars on mannequins, straightening stacks of sweaters, running a hand across the glass cases to remove lint only his eyes seemed to detect. Showcases gaped open as Abel moved from case to case repositioning jewelry, using a lint brush to clean velvet runners.

The sound of a door closing echoed in the stillness. Abel turned and listened. "Sophia?" he called out. All of the salespeople had left thirty minutes earlier. He rushed to the back of the store. The door was closed. His eyes roamed the aisles, the break room, and store room. "Anyone there?" He checked both restrooms, then shrugged. Returning to the showroom, all Abel heard was the droning of the ceiling fans. A breeze licked his face and sent a chill up his spine. He flipped a wall switch and the ceiling fans drifted to a stop.

Certain that his jumpiness was due to an overdose of caffeine and demands of holiday shoppers, Abel went back to buffing and shining. He finally locked up the showcases and turned to leave. That was when the uneasy feeling settled over him. It was hard to describe. He had the distinct feeling he wasn't alone.

After turning off the lights, Abel opened the back door and walked out to his car to unlock the trunk. Gravel crunched behind him. Abel turned sharply, his eyes darting from side to side. The parking lot was well lit and he could see he was alone, but he didn't feel alone. He rushed back inside for the two shopping bags of gifts for his salespeople. His wife did a better job of wrapping than he did. Abel set the alarm, pulled the door closed, then hurried to the car.

12

"Yeah, yeah, it's early. So bite me." Padre pushed past Dagger and made his way into the living room.

"It's also a Sunday," Dagger said as he closed the door, "but make yourself at home. *Mi casa es su casa.*" He eyed the cop's battered briefcase. "Sure hope Santa brings you something a little newer to tote around."

"It's an heirloom. Vintage 1987," Padre replied, setting the briefcase on the coffee table and snapping open the locks.

His voice attracted Einstein who flew to the perch behind the grated door. "AWK, UP AGAINST THE WALL AND SPREAD UM."

Padre responded by pointing a finger gun at the macaw. "Nice furniture," he added, studying his surroundings.

"What did you bring?"

Padre pulled a tape from his briefcase. "The video from the ATM shooting. Being the nice guy that I am, I made you your own personal copy."

Dagger shoved it into the VCR and returned to the couch.

Padre picked up a magazine from the table. It was

opened to a picture of an outdoor pond. "This a new project?" Padre asked.

"Not that I know of. Sara must have left it."

Padre tossed the magazine down and picked up the remote. "I need a fresh set of eyes to look at this. I interviewed the victim. He said he didn't hear anyone. Has no enemies. Yada yada. He's going to make it, but his career as a firefighter is history."

"What's stumping you?"

"Connect the dots," Padre said. "Used to like to figure those out as a kid. Would frustrate the hell out of me when I wouldn't get it right the first time. I'm sure you've never had that problem."

"Never."

"Just watch." Padre held up the remote and pressed the button. On the screen the camera followed the movements of Brent Langley as he jogged to the ATM. The men watched in silence as Langley fumbled with his card and then entered his code. The fireman looked bored and cold as he glanced over his shoulder, then back to the machine. Several seconds later his body slumped against the machine and slid from view.

"Langley heard something. He thought it might have been footsteps but all he saw were leaves dancing around the asphalt."

"I say the guy was hiding behind the ATM and crawled up behind him," Dagger suggested.

"But we still have the mom and kid eyewitnesses."

"Too far away, afraid of being involved, not wanting retribution if gangs were involved. Pick one. You're a bright guy."

"And you are in a pissy mood today." Padre rewound the tape. "Have anything to do with Sara?" When Dagger didn't reply, Padre asked, "Care to talk about it?"

"Nothing to say." Dagger cranked his hand as if to say *just roll tape.*

"Yep. *CAB.*" Padre pressed the play button again. They watched the tape a second time. Padre paused the tape at the point where Brent Langley looked over his shoulder.

"Must have heard something," Dagger said.

Einstein clamored back onto his perch and squawked, "ARNOLD, ARNOLD." The macaw clawed his way up the grated door. "ARNOLD, ARNOLD."

"Shhhh." Dagger waved an arm in Einstein's direction.

"I keep thinking they used a defective camera or something, but, for some reason, that little nagging angel sitting on my shoulder whispers, 'connect the dots.'"

"You should check out who installed the surveillance camera. Might be something intermittent. The camera freezes or the tape skips."

"ARNOLD, ARNOLD." Einstein banged his beak against the grating.

"Whoa, whoa." Padre yelled, flailing one hand in the air and popping the tape from the recorder with the other. "Hang on a sec." He paced a short track in the rug then paused, snapping his fingers repeatedly as if trying to jump start his memory. "That's it." Padre pulled a cell phone from his pocket and dialed.

"What's it?" Dagger asked.

Padre shushed him with the wave of one hand. "Cindy, how's my favorite weekend clerk doing?...Course, I always want something, but let's skip the niceties and get down to business." He was smiling now. Dagger never knew anyone who could get more cooperation from people by being demanding. It never worked for Dagger. Padre continued, "Pull up Arnosky on the computer. Yeah, that's the one. I want to know if he's been released." He covered the mouth-piece as he spoke to Dagger. "I put this guy away five years ago. Could only get him on income tax evasion, but I know he was responsible for a string of thefts, all by using his cameras. If I could have proved it, I would have nailed him for his partner's murder, too." He pulled his hand from the mouthpiece. "I'm here, Cindy." His smile broadened as he said, "I owe you one. Add it to my tab." Shoving the cell phone back into his pocket, the detective said, "Arnosky was released three months ago." He turned to the macaw. "You are an Einstein, Einstein."

"So how did he pull the robberies you couldn't nail him on?"

But Padre had already grabbed his coat and was running out the door.

13

First thing Monday morning Padre left two phone messages for Jeff Crnich. When he didn't receive an immediate return call, Padre kept calling until the receptionist put him through.

"Don't give me 'he's kept his nose clean' crap," Padre barked into the phone. "Guy like him is always looking for another score."

"If I remember correctly, Sergeant Martinez, you were always looking to hang something on Arnosky. I've known too many cops looking for payback."

Padre held up five fingers to Chief Wozniak, who nodded and returned to his office. "Well, sometimes experience will do that to a cop. How old are you, Crnich? Twenty-eight? Thirty? I've been looking into the eyes of liars for longer than you've been out of your Social Services One-Oh-One grad school."

"Well, maybe I want to see the potential in people."

"You haven't been a parole officer long enough to know potential if it bit you in the ass. All I'm asking is that you keep Arnosky closer to you than a nursing baby." Padre hung up and charged into Wozniak's office.

"What did Arnosky's parole officer say?"

"He's nominating him for sainthood."

"You have to handle this one with kid gloves." Wozniak held up a hand the size of a baseball mitt. "I know. I shouldn't have to tell you, but this guy is an expert at pushing your buttons. So, let's play fill in the blanks."

"All of the bank security cameras were installed eight years ago by Guardian Security."

"I'm loving it already." Wozniak drew a circle in the air with his finger. "Keep it coming."

"None of the cameras were replaced after Arnosky's arrest."

Wozniak clasped his hands behind his head and leaned back in his chair. "Ahhhh, yes. I just love it when these guys fuck up."

"Bad news is, just like in the past, we can't prove it."

"You take it slow. Wait until our lab checks out the tape. If needed, we may have to use an outside source, too, just in case Arnosky has gone into high tech that even our experts can't verify. If Arnosky is up to his old tricks, it's going to take patience and lots of it." Wozniak retrieved a theft report from his in-box and flung it across the desk at Padre. "Just to be safe, check this one out. Baylor investigated it early this morning. Had a mega-buck ring lifted from Beckman's over the weekend. According to the owner, the security cameras were installed by Guardian Security seven years ago. The owner's name is Abel Beckman. No sign of forced entry. No one on staff worked Sunday. Mr. Beckman was the one to lock up Saturday night."

Padre smiled at the prospects but Chief Wozniak held up a warning finger. "I know, Molasses is my middle name."

* * *

"Must be fate, Sara."

The voice was like a chilly breeze against naked skin. Not a pleasant sensation but one Sara was personally familiar with—danger. She was curious how he knew her name but then remembered he had been leaning over her shoulder the day she filled out the order form.

Sophia was lining a gift box with tissue paper. Her hands shook as she folded and refolded the sweater. Sara didn't remember Sophia being this nervous before.

"Is everything okay?" Sara asked.

Sophia shook her head. "We had a robbery over the weekend," she whispered, then looked over her shoulder toward a balding man talking in an agitated voice to two salespeople.

"Hope you didn't lose too much," Sara said.

Sophia whispered, "It was the *Rafael*. Mr. Beckman is so upset but we aren't supposed to talk about it." She returned to her folding and boxing up of Sara's purchases.

Sara could feel the stranger's presence behind her, his breath against her ear. An uncomfortable silence stretched while Sara watched Sophia place everything in a shopping bag.

"I included gift receipts in the boxes," Sophia said. She handed Sara her change and sales slip. "Thank you so much for your patience."

"I don't suppose I could interest you in a cup of coffee or hot tea," the stranger said. "There's a café just a couple doors away."

Sara turned and studied the man. He may as well have

added the phrase, *Said the spider to the fly*. She doubted it was by sheer coincidence that he showed up on the same day and at the exact time that she stopped by to pick up her order.

"Not with a stranger," she said.

He leaned against the counter, careful not to lean too close but close enough for Sara to hear him. "You have got the most gorgeous eyes I have ever seen," he whispered, his eyes doing the reptile shift again. "I'm Mitch. Nice to meet you, Sara."

Sara clutched her shopping bag, declining Mitch's offer to carry it. He led the way to the café. While he ordered two cappuccinos at the counter, Sara purchased a pound of Brazil nuts.

It was too late for breakfast and too early for lunch so the café was empty, except for two teenagers huddled over drinks topped with whipped cream. Sara slid into a booth by the window. Mitch set the two cups of coffee on the table and slid in across from her.

"Your weakness?" Mitch nodded at the bag of Brazil nuts.

"They are for Einstein." When Mitch flashed a puzzled look, Sara explained. "Einstein is my boss's macaw. Einstein likes Brazil nuts and cheese curls."

"Cheese curls?" Mitch laughed, the reptile facade dropping away briefly. "Those are expensive birds. Is it a blue and gold?"

"Scarlet. He's beautiful and very smart."

"Is the boss the business associate you purchased those expensive gifts for?" His gaze danced around the café. Sara noticed how his head never moved, just his eyes, as if he were casing the place.

"He keeps Einstein at the office," Sara replied. "Exactly what is it that you do, Mitch?"

His gaze drifted to her face and he smiled ever so slowly. "I'm a venture capitalist." The smile broadened as he added, "I find a venture and I capitalize on it." He chuckled now, lifting his cup in a toast.

She always trusted her instincts and right now she felt tiny electrodes darting across her skin. She was curious what it was about this guy that had her guard up. Her attention was drawn to the window where several doors away Padre Martinez was climbing out of an unmarked car and entering Beckman's.

"I was the one to lock up. I was the last one to leave, Sergeant. My salespeople are honest, hardworking people."

Padre couldn't remember the last time he had heard an employer speak so highly of his employees. Abel Beckman patted his glistening forehead with a monogrammed hankie.

"As I told the investigating officer," Beckman started, "I don't keep the cameras running throughout the day. No need. There's always someone on the floor. All the jewelry cases are kept locked. Tommy sets the recorder at closing time. I dusted that showcase myself, after the staff left." He took another swipe at his face with the hankie. "You'll see it on tape. One minute the ring's there, the next it's gone." Beads of perspiration dotted his upper lip. "I know what this looks like...like I stole the ring myself. I'm sure that's what my insurance company thinks. Never." Now Beckman was stripping off his jacket. "Never has this happened before. Come." He crooked his finger and led Padre down a carpeted hallway to a back office. "The officer this morning took a copy of the tape. I had Tommy make a couple more. I'm sure my lecherous insurance agent will want one."

Padre was surprised at how tidy the office was. The desktop gleamed under the ceiling lights. Cups were washed and sitting upside down next to a coffee maker. Pens were kept in a large cup with a Beckman's logo next to a paperweight in the shape of a diamond.

"Please sit." Beckman stared at the buttons on the VCR. Like a toddler deciphering a block toy for learning shapes, he studied the opening in the VCR and compared it to the size of the tape. Assured it would fit, he tried to push the tape into the slot.

"I think you need to turn it around," Padre said.

"Sorry. Tommy usually handles these new gadgets." Beckman pressed the play button. He started to narrate but Padre held up his hand to silence him.

The one camera in the upper left corner had been strategically placed to focus on the high line items in the showcases and then pan to the front entrance. Padre started to wonder how much dusting he would have to watch until they got to the meat of the tape.

"You are alone at this point?" Padre asked. "All the staff left?"

"Yes." He fumbled with the controls and then gave up.

"It's okay. I can study it better back at the office. How many copies did you make?"

"Take as many as you want. Maybe I'll give them away as Christmas presents."

14

"What do you mean he won't talk to me?" Padre yelled. "How about I just drag the skinny twirp in for possession of stolen goods?"

"Hard to prove. Besides, you know Skizzy breaks out in hives around cops. But he assured me that if he did sell illegal weapons, a sniper's rifle is one he would not have sold to anyone." Dagger added under his breath, "Except me."

Padre walked past the aviary and paused. "What the…" Inside the aviary Sara was seated at a card table eating spaghetti. Einstein sat on a perch next to the table, a lobster bib around his neck and a spaghetti noodle dangling from his beak. The macaw sucked and the noodle whipped around like a frenzied snake, spraying spaghetti sauce on the bib.

Dagger joined him in the doorway. "She pampers him too much."

"Sounds like someone's a little jealous."

"Hardly."

"Only a little more left, Einstein." Sara pushed the plate closer to the bird. "Then hit the shower." Einstein jabbed his beak at the plate and sucked up the last two noodles, whipping a splash of tomato sauce across his back. Einstein eyed the empty plate, then rubbed his beak against her arm. "Maybe tomorrow, if you are good." Sara picked up the plate and bib. "Hi, Padre."

"Einstein eats people food?"

"Of course. He can eat just about everything we eat, within reason." She shoved the door closed with her elbow before traipsing off to the kitchen.

"What did you bring?" Dagger asked.

Padre brought out a file folder from his briefcase. "This is the guy I told you about...Arnosky." He sat down on the couch and spread the papers on the coffee table.

"ARNOLD, ARNOLD," could be heard from the aviary over the sound of water spraying from the shower where Einstein was flapping his wings.

"The guy was a computer whiz. He and his partner, Nate Harding, opened Guardian Security ten years ago. You remember the old Mission Impossible series?"

"Peter Graves, right."

"GUNSMOKE, MATT DILLON," Einstein squawked as he turned several times under the shower.

"That was his brother, Einstein," Dagger said.

"Anyway," Padre continued, "he duplicated what they did on the series. Of course, on the series, Peter Graves would place a photo of a room in front of the camera. That way the security guards would see nothing out of the ordinary while behind the scenes Graves' people were breaking into safety deposit boxes, planting bugs, whatever. Very low tech compared to what they can do now. You get the picture."

Sara folded the card table and carried it out of the aviary. She paused by the couch and glanced at the photos of

Arnosky. After returning the table to the storage closet, she strolled back into the living room carrying the landscaping magazine. She stood behind the couch pretending to read it.

"Harding and Arnosky were geniuses. They installed the systems and controlled the cameras. They robbed museums, safety deposit boxes, home safes. It was the perfect scam. And they got away with it."

Dagger flipped through the pages, scanning Padre's meticulous notes. "Rare coins, art pieces, jewelry from home invasions, cash from safety deposit boxes. If he installed all the security systems, why was it so hard to nail him?"

"No proof. No matter how hard we dug, we couldn't get any concrete proof to take into court. The majority of their customers never had a problem with theft or break-ins." It was an isolated few, and the defense attorney worked her magic with words like *heresay, probable cause*, not to mention *police harassment*." Padre tossed another file folder onto the table. "Arnosky was the brains behind the business. Harding liked to party which ticked off his partner, but he was loyal to the end. Couldn't get Harding to roll over. Died in a car accident a couple weeks before the trial."

Sara walked around the couch, her attention on the photo of Arnosky. She left the magazine folded open on the table, grabbed one of the reports, and sat down on the loveseat.

"The guy's a work of art," Padre continued. "Always one step ahead of us, like he had choreographed the whole damn thing and we were just reading our parts. And that damn smirk of his, like he was saying *you are so damn stupid*. I wanted this guy so bad."

"He was your only suspect?" Sara asked.

"Our Number One suspect. I could feel it in my gut but we couldn't find one shred of evidence." Padre ticked them off on his fingers. "Not one dollar bill with a matching serial number. Not one diamond ring. Not one Monet or Ming vase. No fingerprints. No eyewitnesses. No spit on a coke can, discarded cigarette, flake of dandruff. Nada."

Dagger asked, "What did you finally nail him on?"

"Income tax evasion. Just like Capone. So Arnosky gets to suck on the public trough for five years in a minimum security country club in California. And you know the bend-over-and-grab-your-ankles part of it?" Padre leaned forward and jabbed a finger at the air. "The asshole gets to keep all the money. No paying back taxes to Uncle Sam. Still lives in the high maintenance condo his lawyer kept for him. And the stolen items? Probably sold them on the black market and has that money squirreled away somewhere."

"What did you want Skizzy to do?"

Padre pulled videotapes from the briefcase. "Remember the tape from the ATM shooting?" He walked over to the VCR and shoved in a tape. "Well, we got another one. Beckman's clothing store."

Sara looked up from the file folder. "Guardian Security installed the equipment?"

"Seven years ago." Padre pushed the play button. "The tape confirms that the ten-thousand-dollar ring is sitting on its cushy velvet pillow one minute. Gone the next. Beats the hell out of me how that happened. Naturally the insurance company thinks the owner took it in order to file a false claim. Tape shows no one in the store after Beckman locks up Saturday. No evidence of forced entry."

"What do your experts say?" Dagger asked.

"Other than an inside job? Our lab thinks there's a glitch in the surveillance system. You can see the ring when the camera pans one way. Then you can see it's gone the next. That's why it fits Arnosky to a tee. It's like someone cut and spliced the film. Don't know how or when. It's a puzzle to our lab guys, which is why Chief Wozniak wants me to use an outside source. Your squirrely friend is the first one that came to mind." Padre popped the tape out. "I made you and Skizzy each a copy. Just don't tell anyone where you got them. Maybe you guys can find some flaw in the tapes, something to prove Arnosky is up to his old tricks, that the tapes were manipulated." Padre glanced at the clock on the television set. "How about I take you two out to dinner and you can let me blow off more steam."

"I have a date," Sara replied.

Dagger jerked his head around. "With who?"

She unfolded herself from the loveseat saying, "Your Number One suspect."

"Has the jerk changed much in five years?" Dagger had a clear view of the entrance to Biscayne, a restaurant near the Cedar Point Yacht Club known for its surf and turf.

"See for yourself," Padre said. "He just walked in the door."

Dagger studied Mitch Arnosky. The suit he wore would meet with Sheila's approval, a charcoal gray with a matching shirt and yellow tie. "Where's his Panama hat?" The jacket was boxy, almost as if the shoulders were padded. Mitch didn't look to be a muscular guy. Dagger figured he had at least three inches and twenty-five pounds on the guy.

"Look at him struttin' in here like he doesn't have a care in the world." Padre tossed back bar peanuts with fervor. "Looks like a damn kingpin, mafiosa sonofabitch."

The hostess led Mitch to a table near the fireplace. He stopped and motioned to a table by the window.

Padre opened the menu and grumbled some more. "He's probably ordering filet and I can only afford a burger. Damn, these burgers are twelve dollars."

"Just order a steak, already. I'm buying."

"Steak it is." Padre folded the menu and stared across the bar to the dining room where Mitch was studying the wine list. "Hope Sara knows how fancy schmantzy this place is."

"All I care about is that she has the pin on."

As she entered the restaurant, Padre nudged Dagger with his elbow. "Whoa. Did she stop by the car dealer to have that dress painted on?"

Sara was wearing a mandarin-collared sweater dress in holiday red. From this distance it looked made of angora. Padre was right...it hugged every curve of her body. She didn't just walk, she glided like liquid silver with sure strides, a puzzle to Dagger since the last time she tried wearing three-inch heels she almost fell off them. The dress hit mid-calf with a slit that traveled halfway to China. He noticed she was leaving a gallery of turned heads in her wake.

"Why did I have to make her toss all of her homemade sack dresses?" Dagger took a long pull from the beer bottle. His attention swerved to Mitch who was standing now, holding out a chair for Sara. "The damn guy is practically swallowing her whole with his eyes."

"Look at that shit-eatin' grin of his. If a snake had lips,

its name would be Mitch. I'd keep an eye on him around Sara."

Sara willed her fingers not to play with the rhinestone poinsettia pinned to her dress. Which rhinestone held the microphone and which held the camera she didn't know. At least this high-tech version of audio and visual surveillance was better than having a wire taped under her bra.

"Order anything you want." Mitch smiled at her over the top of the menu.

Sara set the menu down. "Good. I want lobster."

"A woman who knows her mind and speaks it. I love it."

There was no mistaking those reptilian eyes. She had recognized him immediately when Padre whipped out the mug shot. Without even knowing how Mitch committed the crimes, Sara, too, believed that he did them.

"How about wine?" Mitch asked.

Sara shook her head. "Just water is fine." Sara tried to avoid looking around the room in search of Dagger and Padre. Dagger had said they would find an inconspicuous spot which was probably the bar.

"Health fanatic. I can tell you take excellent care of your body. You have a certain shine to your hair that's rare. Must be the water."

"Maybe that's the kind of business to be in…bottled water." She felt like a specimen under a microscope the way his eyes bore into her.

"Maybe my fair lady isn't old enough to drink." He folded the menu closed and set it to one side.

"Which makes the fair lady question why a man of obvious means and availability would bother with someone who isn't of an age closer to his."

"Damn, she's good," Dagger said as he leaned closer to Padre.

"What, what did she say?"

"I don't know why you don't wear the ear piece." Dagger repeated what he had heard thus far.

"You know I can't bug this guy without a court order."

The waitress reached between them and placed two salads on the bar. The receptor on the bar between them was the size of a cell phone. Sara and Mitch could be seen on the video screen. Dagger pressed the mute button and the taped conversation appeared across the bottom of the screen.

"Can't stand looking at that punk's smiling face," Padre mumbled around a forkful of lettuce. "Never raises his voice, never a hint of being agitated or irritated or on the defensive. He had the jury eating out of his hand."

"Obviously not every juror. They did find him guilty."

"You never did tell me what type of research your boss does," Mitch said.

"Whatever anyone wants." Sara leaned forward and whispered, "He makes peoples' problems disappear."

"Really?" He smiled slowly and cocked his head in curious interest. "You mean like getting rid of cheating husbands or thieving partners?"

Sara laughed. "No, nothing like that. More like getting bill collectors off your back, conducting background checks on companies, a lot of research mainly done on the computer. He rarely leaves the office."

"That's pretty evasive. And what is it you do for him?"

"I answer the phones." She laced her comment with disdain in her voice.

He leaned back in his chair and studied her for a few moments. "Seems he's wasting your talents."

"He's pretty cheap. Only pays me seven dollars an hour."

Dagger just about choked on his beer. "Seven dollars?"

Padre laughed and pointed at the words on the screen. "Love that little toy of yours."

"Why don't you quit?"

Sara shrugged. "I'd miss Einstein."

"Go work at the zoo. They've got lots of macaws."

"I tried that. They move you around. One day aviary, the next reptile. I hate snakes."

"At seven dollars an hour, I'm surprised you bought him such expensive Christmas gifts."

"I never said the gifts were for him. I said they were for a business associate."

"Expensive gifts?" Dagger said with surprise.

Padre said, "And I bet you haven't bought her anything."

"I've been busy. Besides, how was I to know she was coming home?"

The waitress returned and deposited their dinners on the bar. They had each ordered a filet smothered with mushrooms.

"I find you fascinating, Sara." Mitch swirled the ice in his glass. "But contradicting. You make near poverty wages, spend hundreds on Christmas gifts," he reached over, grabbed her arm and touched the price tag still attached to her dress and tucked inside the sleeve, "yet you deny yourself."

She studied the price tag she had purposely left on the dress. "I like nice things. I just have to return it tomorrow."

He rested his hand on hers, saying, "You deserve nice things."

"Oh, she's really good. I forgot how damn good she was." Dagger spooned sour cream onto the baked potato.

"Did she really disappear for two months or did you send her off to P.I. finishing school?"

"She's got good instincts. Mitch set off some bad vibes when she met him at Beckman's. She noticed he made a point of seeing her name and phone number on the sales slip."

"A guy would be blind not to notice Sara. If every man who wanted her name and number were arrested, there wouldn't be enough jails."

"Still, Sara was suspicious, especially since the theft of the ring occurred after Mitch strolled into the place. I would think you would be jumping for joy."

"I'll jump for joy when Sara gets him to admit to everything."

Dagger's cell phone rang. "Damn." He pulled the phone from his pocket and checked the screen for Caller I.D. "Skizzy has terrible timing."

"What about you?" Sara asked. "What kind of ventures do you capitalize on?"

"Anything and everything."

"Now who's being evasive?"

A busboy appeared carrying a tray, trailed by their waitress. She set their plates on the table along with a silver cup containing hot butter for the lobster.

"Did you want a lobster bib?" the waitress asked, holding the bib that looked the size of a tablecloth.

Sara immediately assessed how the bib would conceal the audio and video bugs. "No, thanks." The waitress removed the tail from the shell. After she left, Sara asked Mitch, "Have you always lived in Cedar Point?"

Mitch did that half smile of his while slicing into his filet. The steak was rare and swam in a puddle of red juices. He washed down a bite with a healthy dose of martini before responding. Sara winced at the sight of the bloody puddle.

"I left town for a while. Lived in California for a few years." He seemed to speak to the steak all the while smiling as if there were some private joke he wasn't sharing.

"California. Right," Padre spit out. "Golfing at a damn country club prison."

"You're going to get heartburn," Dagger whispered.

This time Padre's cell phone rang. "Damn. Can't we have one uninterrupted dinner?" He checked the display. "It's dispatch. Great." He pulled up the antenna and answered the call. "This better be good." After listening for a few seconds, Padre said, "Yeah, yeah. The body isn't going anywhere. Give me a few minutes."

Dagger's phone rang again. "Skizzy must be frantic about something." He pulled out the listening device and pressed the phone to his ear. "Whoa, slow down." Dagger pressed a finger to his ear to cut down the surrounding noise. "Okay, hold on. I'm on my way." He folded the phone and shoved it in his pocket.

"Now we're both leaving Sara alone with that vulture."

"Trust me," Dagger said. "She can handle herself. And she has a recorder that will pick up what I can't, since I'm taking my toy with me." He picked up the monitor from the bar. "What was your call about?"

"Guy walking his dog by Brighton Pond saw the hood of a car in the water. Looks like there might be a couple people in it."

15

Luther waved Padre over to a corner of the shore not occupied by official vehicles. "Sorry to interrupt your dinner."

"I was done eating anyway and I hope I don't give it back up."

"Let's go sit in my wagon while they tow the car out." They climbed into Luther's station wagon and he turned the key to crank on the heat. "Divers saw two victims, a man and a woman. They looked to be in their sixties, the divers said. Maybe they took a wrong turn. Don't know."

Floodlights had been set up around the peripheral area. Padre could see the hood and a portion of the back windows jutting from the water. Brighton Pond was used for boating and fishing in the summer but it was too murky for swimming. Residents had nearby Lake Michigan for that.

"They say how long the car might have been down there?"

Luther shook his head. "Water's too dark, the bodies are pretty well preserved in the frigid water. I'll know more when I get a look-see." He turned the overhead light on and read from his notes. "The responding officer pulled up the plate info from his mobile data terminal. The car is registered to a Doctor Seymour Cohen."

"Cohen? I believe a neighbor filed a missing persons report on them."

"Must be one and the same. He and his wife, who we assume to be the passenger in the vehicle, live at eighteen-forty-three Prescott Drive. According to the Department of Motor Vehicles, Doctor Cohen is sixty-eight, which, according to the divers, fits pretty close to the age and description of the victim."

The tow truck coughed and sputtered as the front wheels clawed for traction on the frozen ground. Finally, it found gravel and lurched forward, dragging with it a late model green Lincoln Town Car. Once free of its watery tomb, the car was quickly surrounded by technicians. The yellow crime scene tape fluttered in the breeze.

"No skid marks," Padre pointed out as he viewed the area from the warmth of Luther's front seat. "No bashed-in guard rails or signs he was run off the road. Maybe the driver had a heart attack."

"Maybe the poor bastard had some terminal disease and the wife couldn't live without him. Suicide pact."

They were silent for a while as the techs scoured the area. Padre's gaze drifted to the ball of light hovering over the treetops. It was almost a full moon. It was tough to concentrate on current cases when his mind was still reeling from the Paul Addison case. How had it really affected Sara? She looked fine, physically, but she was different in a way. That fragility and innocence she had exuded before was gone. Maybe being away and on her own for two months had matured her. Or maybe the harsh reality that there were people who made up their own rules in life had toughened her to the real world.

Luther gave his arm a nudge. "Techs are done. Are you ready?"

"Yeah. Maybe I'll be home in time for the news."

"What is the ..." Dagger never finished. Skizzy grabbed a handful of leather and pulled Dagger inside the pawn shop.

"Shhhhhh." He held several fingers to his lips and slowly scanned the sidewalks and streets through the splayed blinds. "Downstairs, quick," Skizzy whispered. He turned and shoved Dagger toward the back room.

Skizzy scrambled down the stairs like a life-sized crab, bracing his arms against the wall and railing. "Quick, quick."

Dagger shrugged out of his coat and tossed it over a chair. "Do you know how late it is?" He eyed his friend with the intensity of a scientist analyzing a new discovery. Skizzy's hair stood on end like a wiry halo. His eyes seemed tethered on tight bungee cords, able to zip back into his head at a moment's notice. And he paced in a tight circle in front of his mainframe.

"They know. They found me. I don't know how...still trying to figure that out. I just noticed it this afternoon and confirmed it right before I called you."

"Okay." Dagger kept his voice calm and even. No sense agitating the already agitated. "Why don't you have a seat and tell me what it is you noticed." Dagger dragged a chair next to the computer.

Skizzy sank onto the chair behind the keyboard. One hand pulled at tufts of hair above his ear, twisting and twirling strands around his fingers. He took a deep breath.

His hands flew to his mouth, then hovered over the keyboard, not sure where to land.

"Slow, Skizzy. Calm and slow."

"Okay, okay." He took another deep breath. "Once a week I change my route, you know, the relaying and spoofing."

"Layman's terminology, Skizzy."

"Okay, okay. I mask my IP address so it can't be traced. In relaying, I'm using a chain of servers so my route is more convoluted and indirect. No one knows where I'm located. If someone tries to trace my signal back to me, it takes them forever because my signal is zig-zagging throughout the globe, so you can see how hard it would be to find me."

Dagger nodded, even though he knew Skizzy could scale down the techno-babble even more.

"Anyway," Skizzy continued, "the last relay was a ranger station in a Scandinavian country. Then there was a laboratory in New Zealand. Well, when something like that happens, I've programmed my computer to shutdown and return to a default route but I didn't notice until an hour ago that I was running my default route."

Dagger's head was swirling. "Bottom line, Skizzy."

Skizzy brought out the evening paper and pointed at a story on Page 23. "The story says lightning struck the ranger station, even though there wasn't a storm. Freak of nature they call it. Well, naturally, I don't believe in freaks of nature. There's always a reason."

"Maybe another hacker who has met his match decided to show you how good he is."

"No, no." Skizzy's fingers flew across the keyboard. Dagger rolled his seat closer to the monitor. "Look." Skizzy pointed at the screen. "I hacked into the satellite relay from Big Brother. Watch. I'll even put it in slow-mo for you." On the screen a brief stream of light bolted from the sky followed by a burst of fire. "That was no lightning bolt. It went straight. You saw that, right?" Dagger nodded. "Same thing in New Zealand. Watch." Skizzy tapped a few more keys. "This multiple relay just happens to bypass through the Gemini Laboratory in New Zealand." In slow motion, an identical bolt of light fired from the sky, incinerating the tower at the laboratory.

"That was what? A laser?" Dagger leaned over and punched a few of the keys. "Where did it originate?"

"Another satellite." Skizzy's voice changed. It no longer had that edge of insanity. It was quite sane, a little sinister. "Someone's trying to find me."

"Big Brother already knows you exist, Skizzy. The question is, why now? What prompted someone to trace you? Has to be another hacker."

"No, not another hacker. No one is that good."

"Come on, Skizzy. There are high school kids who can send a virus through the network to foul up the most secure systems."

"This is different. These people knew the minute I broke through their firewall." He stood and paced a tight circle behind his chair, his arms wrapped tightly around his rail-thin body. "They won't stop. What if they discover my default? What if they already traced it back to me?"

"Skizzy." He grabbed a bony elbow and steered his friend back to the chair. "Maybe what you need to do is concentrate on finding out what prompted the attack. Think. What were you working on?"

"Nothing important."

"Think."

Skizzy's fingers plunged into his scalp, kneading and twirling his hair. More hair was out of the ponytail than in. His body started to rock. "I can't think," he mumbled.

"What was the last thing you were working on? Did someone give you a job to do?"

Skizzy shook his head. "No one but you."

"Me? I didn't ask you to check on anything."

"Girlie."

"Sara?"

Skizzy nodded. "She asked me to check on a company called BettaTec."

Sara hung up her coat and checked the time on the microwave. Eleven o'clock. Not wanting Mitch to know where she lived, she had purposely insisted on driving herself. As she moved to the living room, she fumbled through her purse for the tape recorder, then unfastened the pin from the dress collar. Out of the corner of her eye she saw Dagger sitting in the dark, a stream of dim light dancing through the pass-through and across the couch where he sat.

"He was pretty much guarded most of the night. I don't know at what point you and Padre left, but here's the tape." She set the recorder and the pin on his desk.

"Have a seat, Sara."

There was a certain sound in his voice, or maybe the way he was sitting in darkness, that gave his words an eerie tone.

"He didn't touch me, pops." Sara started to climb the stairs.

"Sit down, Sara." He enunciated each word slowly.

Sara didn't like the feeling washing over her—anger, distrust, danger. Even her two-month absence couldn't produce this reaction from Dagger. She didn't like the look in his eyes as she approached. She slowly lowered herself onto the loveseat.

Dagger uncrossed his legs and leaned forward, forearms on his knees. Tape was wrapped around both hands and perspiration drenched his sleeveless sweatshirt and dripped from his hair. His eyes were dark and feral. Sara flinched at the sound of his voice.

"I told you to let it go, Sara. But you disobeyed me."

She blinked in confusion. "What are you talking about?"

Then Dagger told her about Skizzy's attempt to penetrate the firewall at BettaTec and the squirrely guy's subsequent paranoid hysteria. "I told you to let it go, Sara. Instead you involved Skizzy."

"You wouldn't answer my questions."

"For a reason." His voice rose and he stole a quick glance toward the aviary. "These are dangerous people. Skizzy tried hacking into their system and was detected."

"You said his computer identified the interruption and switched to the default."

Dagger pounded his fists on his knees as he bolted from the couch. "One ranger station and a laboratory were incinerated. Lucky for you there wasn't anyone in them at the time."

"What?" Her fingers gripped the cushions as she digested the chain of events that started with one word—BettaTec.

"People could have been killed. I can't imagine the

destruction if Skizzy's computer hadn't detected the pene-
tration."

"But how?"

"Their computers picked up Skizzy's presence and..."

"From the satellite," Sara gasped, remembering the map
with the blinking lights. "The blinking lights are satellites."

"It's your fault. You shouldn't have gotten involved."

"Don't lay this at my feet." Sara stood, her hands balled
into tight fists. "If you had only told me..."

"NO. Keeping the information from you is the only way
to keep you safe."

"I can take care of myself."

"Not from them," Dagger yelled.

"Who is them?" she yelled back.

But Dagger opened the front door and charged across
the yard to the garage.

Sara stood by the door and watched as he entered the lit
garage. She soon heard the thumping of the punching bag.
Dagger was letting loose his anger. Forget tai chi. His anger
was beyond the help of deep breathing.

16

The next morning Dagger was thumbing through one of the landscape magazines on the coffee table when Sara padded down the stairs.

"Sara." He tossed the magazine down. "We need to talk."

She hesitated, her gaze dropping to his knuckles. They looked battered and bruised. She looked down at her own knuckles raw from her nervous habit of chewing on them the way most people chew on their nails.

"We're going to play a game."

She rolled her eyes as if to say *I'm a little too old for games.*

"We're playing Twenty Questions."

There was caution in her smile as she took a seat on the couch, tucking one leg under her. "Twenty?"

"Figure of speech. I'm not that generous but we can do five. We each get five questions to ask."

"Me first?"

"Ask away." Dagger crossed one ankle over his knee and waited. Her first question didn't take long.

"Where were you born?"

"Only yes or no answers." Dagger needed to set some ground rules fast.

"Were you born in the States?"

"Yes." Dagger thought he would start out with the easy questions. He'd had all night to think of his five. "Do you have any brothers and sisters?"

"No." Sara stared at him, brows hunched in thought, as she searched his features for clues. "Did you work abroad?"

Dagger had anticipated this question. After all, she had seen the BettaTec map and the various lighted dots in foreign countries. "Yes." He studied her face, youthful and innocent in the light of day. Last night she was a paragon of wisdom and sophistication. The contradiction sometimes made his head spin.

"Your turn," Sara prodded.

"When I take a phone call, can you hear both sides of the conversation?" Dagger had always been curious about her enhanced hearing, but she had never let on that she was eavesdropping.

Sara's right knuckle found its way to her mouth but she pulled it away and clasped her hands in her lap. "I don't mean to…"

"Yes or no answer." Dagger flashed a perfect *gotcha* smile.

"Yes. But I don't mean to."

That was something Dagger hadn't considered. His brain raced to remember prior phone conversations, especially emotional ones with Sheila when they were still dating.

"Did you work for BettaTec?" Sara asked.

Dagger had expected this question. There wasn't any need to avoid it or lie. "Yes." Having stipulated yes or no responses, he was sure he could satisfy her curiosity yet keep her from asking for more detail than he was willing to give. He asked, "If you could change the way you are, would you?"

Sara's gaze slowly dropped and her brows scrunched in thought. Dagger could tell she had not expected the question. And the long silence told him she was doing some soul-searching.

"No," Sara replied. Her next question came quickly, and was cloaked in a glare of curiosity that made him uneasy. "Is your real name Chase Dagger?"

Dagger just stared at her. He didn't blink or grimace, just stared. This question had come out of left field and he wondered why she would ask it. "Yes."

She cocked her head and narrowed her eyes in doubt. Dagger pulled out his wallet and flashed his driver's license.

"Skizzy can make a dozen aliases. How do I know that's the right one?"

"Is that another question?"

"No. My next one is whether BettaTec worked for the government."

"You're going out of turn but that answer is also no." He smiled now, thoroughly amused that in her quest for information she had used up all five questions. "You're out of ammo." He settled back with arms stretched out across the back of the couch. "And I have two more." His smile slowly faded and her look changed from disappointment to apprehension.

Dagger's left hand moved to a manila folder on the loveseat next to him. He flipped it open. In a tone that sounded like a lawyer's doing a cross-examination, he asked, "Did you kill your parents?"

Her breath seemed to catch in her throat and she whispered, "I don't like this game anymore." Sara bounded off the couch to the plate glass windows, arms folded, anger rising like steam.

Dagger knew Sara's grandparents had moved her around a lot. He also knew there could be no witnesses, that the wolf would kill to keep Sara's secret. Dagger was safe because he had saved the wolf, as had Ada. But what if Sara's parents had witnessed her shape-shifting? Was that the real reason they had died?

He picked up a piece of paper and went to stand next to her. The newspaper article was from a small town in northern Montana. Sara's gaze flicked to the headline, which read "Fire Kills Couple — Hate Crime to Blame." The article was from thirteen years ago. After a passing glance, she carefully turned her attention to the view outside the windows. But Dagger could see her hands clasped tightly and her bottom lip quiver.

He held the article up and read aloud.

An angry mob descended on the home of Michael and Jeanine Gallagos late Friday evening in Medicine Lake, a small town outside of the Fort Peck Indian Reservation.

"That makes you Assiniboine, right? Or maybe Sioux?" Sara had always been vague in the past whenever anyone had asked of her ancestry. Dagger thought the Assiniboine were originally from Saskatchewan, Canada, and northeastern Montana. That fit with the other bits of her past he knew, and he had heard that they and some Sioux bands had been at Fort Peck. He thought it was a pretty good guess.

"Mixed blood."

Dagger examined yet again the almond shape of Sara's eyes with their turquoise color. Not what white men expect to see in Indian maidens. "Must have been hard to fit in."

She remained silent so Dagger continued reading.

Authorities could ascertain no apparent reason for the attack other than a hate crime against a Native American family. But Native Americans from the nearby Fort Peck Reservation believe the town had been agitated by rumors that either Michael or Jeannine Gallagos was a manitou, a mythical being with the ability to shift into animal forms. It was estimated that nearly five hundred residents took part in the attack. The body of their six-year-old daughter, Sara, was never found. Although reports say the remains of the bodies looked as if they had been mauled, the medical examiner was unsure whether the intense heat...

"That's enough," Sara said in a quiet voice.

Leaning close, he whispered, "Sometimes memories are just too painful to recall. Sometimes things beyond your control occur that constantly remind you of those memories." Sara gave a perceptible nod. His whisper was even softer this time as he edged closer. "Is that why you're afraid of crowds, Sara?" He saw her swallow and wrap her arms tightly around her body. Once he found the article, he was sure that event was the root of her phobia. Each time she was around too many people, she was probably reminded of when she was six, when the angry crowds pressed closer, driving her and her parents back into their home where they were trapped. He imagined a frightened girl, small enough that even a crowd of forty would seem like a thousand.

"I don't remember much of what happened. Sometimes I thought I was dreaming. You know how sometimes you fly in your dreams. I didn't know it was actually happening so I paid no attention that people might be watching. But the wolf knew. I would wake up in my bed naked, the sheets bloody. All my parents tried to do was protect me from people who didn't understand."

Tears fell in tiny rivulets and she leaned against the window frame as though needing support. "There were so many people." Her voice quivered, the emotions of that day still clear in her mind. "It was my father they wanted. They thought he was the one who was doing the killing. My mother told me to run but there were people trying to break in through the back door. The only place for me to go was up to the attic. I smelled the gasoline long before the smoke started rising. There was just one window in the attic. I didn't even have to think about it. Just shifted and hid out in the forest. It was a safe place to be, in the trees. I don't know how long I stayed there, but I eventually found my grandmother on the reservation. She'd heard about the fire and thought I died with my parents. You could imagine her shock when she started to hear my voice in her head." Sara blinked causing another rivulet of tears to descend. As she thought of Ada, Sara managed a brief smile. "She thought our ancestors were talking to her."

"It hurts when people go behind your back digging up information," Dagger said as he pressed a hand against the window frame.

She gave another perceptible nod, then turned and looked up into his face. "I can do more than hear your phone conversations, Dagger. I can sense fear, anger, uncontrollable rage in people. The beating of lovers' hearts as they spot each other from across a room. I sense the same beating of Sheila's heart when she sees you, but your heart is cold around her. And I also sense a frightening reaction in you whenever I mention BettaTec."

Dagger reached out and traced her jaw line with his fingers, erased a tear from the corner of her eye with his thumb. His hand moved to cup her face and he stared into her eyes for a telltale flinch. There was a time he couldn't come near her, she had been that afraid of people. But the fear he saw in her eyes today wasn't a fear of him. Sara was afraid *for* him. This made the answer to his fifth question even more important.

"Would you kill for me, Sara?" He watched her eyes carefully because the speed and truthfulness of her response was the key.

"Yes," she replied immediately.

He believed her.

17

"It's been a long time, Sergeant Martinez. You've lost a few more hairs."

Padre poured himself a cup of coffee and sipped it as he prowled the interview room.

"I'm sure there is an excellent reason why I've been dragged out of bed so early in the morning." Mitch pulled a chair out and slinked into a comfortable position.

"How nice of you to cooperate, Mr. Arnosky."

"I aim to please Cedar Point's Finest. I expected no less than to be in your cross-hairs whenever some little old lady splits a hangnail."

"You've been out for three months, Mitch. What have you been doing with yourself?"

Mitch rocked back on the legs of the chair, hands clasped across his stomach. A hint of a smile played across his lips but it was his eyes that mocked, crinkling at the corners and blinking lazily, like a man wrested from a two-day nap.

"I enjoyed the sunny beaches of California for several weeks. Did you know the sun shines ninety-eight percent of the time? And women wear nothing more than dental floss on the beach."

"It's not like you were doing hard time, Mitch."

Mitch smiled at that, full-lipped this time, thoroughly amused.

"Thought for sure you'd go to the Cayman Islands to visit all your money." Padre knew Mitch had made a reasonable profit from his computer business, for which he had neglected to pay taxes. But Padre also knew the jewelry and other valuables Mitch was suspected of stealing probably made the man a millionaire.

"I had a good business going, Detective. I've paid my dues to society. So why are you busting my ass?"

Padre stopped his prowling and took a seat, pushing the chair back until it touched the wall. "Where were you last Thursday night?"

Mitch dropped his gaze to the cup cradled in Padre's hands. "Got anymore of that?"

"No. Where were you last Thursday night?"

"My. You've lost your manners, Padre."

"It's Sergeant Martinez, and answer the question."

Mitch's gaze swung up to the spot over Padre's shoulder, the wall with the two-way mirror. "Let's see." He stretched like a cat, clasping his hands behind his head. "Last Thursday. I had dinner out, Juniper's, I believe. Had a steak with garlic mashed potatoes." He paused and cocked his head. "Not as good as the prison food mind you." The smirk played across his face. "Let's see, what else. I had two beers and was home by nine o'clock. Anything else you want to know? Oh," he added, "and sorry, no witnesses after the restaurant. I went home alone and I listened to some classical music."

"What about Saturday night?"

"My, my, Sergeant. You are really taxing my brain here."

Padre finished his coffee and pushed the cup aside. He wanted to reach across the table and wrap his fingers around Mitch's neck.

"But it's such a huge brain, Mitch, to match your ego. I bet you know exactly where you were." Padre grinned and hoped it didn't look as forced as it felt.

"I did some Christmas shopping."

"For me, *mi amigo*? You shouldn't have." Padre's smile faded. "Who could you have shopped for, Mitch? Your partner is dead. You don't have any living relatives."

"For me, of course."

"Where did you shop?"

"All over."

"Did you happen to shop at Beckman's?"

"That was Saturday. I had my eye on a cashmere sweater and a gorgeous young woman who was shopping there."

"Not on jewelry, like a ten-thousand-dollar ring?"

"I'm not a ring man." His face grew serious, like a snake shedding its happy face. "Cut to the chase, Sergeant. What are you accusing me of?"

"There was a shooting at the ATM at Sheffield Trust and Savings Thursday night."

"I read about that. A fireman was shot."

"Then the ring was stolen on Saturday night. In both instances, Guardian Security equipment had been in use, equipment you had installed."

"And, what? The film was fuzzy?"

Padre glared across the table. Mitch hadn't changed

much. Prison changes everyone. Whether it shows up in weight loss, sallow complexion, bitter attitude, circles under the eyes from lack of sleep. If anything, Mitch may as well have returned from a cruise. He looked well-rested and physically in great shape. Padre couldn't detect one strand of gray hair on the guy's head.

"There seem to be computer glitches."

"I only installed the computers. I didn't maintain them."

"But you did install them."

Mitch blinked lazily and sank back against the seat. His sigh was loud and drawn out. "Are we back to this again, Sergeant? Are you still trying to accuse me of somehow sabotaging the cameras while I kill, maim, and pilfer? You need a life or maybe a different line of work." He stood and shoved the chair back with the grace of a man helping to seat a woman in a restaurant. "If we are done here, I have things to do. And next time, I bring my lawyer."

"I'll be in touch," Padre called out. He watched the door close and shook his head. "I want that search warrant," he said to the empty room but speaking to Chief Wozniak who was watching from behind the mirror.

"We're working on it," the chief said as he entered. "Go slow on this one." He hefted one sizable cheek onto the table. "Tell me about the vics from last night."

"They were our missing couple, Ruth and Seymour Cohen. According to the neighbors the Cohens were quiet, enjoying retirement, a loving couple. No hint of squabbles, no raised voices coming from the house. Last time the neighbors saw them was a week ago Monday. The Fentons to the north say Seymour rolled his garbage to the curb at eight o'clock. That's how they know it was a Monday. It was also Ruth's monthly bridge club meeting at the home of Karen Vogel. Mrs. Vogel says Ruth left around nine-thirty. Seymour called a little after eleven looking for his wife."

"Could have been a cover."

Padre nodded. "That crossed my mind." He motioned for Wozniak to follow him as he ambled back to his office. "Luther will run some tox reports, see if the old man was drunk. The car has been towed into the garage and I'll have the tech reports soon." He shuffled papers into neat piles before taking a seat.

Wozniak braced his body against the doorjamb. "What about the house?"

Padre said, "I'm on my way right after I talk to Luther. I took a look at the car. Doesn't look like it was hit from behind or that the brake line had been cut. No suicide letter in the car but maybe there's one in the house or on his computer, if he uses one."

"What about kids or neighbors with keys to the house?"

"According to the Fentons, neither the son in New Jersey nor the neighbors has keys. Even the cleaning woman doesn't have keys."

Wozniak rapped his thick knuckles against the wall. "Keep me posted."

Luther stood between the two examining tables with a clipboard in his hands. Seymour was laid out on one table, Ruth on the other.

"What?" Padre stared at the bodies. "No autopsy?"

"Can't," Luther replied with a sigh. "They are Orthodox Jews. They don't allow autopsies. And I have to release the bodies immediately."

"That's just wonderful." Padre tapped his notepad against the palm of his hand. "What can you tell me?"

Luther pulled the sheet down to Seymour's waist. "Cold water slowed the decomposition rate. Neither victim was wearing a seat belt. No bullet wounds or lacerations. There is a bruise on the husband's head. Might have hit the steering wheel although it doesn't appear the car hit the water at a noticeable speed. It was almost like it rolled in."

"So he could have been struck with a blunt object?"

"Possible. It's possible he drowned but I think she might have been dead before she hit the water. Possibly a heart attack."

"How long had they been in the water?"

The M.E. stared at Padre's notepad and smiled. "Bet you got it down to the hour and you are just testing me." Luther pulled the sheet up to Ruth Cohen's thighs. "Class is in." He pointed at the feet, which were dainty but distorted with bunions and nodules. "The skin has not separated from the underlying tissues, which usually occurs five to six days under normal temperatures." He pulled the sheet away from the side of her body and held up one of her hands. "The nails on the hands and feet have not separated. Body has not been through the typical swelling and there wasn't much damage done to the tissue when removing the body. Given the temperatures, the shady area of the pond where the sun wouldn't change that temperature drastically, I'd say they died eight days ago between ten and midnight."

"Damn." Padre checked his notes with a shake of his head. "That's amazing. How the hell did you do that?"

"Excellent training." He straightened the sheet on Seymour. "Mensa I.Q." Then the sheet on Ruth. "And my aunt belongs to the same bridge club as Ruth."

"Aw, jeez." Padre turned a three-sixty, notepad and pen tossed into the air. "There goes your reputation."

"And before you ask, my aunt says the Cohens were a perfect couple, never argued except on which landscaping service to use. Both were in good health so that rules out double suicide or murder-suicide."

"He could have had a seizure or something," Padre said, retrieving his notepad and pen. "Could have had a stroke at the wheel, maybe tried to pull over but passed out."

"Let's face it, that road is not a direct route to their home and they aren't at an age to park in Lover's Lane. Besides, maybe one person might not use a seat belt, but both?"

"Now who's playing homicide detective?"

Luther smiled at the detective and crooked his finger. "Can't do an autopsy but I do have all six of my senses. Follow me." Luther pressed his hands on the sides of Ruth's face and bent down, took a whiff. "Smell," he told Padre.

Padre hesitated, looked at Luther as if he were nuts, then bent over and inhaled. "Garlic? What did she eat, a bottle of it?"

"Can't check stomach contents but..."

"Whoa, wait." He cocked his head and sifted through his brain file. "Arsenic?"

"That would be my guess." He crooked his finger again and motioned for Padre to follow after instructing an assistant to place the Cohens back in storage. Luther led Padre into the lab. "I did take hair and nail samples." He punched a few keys on the computer, then pointed at the monitor. "If she had been poisoned over a long period of time, it would have shown up. If it was recent, I'll need to do another test."

"So now we are back to murder-suicide."

"There are some things women won't tell even their closest friends. So maybe a search of the house might turn up a suicide note. Maybe they were in debt up to their dentures."

The number of cars parked in the driveway was Padre's first hint that he had a welcoming committee. He pushed the door open and stood with fists jammed onto his hips.

"What the hell is going on?"

A parade of black suits trailed through the house oblivious to his question.

"Hey!" Padre tried again, holding up his shield. "Sergeant Jerry Martinez, Cedar Point P.D. How did you get in here?"

They were like ants, disappearing through a doorway and coming back with goodies in their hands. One was carrying a computer.

"Hey." Padre hustled to block the man's way. "You aren't going anywhere with that." He pulled his Sig Sauer and aimed it at the man, who paused long enough to gaze briefly at Padre, then the gun, then proceeded to the front door. Padre beat him to it and slammed it shut, rattling the pictures on the wall and bringing the other ants in black suits to a halt.

"Now, before I fire several holes into the ceiling, and lord only knows if they will bounce back at you, I want everyone out. I'm investigating the death of Ruth and Seymour Cohen and you are disturbing possible evidence."

A bald man weaved his way between the suits and made a signal with his hand. His followers set whatever they were carrying on the ground. Baldy reached into his pocket.

"Hold it." Padre turned his gun on him. "Slow and easy."

"Just getting my I.D."

A black man in an equally dark suit emerged from a hallway and reached into his pocket.

"Agent Jack Calley, FBI," Baldy said.

"Mason Jones, CIA," the black man said.

A tall man in full military garb with more medals than Padre had ever seen pulled up behind Calley and nodded. "DOD," was all he said.

"Department of Defense? What the…" Padre holstered his gun. "Okay, Lucy. You gotta lotta 'splaining to do."

Each man looked around the room and nodded, at which time all the suits picked up their boxes and computers and headed toward the door.

"Hey." Padre looked at the three men in charge. It was then he noticed a fourth person was sitting in a chair in the corner. At first, all he saw were shoes and slacks. Then the slacks straightened and she emerged from the chair. She was striking in her pin-striped power suit. Dark hair cut short, skin like rich caramel. Her mouth smiled but her eyes were piercing.

"We're done here," she announced.

"Done?" Padre watched the last of the ants leave. "I don't suppose anyone found a suicide note or anything else I should know about?"

"No," she replied simply, as she followed the men out of the house. No one needed to introduce him to Carmella Estrada, the president's National Security Adviser.

The man in military garb handed Padre his business card. "But it WAS a murder-suicide. Right, Sergeant Martinez?" He held his gaze for several seconds before walking out of the house.

Padre shoved the door closed, then studied the name on the business card—General William J. Lorenz. "Great," he huffed, shoving the card into his pocket. The living room had not suffered the wrath of their search and destroy mission. If they had been searching for something, they were neat about it. Cushions weren't pulled out, drawers weren't left open. But then, this didn't seem to be the room they were interested in.

He made his way down the hallway. The kitchen was clean, dishwasher filled and run through a wash cycle. Several take-out cups sat on the counter. Padre touched a half-filled cup. It felt cold. The suits had been here awhile, more than an hour.

The study was a different story. The bookcase was empty, drawers were turned upside down but the contents weren't anywhere to be seen. The desk was devoid of its computer equipment. All that was left seemed to be the framed degrees on the wall. Doctor Seymour Cohen had been a physicist and systems design engineer.

He continued down the hall, past the bedrooms, bathrooms, and an exercise room to what looked like a sewing room. The last room was a laundry room. Padre returned to the study and took a closer look. The suits had boxed up and taken every piece of paper in the place. But Padre recalled neighbors saying that Cohen was retired. If that were true, why on earth would they want Cohen's equipment and papers?

Padre stepped further into the room, kicking something hard and square. On the wall next to the bookcase was what was left of a keypad. There was also a vertical crack in the wall with gouges about waist high.

"You boys didn't know the code so you pried it off."
Padre dug his fingers into the gouge and pulled. The wall
came away easily to reveal a large room with empty shelves,
empty walls, empty tables. It was a wonder the stark white
tiles were still on the floor and the overhead work lights
hadn't been removed.

"What on earth kind of experiments did you do here,
Doc?" Padre asked the empty room.

"Just tell me good news. If it's bad, go bother someone
else." His fingers flickered in a move-along motion.

"Oh, you're gonna like this." Kiley placed a report on
Padre's desk and pointed a chubby finger at the image.
"That is a print we pulled off the hood of the Cohen vehicle." He wiggled his eyebrows up and down. "Ready?"
Kiley looked like Baby Huey had jumped off the comic
pages. He was pink and pudgy with a wisp of hair above his
forehead. And his eyes were huge, as though in perpetual
awe of everything around him.

"What have you got?" Wozniak lumbered into the room
and hovered over the tech's bulk. The scent of chemicals and
cough drops floated around the tech like a cloud of gnats.

"Prints off the Cohen car," Kiley replied.

"And you got a match?" Wozniak sounded hopeful.
Padre was doubtful.

"Do we ever." Kiley placed another report next to the
first one. "Perfect match."

The two men crowded around Kiley's index finger. The
print he was pointing to belonged to Mitch Arnosky.

18

Chief Wozniak's broad face pinched as he looked at the report. "You're sure there's no mistake?" He glared at Kiley.

"As sure as you are that I'm the best tech in Cedar Point." Kiley grinned. It wasn't an arrogant bluster. Kiley prided himself on doing his best.

"Slow, need I repeat that four-letter word," Wozniak cautioned Padre.

"Molasses is my middle name."

"Kiley," Wozniak said, "get your techs over to the Cohen house and have them give it a thorough going over."

"Already on it. To their credit, the Alphabet Boys wore gloves so they shouldn't have left a herd of prints." Kiley gave a wave and left the office.

"What about the tapes from the ATM and Beckman's, Padre?"

"Haven't heard from the lab yet."

"And your outside source?"

"I'll check this afternoon. Can't be that difficult to detect if someone tampered with the tapes." Padre leaned back with a moan and covered his face with his hands. "Surveillance." He stared at the chief. "The Alphabet Boys took Cohen's security equipment. I just wonder if it was installed by Guardian Security."

"Wouldn't he have a receipt at the house?"

"Gone. Everything boxed up and off to wherever the government boys take these things."

"Check court documents. Six years ago when Arnosky was arrested I know they had a list of Guardian Security customers. Just don't drag Arnosky back in here until we have more to go on. You know he'll be hauling his lawyer with him."

"Give a guy a little time, why don't you." Skizzy gathered up the tapes and dropped them into a box.

"You're fast," Dagger said. "Faster than the P.D. techs, so don't make a liar out of me."

"Stroke, stroke."

"What did you find?" Dagger leaned his elbows on the counter and studied the watches in the showcase. He couldn't believe some of the things people pawn. Pocket watches, pearl-handled switchblades, even a metal Santa Claus Pez dispenser.

"They are all clean. No hankie-pankie, no dubs, no spy-spoof stuff going on." He dropped the last of the tapes into the box and pushed the box in Dagger's direction. "Sorry."

"If there were something there, you would have found it. At least we know they are legit."

Skizzy cocked his head to one side. "You weren't hard on girlie, were you?" When Dagger didn't answer, Skizzy's shoulders sagged. "Dang it. You shouldn't go blaming her. How was she to know what's off limits and what isn't? Hell, I don't even know the boundaries yet."

"She ignored my orders to leave it alone."

"Orders, smorders. She ain't a damn dog you're training. Besides, it's her birthday. You don't go making people feel bad on their birthday."

"Today?" Dagger tried to recall if he had ever been told Sara's birth date.

"Soon. December twenty-first, I think. Right before Christmas. She'll be nineteen. That much I remember."

"Tell me something, Skizzy. Has Sara asked you anything more about BettaTec?"

Skizzy shook his head. "You musta put the fear of god in her."

Dagger picked up the box of tapes before glancing at his squirrely friend. "What about you?"

"Uh, uh. I ain't going near something that can incinerate me."

Dagger set the box back down and thought about the incinerated ranger station and laboratory. "Did you ever review exactly how far into their firewall you got before all hell broke loose?"

"Nothing that made sense. Some kinda list of countries, names, maybe customers, and target dates. It was all coded and my computer had just started deciphering it when WHAM, everything shut down. Weird." He shook his head, freeing wiry hairs from the rubber band. "What is it? Some covert company working for our government?"

Dagger shook his head. "Just be glad it's over with."

The clerk looked up from her roast beef sandwich. She didn't know why she was alarmed. Above her was a ceiling vent, but the heat always turned on and off sporadically throughout the night and never before left her with this uneasy feeling. Out of the corner of her eye she saw the door to the stairway quietly snap shut. It was the hour, she knew. Working the night shift in Homicide often gave her the creeps.

Jayne turned back to her roast beef sandwich and *Soap Opera Digest* and thanked her lucky stars that she didn't work in the morgue. She had just reached the VCR Alert section of the magazine when something passed in her peripheral vision. Turning, Jayne's eyes danced around the reception area. Maybe it was an insect, something that flew past and caught her attention. She liked her job, which involved inputting reports into the computer. The night shift gave her the uninterrupted time necessary to clean up the backlog. The two third-shift detectives were out to lunch. But right now she wasn't feeling alone. She felt eyes on her, and she couldn't shake the feeling.

Sugar was the culprit, she thought, as she stared at the can of Pepsi and empty package of Twinkies she had indulged in a little more than an hour earlier. She flipped the page in the *Soap Opera Digest* and checked out the cosmetics secrets of Catherine Hickland, then the fashion tips from Linda Dano.

A faint scraping and screech came from one of the offices. The building was old and creaked and groaned all night long, but the sounds were especially unnerving tonight. Setting her sandwich down, Jayne walked to the center of the room. She listened for several seconds but didn't hear anything.

"Eddie? You there?" Jayne didn't think any of the detectives had returned but she wouldn't put it past them to play a trick on her. She kept looking over her shoulder as she walked back to the reception desk. With a shrug, Jayne sat down to finish her sandwich. Ten minutes later she tossed the empty sandwich wrapper in the garbage and was just settling back to finish the magazine when, again, she saw something in her peripheral vision. She turned just in time to see the stairway door slowly close.

19

Impatience got the best of him, so the next morning Padre invited Mitch and his attorney for a little one-on-one. The attorney was a dour-faced woman who started every morning furious at the sun for shining, the alarm for ringing, and every person she met for sucking on her oxygen.

"Attorney Angie Garafalo, how nice to see you again." Padre smiled broadly and held out his hand. The attorney looked at it with as much enthusiasm as one would look at a pile of dog shit.

"What is this, Sergeant? Be kind to female attorneys week?" She turned to Mitch who had followed her into the conference room like an obedient schoolboy. With just a nod from her toward the chair, he sat down. Without asking, she walked to the coffeepot and poured two cups. "Make this quick, Sergeant Martinez. I have a busy day."

"As we all do, Miss Garafalo." Padre didn't know why she hadn't applied to the FBI. She already had the closet of dark suits and the personality of a robot. He kept his hands clasped on top of a folder in front of him.

Padre turned his attention to Mitch. "Seymour Cohen. Does the name ring a bell?"

"Seymour Cohen. Cohen." Mitch stared at the ceiling in thought and then turned to his lawyer, shaking his head and shrugging a shoulder. "Can't say that it does."

"Ruth Cohen?" Padre tried again.

"Cut to the chase, Sergeant. I read the papers," Angela said. "The Cohens were found in their car, partially submerged in water. Murder-suicide. What does that have to do with my client?"

Padre pulled an envelope from the folder and slid it across the desk. "I have a search warrant for your premises, Mr. Arnosky."

Mitch grinned and turned to his attorney. "He's at it again."

"On what grounds?" she asked.

"Guardian Security installed the security system in the Cohen residence." Padre had found the list of customers in the court documents, as Wozniak had suggested.

"Guardian Security had a laundry list of customers," Angela replied. "You don't expect him to remember every name."

Mitch leaned over and whispered something to his attorney.

"His partner also installed a number of units. It could have been one Nate Harding installed," Angela added.

"Yes, how convenient Mr. Harding isn't here to corroborate his story."

Angela started to speak, but Mitch raised his hand. "It's okay. Let him search my house. I have nothing to hide. Then I want to sue his sorry ass and the department's for harassment."

"Really?" Padre smiled. He turned to Angela. "Want to

ask your client how his fingerprints ended up on the hood of Cohen's car?"

Angela didn't lose her poker face. She turned to Mitch and jerked one eyebrow up as if to ask if he were holding out on her.

"He's lying," Mitch said. "If it's there, he planted it."

"It was in the papers, Sergeant," she said. "The car was submerged. You can't get prints off of anything that has been in water. Nice try. Are we done here?" Angela grabbed her briefcase.

"It wasn't completely submerged," Padre replied with the calm of a man who had all morning to talk evidence and case files. "A portion of the hood had been left exposed."

"Exposed to the elements? Come on, Sergeant. You can do better than that." Angela started to rise.

"Sit back down," Padre ordered, which elicited a *how dare* you look from the attorney. "The medical examiner says the Cohens died anywhere from seven to ten days ago."

"No," Mitch said.

"No? I haven't asked the question yet."

Mitch whispered to his attorney. Angela pinched her lips even tighter, then turned her wrath on Padre. "Can you remember what you did and where you went three days ago let alone five or ten? I sure can't."

"He better start making his list and checking it twice," Padre said, smiling. "He can stay here and compose it while me and Cedar Point's Finest go and tour his fancy digs."

"It's harassment," Mitch spit out.

This time Angela silenced him with a dour glare. "You go do your parade of homes, Sergeant. Meanwhile, I'm going to personally take a look at the chain of command on the evidence log to determine exactly who was near the car after it was brought into the garage. You are not going to get away with harassing my client the way you did six years ago. Not this client or any other." She tugged on Mitch's arm and they rose to leave.

"While you are there," Mitch said with a grin, "could you toss in a load of clothes? Warm water only and no bleach." His eyes blinked slowly and never strayed from Padre's face as he followed his attorney out of the room.

It shouldn't have surprised Padre that the news cameras and reporters were camped outside Headquarters. Attorney Garafalo was known for quiet publicity. She would drop subtle hints to just a couple of people. Then things would get blown into a full-fledged photo-op with reporters from stations and newspapers. Garafalo's surprise reaction at the response from the media would be genuine, but it never stopped her from having a prepared statement. By the time Angela Garafalo was done, her clients were painted as innocent victims verbally bludgeoned by over-anxious police eager to make a name for themselves.

Padre avoided the nest of hornets by retreating to the basement and out the rear doors. Unfortunately, the one person who had pulled up to the front door and was swarmed by reporters was the chief of police.

"You okay?" Dagger stood in the doorway to the greenhouse where Sara was watering hanging baskets. He didn't know how she got so many plants to bloom in the winter.

Sara looked up from her watering and graced him with a flash of turquoise. A smile played on her lips as she pinched off a yellow leaf from a philodendron.

"Are *we* okay?" Dagger was always amazed at her resilience. She never carried a grudge, never remained angry. It was one of those Indian characteristics she couldn't explain to him. "It's who we are," was the best she could do. His reaction after her return had only confused her, it hadn't angered her.

Sara snipped off a pink rose and inhaled its aroma. "Remember the time you scared the heck out of me with your robot spider?"

Dagger remembered that day. Sara thought she had seen something crawling across the floor, then the black bug with bright red eyes came charging across the couch at her. "Yeah. That was good."

Sara handed him the rose, a strange gleam lighting her eyes.

"Thanks," he said. "I never received flowers before." He reached for the rose and saw her hand. Her long slender fingers shifted to talons and then back to fingers. "HOLY FUCKIN' SHIT." He dropped the rose and fell back against the wall.

Sara laughed. His face must have drained of all color because she couldn't stop laughing. "Payback is a bitch, isn't it?" she managed to blurt out while holding her stomach and staggering to the kitchen table.

"How did you do that?" Dagger didn't move away from the wall, couldn't. He wasn't quite sure of what he saw.

"It's partial shifting," Sara said when she finally calmed down. "It takes a little more concentration than total shifting. Kind of neat, isn't it?"

"It got my heart pumping." Dagger picked up the rose and walked over to the table. "Just don't do it again." He handed her the rose just as he spotted a car rambling up the

weather report.

Dagger stepped over Sara and moved a magazine to sit down. He was puzzled at yet another landscaping magazine left opened to a picture of an outdoor pond. "Any idea what the Alphabet Boys wanted at the Cohen's?"

Sara said, "Alphabet Boys?"

"FBI, NSA, CIA, you name it, it was there. Oh, and DOD."

"Department of Defense?" Sara's eyebrows scrunched. "I thought you said Doctor Cohen was retired."

"That's what everyone said."

"Maybe upon hearing of his death the Alphabet Boys just wanted to make sure he didn't have any sensitive material lying around," Dagger offered.

"Place was totally cleaned out so what was in that lab is a mystery. Neighbors know nothing. The rabbi knows nothing. Here we go." Padre pointed the remote and turned up the volume on the television.

On screen, Attorney Angela Garafalo was fielding questions about Mitch Arnosky's alleged involvement in the shooting at the ATM and theft at Beckman's. Mitch stood quietly beside her with his best *I'm innocent* look. He even let a few sparks of anger flash across his face.

"The police department could only try my client for income tax evasion. That was how flimsy their charges were six years ago. Mr. Arnosky has served his time. He was even released on good behavior after five years," Garafalo stated. "If it wasn't for Sergeant Martinez's relentless harassment of my client, Mitch Arnosky would be able to put his past behind him and lead a normal life. These charges are fabricated by a detective who is irate that he could not get trumped up charges to stick before and is hell bent on pinning anything he can on him now. That's all I have to say."

This was followed by several "no comments" from Mitch.

"She timed this perfectly," Padre said. "Now watch how Chief Loughton pulls into his parking space and is swarmed by the reporters. This is when I split, man."

On screen, Loughton looked blind-sided by the questions and was visibly puzzled and angry at the reporters. After a number of "no comments," he shoots an angry glare at Attorney Garafalo.

"I wouldn't have put it past her to somehow know when the chief was going to be back in the office and time it so he stumbled into her little press conference." Padre clicked the remote and the television turned off. "What about Skizzy? Did he find anything useful in those tapes."

Dagger shook his head. "Skizzy said they were clean. He didn't detect any foul play, no splicing, dicing, whatever."

"Shit. How the hell is Mitch doing it?" Padre's phone rang and he dug around his pocket for it. "Martinez," he said with a little more irritation than necessary. "Okay, give me twenty." He folded the phone and shoved it back in his pocket. "Something jumping back at the office. My presence is requested by the big boys."

20

"That's really amazing," Padre said as he stared at the man seated across from him. "Moby Dick never moved that fast when he was investigating a case. Now that he's in Internal Affairs, he's faster than flies on a three-day-old corpse."

"That's enough," Chief Loughton said. "Just turn in your shield and gun, Martinez. You're on paid leave until further notice."

Richard Moby shoved the chair back and stood. "Maybe it's because dirty cops make more dumb mistakes than the criminals. They're easier to catch."

Padre shot out of his chair.

"I said that's enough." Chief Loughton paced the room in three-hundred-dollar loafers. Padre watched him, wondering if Loughton's concern was really for the welfare of the department. Elections were coming up next May, and if this incident were to affect the mayor's re-election, it would also affect Loughton's re-appointment.

A quick look at Wozniak's face made Padre choke back any additional comments. Wozniak turned his gaze to the floor, hands jammed in his pockets. Even his buddy, the man who'd attended the same seminary as Padre, was at a loss for words. He couldn't look Padre in the eye.

"Your shield and gun, Padre," Wozniak said quietly, keeping his eyes trained on the floor.

Padre unsnapped his holster and placed it on the table. This was followed by his shield, which slid across the table and rapped against Moby Dick's fingers.

"Now I have to go prepare a statement for the press. It will be short and sweet," Loughton announced. "You, on the other hand, Martinez, are not permitted to speak to the press. I don't want to see your face on the news or hear your voice on the radio. Got it?"

Padre just glared and wondered how the chief's hairdresser got his hair to fluff out like a chia pet.

"Martinez," Wozniak said, a hint of warning in his voice.

"Got it."

Loughton left, trailed by Richard Moby who gathered up Padre's gun and shield with unconcealed glee. Once the door to the conference room closed, Padre sank onto a chair. Wozniak took a slow stroll around the table before sitting down.

"If you didn't write it, how did it happen, Padre?" Wozniak was referring to an E-mail Padre allegedly wrote to Kiley ordering him to make sure Mitch's fingerprints showed up in Cohen's house. Padre's E-mail had gone so far as to suggest they show up on the control pad for the burglar alarm. Attorney Garafalo had been quick to point out that Padre was the first person to inspect the Cohen vehicle after it was towed into the garage, so he had ample time to plant a print on the hood. And a speedy search through Padre's desk reaped Mitch's print duplicated onto a latex finger, a finger that could be used to leave Mitch's prints just about anywhere.

"I can't explain it, John. You know me. I wouldn't do something that stupid or that unlawful. How convenient for Garafalo to find exactly what she wanted and search exactly where Arnosky told her to search."

Wozniak covered his face with his hands. "Give me something, Padre. Give me some explanation as to how this could happen. And don't say Mitch installed our security cameras because these are not Guardian Security cameras."

Padre couldn't think. He knew Mitch was behind this but didn't know how he did it. "I need some time."

"You've got plenty of it."

Padre nodded.

"Take the garage doors by the locker rooms. Somehow the press already caught wind and they are camped outside the front doors."

"I gotta break my pattern. I'm getting too easy to find," Padre whispered.

"Well, I'm just smarter than the average cop." Dagger weaved his way between the pews and took a seat in the balcony next to Padre. The altar below was lit with candles and surrounded with poinsettia plants. St. Michael's was the largest Catholic church in Cedar Point and a place Padre often sought refuge when he wanted to think.

"I take it you saw the news."

Dagger said, "Oh, yeah. It played over and over and..."

"I get your point."

"Do people really talk to you here?" Dagger asked. Padre flashed him a puzzled look. "You know." Dagger pointed skyward.

"Most times this is like going to a shrink. You end up

asking and answering your own questions, solving your own problems."

"So this is mainly a sanctuary, a place to hide out until *the man* returns your phone call."

Padre chuckled and shook his head. "You are going to burn in hell, my friend."

"I thought this was hell. Name me one person you know of who isn't suffering."

"That's easy...Sara." Padre saw the change in Dagger's face. "Uh oh. I don't like that look."

"She's got some issues she's working on."

"So you two finally talked."

"A little but she's still holding back on something. I can't drag it out of her, Padre."

"Well, don't blame *the man*. As I've said before...he's a hands-off kinda coach. He gives you the rule book and at the end of the game he'll tell you if you played well."

Dagger lifted his face to study the solid oak wainscoting and Sistine Chapel-type painting on the ceiling. They sat for several minutes watching parishioners below. Then Dagger told him that Sara received another call from Mitch.

"I'd feel a hell of a lot better if she stayed away from him."

"Me, too, but she wants to keep busy and right now she is our best insight into his devious mind." Dagger looked around the balcony seats. "So, these your new digs?"

"Father Frank has a room for me. I sent the wife and boys out of town. They are due for Christmas break soon, anyway. I'm sure the press would be pitched outside my house for a while and I don't want them subjected to that. And here, Father Frank has assured me the utmost secrecy. As far as anyone knows, I went out of town with the family."

"What do you want me to do, Padre? Just name it."

"I don't know what you can do. I didn't send the E-mail to Kiley. He didn't want to help out I.A. but I know he had no choice. And I have no idea how that latex finger got into my desk drawer."

"Maybe Mitch is getting some help from the inside."

"Chief Wozniak reviewed the surveillance tapes from the entrance. No unauthorized personnel had entered Homicide and we both trust the other detectives. Besides, the E-mail was supposedly sent at seven-thirty in the morning, a time I'm usually in the office. But I swear I didn't send it."

"It's very easy to have the computer hold mail until a designated time. Someone could get in there at two in the morning, type the message, and specify a time."

"It still doesn't explain who would have gotten past the desk clerk and into Homicide, much less learn my password."

"For an experienced hacker, it's nothing to learn your password."

"You're not hearing me, Dagger. It came from my computer. Explain that to me."

"And you're not hearing me. I know Skizzy could access your computer from the convenience of his bunker. Piece of cake. Just turn me loose, Padre, and I'll get you your answers."

Padre laughed at that last comment but his eyes didn't smile. He was frustrated and furious. "Seems to me you have never waited for my permission to *turn loose,* my friend."

21

The wolf tore through underbrush, leaped over creeks, and bounded across foot trails as it raced through a forest just east of the city. Guardian Security had been housed in a warehouse tucked in an abandoned industrial section on the outskirts of town. Mitch and Nate had favored the isolation. Although six years before the authorities had stripped the place clean in their search for evidence and confiscation of any assets, the warehouse had remained as abandoned as its neighboring surroundings.

Just before breaking into the open, the wolf leaped up, shifting into the gray hawk before landing on a thick branch. The wolf's acute sense of smell switched to the hawk's visual acuity. A rodent scurried between the buildings a block away, pausing long enough to sniff the ground, then scratch at the hard-packed sand. The hawk saw a spill of glowing liquid in ultra-violet as the rodent relieved itself.

In the distance a set of headlights slowly grew in size, appearing to float on the horizon. The hawk's keen eyesight saw Dagger behind the wheel of the Lincoln Navigator. It watched as the vehicle pulled up to an opened bay, leaving the headlights shining on the interior of the building.

With rapid wing beats the hawk emerged from the forest and soared over treetops, glided past the row of buildings, and lighted on a windowsill. The hawk's eyesight pierced the darkness beyond the windows. Every light in the warehouse may as well have been lit.

Half the building was one story with a vaulted ceiling. Grated pallet rackings stood empty against two walls. Two floors of businesses comprised the other half of the building. Guardian Security had been located on the top floor.

The hawk's attention was drawn to the figure climbing the open stairwell. A small pen light illuminated the area with the intensity of a strobe light.

Could you be less noticeable?

Jeezus, Sara. Dagger stumbled on the stairs. Sometimes when he heard her voice in his head it sounded almost as if she were right behind him. *Didn't I tell you to stay home?*

I have a new mantra—hear no one but yourself. I believe you taught me that.

That only applies to me.

Well, either way that halogen beam can probably be seen from downtown.

That's fine. There isn't anyone around for miles.

Dagger reached the second floor and paused. The beam traveled down a long hallway searching the shadows. Two doors to his right gaped open. According to the floor plan in the file, the bathrooms and a break room were down this hall. Padre always kept a copy of his case files, and the one on Guardian Security was thick. Since the police had already searched Mitch's condo, Dagger realized from the file that no one had checked out the deserted offices.

Dagger swung the beam to the archway straight ahead

and stepped through. Walls were barren and the floors weren't any better. There was little left to hint that the office had once been occupied.

The halogen beam washed over the walls toward the window where the hawk perched on the outside sill. The beam showed the intensity of the hawk's turquoise eyes.

Just stay put. Do you see anything out of the ordinary?

No, not even a wall safe.

Dagger aimed the light at the corners of the room. *What about cameras?*

Nothing I've detected.

The beam settled on the faded squares on the wall, places where pictures had hung. Dagger imagined that Mitch had spared no expense in decorating his office. The floor was marble in a grade that would put Sheila's condo to shame.

Makes no sense, Dagger told her. *The floor plan showed a much larger office. Hell, the entire floor. Yet...* He walked over to the far wall and slowly ran the beam over every square inch. The wall was detailed with vertical decorative molding every four feet. *There has to be a door here that we just can't see with the naked eye.* Dagger paced the wall, stopping every few feet to push, prod, and knock on the wall. Next he aimed the light at the floor to search for foot-prints trailing into or out of the wall.

This makes no...

Don't move.

The panic in Sara's voice brought every hair on the back of his neck to attention. Dagger held his breath as his eyes searched the distance of the beam for something with teeth or claws.

What is it?

Someone is standing in the doorway.

Within a time span too quick to calculate, the flashlight moved to Dagger's left hand and his right hand wrapped itself around a Kimber .45. He spun around and shone the light in the doorway. No one was there. But that didn't explain the tiny pinpricks dancing across his skin.

Where did he go? Dagger asked.

He's still there. You've got your light right on him.

"Anybody there?" Dagger called out. "I'm armed." His eyes scanned the twelve-foot wide archway and beyond but he still couldn't see anyone. He stepped out into the hallway and shone the light down the aisle.

Where is he, Sara?

He's...I don't believe it. He disappeared.

Dagger grimaced. *If you are making this up to see my hair turn gray, I just have one thing to say—payback is a bitch.*

Dagger, I wouldn't joke about something like this. I swear someone was there.

He jammed his gun back into the belt holster and made his way down the stairs. He knew he didn't see what Sara saw but that didn't stop him from making a wide arc with the flashlight on his way down the stairs.

Sara always beat him home. Usually she was showered and changed by the time he pulled into the garage. He found her sitting in front of the bay window in her bedroom, fingers combing through long, wet hair.

He slid to the far side of the cushion. Sara was stretched out on the window seat cocooned in an afghan, back against the wall, gazing out at the huge ball of light hovering over the treetops. How soon until the moon was completely full, he wasn't sure. Instead of noting a day of the full moon, he found himself noting the minutes. After all, the moon was only full for three minutes. Dagger had learned that from the late Professor William Sherlock.

"Do you think about it often, Dagger?" Sara had a faint listlessness to her voice as she stared up at the ball of light.

"Sure," Dagger said. "About three days before a full moon and three days after. I don't think I really sleep on the actual day of a full moon. I just watch Einstein for any changes in him."

"Hmmm." It was more a sigh as if the subject were as unimportant as the weather.

Dagger studied the young woman as she leaned back against the wall. She looked as calm and serene as if she were seated in a canoe drifting down a scenic river, one hand rippling the water, thoughts unencumbered.

"Padre has felt the same way," Dagger continued. "He and Marty spend hours going through case reports from across the country during that same post full-moon period just in case..." He let his own thoughts drift to that night, the hospital, Sara's empty hospital bed.

"Why did you leave, Sara? I promised your grandmother I would watch out for you, keep you safe. When I saw all that blood...I thought Addison killed you."

She turned her head slowly from the window. Her voice was barely above a whisper when she said, "He didn't do it to me."

The realization of what she said hit him in a flurry of images. Her dress, the blood. She had almost been eviscerated. But if Addison hadn't done it, then...

"My god, Sara." He reached out to her. She recoiled, pulling her knees up to her chest and turning to face the window.

"I'm not sorry, Dagger." But there was a quiver in her voice that told him otherwise.

"But you can regenerate. I've seen it."

"Arms, legs, but definitely not organs."

Dagger couldn't imagine, in wolf form, the split-second decision Sara had made. A decision she now had to live with.

"Why, Sara?"

She leaned her head against the wall and sighed heavily. Her gaze drifted to the ball of light in the sky. "Do you know how some people claim to see their lives pass before their eyes right before a car slams into them? When I saw Addison shifting into those horrible creatures as he was dying, I saw my future pass before my eyes." She turned her attention back to Dagger and he could see tears welling. "I thought, what if I'm the anomaly, not Addison? What if I was supposed to be like him, passing on this evil from generation to generation, affected by the full moon?"

Dagger couldn't begin to imagine the emotional conflict she had gone through. No one could have. "Don't you think that was a little extreme, Sara?"

She shook her head no. "My people never pray or perform sacrifices for personal gains. For the good of all our relations, I sacrificed my fertility. *Mitakuye oyasin.* That's what I always heard. I had to do it. *We are all related.*"

Dagger moved to her side of the window seat, nudged her away from the wall and sat down. When he wrapped his arms around her, Sara stiffened and gathered the afghan tighter around her shoulders.

"Other than Addison," Sara said, "I only knew one other shape-shifter...Micha. He was an elder who had helped me in my youth. He was a shape-shifter like me, but his actions weren't always good. I was nearly sure he had told me the gift could be passed on. But it had been years since I had seen him."

"So that's where you went? To find him?"

"Yes. I had so many questions that no one else could answer."

"Did he help?"

Sara shook her head. "All I found was a grave."

"I'm sorry, Sara. And I'm sorry I've been hard on you." Dagger ran his fingers through her damp hair, inhaled the subtle smell of lavender. "You have the most unbelievable gift and you use it to do good. Your grandmother was intuitive. She knew you had to be protected and for some reason she chose me for the job."

Gradually her body relaxed and she finally let him pull her closer. She rested her head against his shoulder, and after a brief silence, Sara asked, "Did you ever stop to think, Dagger, that maybe Grandmother meant for me to protect you?"

22

The next afternoon Chief Wozniak asked Dagger to meet with him and Padre at Saint Michael's.

"What's the emergency?" Dagger asked as he followed Padre down the hall to his cramped quarters. Dagger shuddered as he eyed the twin bed, nightstand, and three-shelf bookcase. "Don't you get claustrophobic in here?"

"I've lived in smaller places."

"A jail cell is bigger than this place."

"You learn to live on very little in the seminary and you take a vow of poverty."

"No, it's the nuns who live a vow of poverty. I seem to remember the Catholic Church owns more property than any other institution. I'm surprised the National Organization for Women hasn't started picketing Rome."

Padre raised his eyes. "It's in the house of the Lord he says these things."

Dagger looked around for a place to sit. "I hope you don't intend for all three of us to sit on your bunk bed."

"Such a cry baby. Follow me." Padre led him down the hall to the kitchen, which was large enough to prepare meals for an army. The solid pine table could accommodate twelve people comfortably and the stove had enough burn-ers for an eight-course meal.

"Aye, Father Jerry, what will you be having?" The moon-faced woman with the Irish lilt to her voice was armed with an oven mitt and wooden spoon. Her bib apron had a collage of stains.

"Please, Rebecca, just Jerry. We don't want Father Frank to think he's being dethroned." Padre motioned to a chair across the table as his nose lifted to inhale the aromas of cinnamon and nutmeg. "Apple strudel?"

"Aye. She'll be coming out of the oven momentarily." Rebecca's splash of freckles matched the color of the hair piled on top of her head in a tight bun. What strands man-aged to untangle themselves were the color of cotton. Without asking, Rebecca set out cups and saucers, plates and forks.

"Find anything interesting in my notes?" Padre asked.

"I've sorted everything out," Dagger replied. "Been through the tapes again. It will be hard to trace the money, but I have Skizzy checking into any info on the rare coins and jewelry. Don't hold your breath. All of that could be long gone."

"I know but I'm grasping for a lifeline here."

Dagger told him about his trip to Guardian Security.

"You're spinning your wheels, Dagger. We couldn't find anything six years ago after Mitch was arrested. Even then, he claimed it was all his partner's doing and he knew noth-ing about it. He's playing the picture perfect citizen right now."

"Still…" Dagger took a sip of the fresh-brewed coffee and thanked Rebecca with a nod. "I couldn't get into the back half of the building."

"It was used for storage, then someone was thinking of renting the building so they closed up the one entrance and put the entrance in the hall. That person backed out and someone else did work on it but nothing ever happened. The other buildings were cited for asbestos and no one wanted the expense of bringing the buildings up to code. So the entire two-block area has been empty for years. Mitch's old building is the only one okay for occupancy but no company wants to be isolated out there."

The back doorbell jangled just as Rebecca was pulling the strudel out of the oven.

"I'll get it," Padre said.

"No." Rebecca set the strudel on a cooling rack. "You never know who it might be. Can't take chances, Father Jerry."

"Father Jerry," Dagger chuckled. "I don't think I could ever get used to that."

Chief Wozniak ducked as he walked into the kitchen. "Something sure as hell smells good."

Padre waved his hand at the air. "I give up. No one has respect for the Lord's house any more."

Wozniak gathered Rebecca into a bear hug. "How's my Becca doing?"

"Now John, you stop that." Her face turned crimson as she pushed him away and straightened her bib apron. "You'll be looking for Wife Number Four if you keep that up."

John shrugged. "Maybe you'll be ready then."

Rebecca giggled in schoolgirl fashion. "Go sit yourself down." She continued to giggle as she cut the hot strudel.

Once everyone was served, she made a quiet exit.

Wozniak tossed a set of stapled papers on the table near Padre.

Dagger spent several minutes studying the chief's face. It wasn't often he broke bread with Padre's boss, much less strudel. But frustration and fatigue were etched in the tiny lines around Wozniak's eyes and the crease at the bridge of his nose.

"Mitch's lawyer has filed a lawsuit against the department," Wozniak reported, "and you for tampering with evidence, defamation of character, intent to commit fraud, and a whole laundry list which, she claims, can get you fifteen to twenty. Sorry, Padre."

While Dagger was visiting Padre, Sara was checking the Internet for local sources for arsenic. She was seated on the couch, the laptop on the coffee table. According to some of the sites, you had to obtain a permit to purchase certain poisons. Arsenic was also a naturally occurring element in soil in certain parts of the country and high toxic levels could be found in ground water.

Her eyes scanned down one of the permit forms. "Certain poisons such as arsenic, cyanide, and benzine require a Record of Transaction." Some of the categories included storage and planned use of the poison. "Right, like someone who wants to poison someone is going to list the use." Her fingers drummed the couch as she stared at possible other sites to research. Without even thinking, her hand moved the cursor back to the search line. She wasn't sure why she did it. She knew she shouldn't but her fingers typed BETTA in the search line. Sara definitely wanted to stay

away from anything to do with BettaTec but she was curious why it wasn't spelled B-E-T-A. She was trying to think
of what other words of description to use when she acci-
dentally hit the ENTER key. Over two-hundred-thousand
hits were listed.

"What on earth?" Sara examined the first twenty entries.
Most referred to fish. She moved the cursor back to the
search line and typed: BETTA +FISH. This narrowed the
search. She picked a random entry and clicked on it. As she
read, Einstein plodded across the floor to the bookshelves,
his long, colorful tail dragging behind like a feather duster.
He wasn't bothering to fly. It was as though he were trying
to sneak out of his room.

"Einstein, what are you doing?"

The macaw didn't reply. He just clamped his beak onto
a DVD and pulled it off the bookshelf.

"Einstein, no." Sara jumped from the couch and ran over
to the bookshelf. Picking up the DVD, she noticed it was an
Arnold Schwarzenegger movie.

"ARNOLD, ARNOLD." Einstein flew to the perch
behind the couch.

"Okay, but you be quiet. I have work to do." She placed
the disc into the DVD player and pushed the play button.
The movie Einstein had selected was *Predator*. Sara hoped
it would keep him quiet for a while.

As she skimmed through one of the sites, Sara learned
that a Betta fish was from the species Anabantoidei and sci-
entifically known as Betta Splendens. The pictures showed
fish in a variety of eye-catching colors with swooping fins.
The Betta was considered the peacock of the fish tank. It
had a labyrinth breathing system, meaning it needs to come

up for air like whales and dolphins. Although she found the information fascinating, she didn't think it had anything to do with BettaTec until several words caught her attention—Siamese Fighting Fish and aggression.

Sara pressed the BACK button to return to the search list. She then selected one entry that specifically mentioned the temperament of the Betta. It stated that the males are very territorial and have to be kept in their own containers away from other males and even females. Their main behavior is fighting and they rely on instinct rather than deductive thinking. Scientists believe the aggression is linked to certain pheromones and chemicals that control their social behavior. One picture showed a Betta displaying its gill covers and fins extended, a behavior that occurs even when it sees its own reflection in the glass. This is termed *display behavior*, which scientists believe is hard-wired in the Betta. Sara still couldn't see what it had to do with BettaTec. It wasn't illegal for companies to have communication satellites. But there weren't any satellites, to her knowledge, that use laser defense technology, unless one listens to Skizzy, who believes it's Big Brother.

Sara glanced at the wide-screen TV. The movie was one she hadn't seen before, and although she tried to focus on her computer, the movie kept pulling her attention. It was a few years old and Arnold was off on an island somewhere trying to rescue Marines from a downed helicopter. One by one his crew was being killed by animals or cannibals, she wasn't sure yet. It was definitely a man's film, with all the blood and guts. After what she had been through with Addison two months before, a movie about men being disemboweled was not making her lunch sit too well.

Other than a few tap dances on the perch, Einstein appeared mesmerized. It was obvious he had seen the movie before but Sara wondered why he yelled out ARNOLD after watching the surveillance tapes. What did one have to do with the other?

She turned back to her computer. Another interesting sentence caught her eye:

Scientists have been studying the aggression aspect of the Betta since the 1930s as it relates to the aggression and social behavior of man.

She doubted BettaTec had anything to do with breeding and selling fish. Maybe the owner liked the fish. Maybe his kids owned Bettas.

"Focus, focus," she told herself and went back to searching for possible sources for arsenic. One tidbit of information sounded promising. It said that arsenic has been found stored in old farmhouses and basements of antique stores.

She leaned back against the couch cushions just in time to see another one of Arnold's men disemboweled. But then the culprit was discovered.

"ARNOLD, ARNOLD," Einstein squawked.

On screen, the trees came alive. The killer was an alien who could blend into the background and become completely undetectable. A chill zig-zagged up Sara's spine as she watched the alien show his true form and then disappear into the background again. She fumbled for the remote and fast-forwarded in an attempt to find similar examples.

She pressed the stop button, then slipped the videotape from the ATM into the VCR. "Tell me what you see,

Einstein." All Sara could see on the screen was Brent Langley walking up to the cash machine, punching the keypad, looking over his shoulder, and a few seconds later crumbling to the ground.

"ARNOLD, ARNOLD."

"I don't see it, Einstein." Sara studied the macaw, then rewound the tape. "I wonder." She didn't want to shape-shift in front of him. It might traumatize the macaw. But during her two-month sabbatical she learned how to hone her skills of calling on the senses of the hawk and the wolf without shifting. She focused on the hawk and instantly had its eyesight. On screen Brent Langley was no longer alone. Someone was walking up behind him. It was a shimmer, a slight change in the landscape but still in the shape of a figure, though faceless. Just like last night!

"How could it be?" Sara alternated from human vision to hawk vision and felt an excitement growing. She grabbed the phone and called Dagger.

23

"How did Dagger manage your escape from the church?" Sara asked as she led Padre to the living room.

"He stashed me in the back of the Lincoln."

"No one followed you?" Sara pushed in the *Predator* tape.

"Nope. No press, no I.A." Padre looked puzzled as the Schwarzenegger movie started playing.

"Sara, you had us rush back to watch a movie?" Dagger asked.

She pushed Dagger onto the couch next to Padre. "Yes. I've never seen the movie before but Einstein pulled it from the bookcase and was yelling out Arnold again, like he did when Padre showed the tapes from the ATM and Beckman's. Padre assumed Einstein was referring to Mitch Arnosky."

Padre said, "He was."

"In a way." Sara fast-forwarded the movie, then paused it at the first appearance of the camouflaged alien.

"This is what Einstein is seeing when he watches the ATM tape. He is seeing someone camouflaged somehow, blending in so well with the background that nothing, not a

153

camera, not even the human eye can detect it." As a sudden afterthought, Sara quickly flicked her gaze to Dagger to make sure he understood her meaning.

"I don't think we can put Einstein on the witness stand, Sara," Padre said. "Besides, I've never heard of such an invention."

"Einstein's eyes are like a zoom lens on a camera," Sara explained. "Birds can see things in a larger color range than humans. We just have to trust that something is there."

Dagger walked over to the desk and tapped the spacebar on his computer. "Let me get Skizzy on the speaker."

"Oh, yeah," Skizzy said. "I remember that movie. Government was on another covert mission and ended up being one-upped by an alien."

"Focus on the alien, Skizzy."

Padre piped up in the background. "And this is my defense?"

"Let me check into things and I'll get back to you. Going to be there awhile?"

"Make it yesterday."

"Yeah, yeah. You never change."

Padre thought about that for a moment. "That's ridiculous. There can't possibly be any type of apparatus that can camouflage someone."

"Brent Langley described hearing someone," Dagger said.

"SomeTHING," Padre corrected him. "He said leaves were blowing across the asphalt."

"Might be worth it to get him to think a little harder about that," Dagger suggested.

"Well, there is Jayne," Padre said. "She was working the

night before I supposedly sent Kiley that E-mail. We should probably talk to her again." He shook his head slowly. "If that sonofabitch Mitch is behind this, I'm going to nail him."

"No, you're lying low," Dagger cautioned. "Don't let him get to you." He walked over to the bar and pulled out two beers, handing one to Padre. "Stay for dinner. I'll order Chinese."

"No. I'll defrost spaghetti sauce," Sara offered.

Padre grabbed the remote and pressed the play button. "Let me know if you need a hand. I'm just going to watch the rest of the movie."

When he entered the kitchen, Dagger closed the shutters to the pass-through. He waited for Sara to set the pot of water on the stove to cook the noodles while he pulled out the fixings for the salad.

Sara tugged at the shutters and peered into the living room. Padre was lying on the couch watching the movie. She closed the shutters and stood close to Dagger as he ripped lettuce into a bowl.

"I saw it, Dagger. I used the hawk's vision and could see what Einstein sees." She pulled a container of pasta sauce from the freezer and took off the lid.

"You shifted in front of Einstein?"

"No. It's like the time you were dangling by a rope from the catwalk. I saw the rope as if it were just inches from me." She placed the container in the microwave and punched the defrost button.

Dagger shuddered as he remembered how the bullet from Sara's gun hit just inches from his fingers.

"The acuity of the hawk is eight times better than a

human's," Sara reminded him.

"Don't brag," Dagger said, eliciting a smile from Sara. "Did you actually see Mitch at the ATM?" He sliced the cucumbers on a cutting board while Sara brought out a bottle of Italian dressing.

Sara shook her head. "Only the figure of a person, the same thing I saw last night at Guardian Security. He was standing there, close enough to kill you and you didn't see a thing."

By the time they finished dinner and a bottle of wine and cleaned up the kitchen, Skizzy had finished his research. They carried their coffee cups to the living room in time for Skizzy's call.

"It seems some high-ranking general saw that movie and told his men, 'I want one of those.' So they devised a prototype," Skizzy explained, his voice blaring through the computer speakers. "I'm going to send you some photos. You ready?" Padre and Sara stood behind the wooden partition next to Dagger's desk. "Okay, this first picture is of an Abrams tank. In the first picture you see it. In the second picture you don't. It's draped in some type of electrically conducting cloth covered with reflective sensors. These sensors read what's behind the object and transfer the image to the front. Now watch the second example. Here we have a Special Ops boy. Now you see him...," they could hear the tapping of keys, "now you don't." On screen the soldier seemed to disappear.

"If you look closely, though, you can still see him," Padre pointed out. "It's distorted enough that you know something is there."

"Right," Skizzy replied. "It was a top secret job that

only a handful of people knew about and only one scientist had been working on. The cloth covering the tank and the S.O. are heavy so they've been trying to perfect it."

"Heavy. Damn thing makes the guy look like the Michelin Man," Dagger said.

"Well, according to the Defense Department," Skizzy continued, "the project was scrapped."

Dagger pointed at the project title. The screen said NOCM. "What's the project called? Knock Em?"

"No, no," Skizzy laughed. "It's *No See Em*, like those little chiggers in Florida that bite the hell out of you. Had them in Nam, too. You can probably fit a dozen on a pin-head."

"Damn," Padre said in a quick burst of realization. "The Alphabet Boys."

"What?" Skizzy's voice squealed over the speaker.

Padre asked, "Does any of your research show the name of the scientist who had been working on this project?"

"Yeah. A Doctor Seymour Cohen."

"That explains a lot," Dagger said. "Cohen might have been retired but that doesn't mean he wasn't trying to perfect his little invention."

They thanked Skizzy and ended the call. Dagger printed out the information Skizzy had transmitted.

"Can you find out how much the FBI, CIA, and all the rest got from Cohen's house?" Sara asked.

"They are all tight-lipped," Padre replied.

"The fact that they are no longer in town probably means they found what they were looking for." Sara gathered up the empty coffee cups and set them on the bar.

"Maybe." Dagger thought about that for a moment. "Or

maybe all they got were the notes. Maybe they didn't know
Cohen had the new prototype. I'm sure they wouldn't have
left it lying around."

"What's the flaw other than being heavy?" Padre asked.

Sara glanced at Einstein in the aviary. "If Einstein can
see him, I bet thermal imaging can, too."

"Damn." Padre pounded the top of the railing. "You are
just too damn smart. Does Dagger pay you enough?"

"Don't give her ideas." Dagger stood and stretched.
"Let's work on a Cohen/Mitch connection, Padre."

"He spent time in the Cohen house installing the security
cameras. He probably saw papers lying around or monitored
the doctor working on his project. Mitch could have been
watching Doc from the comfort of his home or office and saw
the possibilities of the NOCM project, maybe heard phone
conversations between Cohen and the government boys.
Then he gets arrested, off to vacation land, and has five years
to think about it."

"So you think he might have caught Doctor Cohen and
his wife at home and stolen the suit?" Sara asked.

Padre rubbed his chin as he walked back to the couch.
But he didn't sit down, just stood there thinking.

"Cohen wouldn't have given it up easily," Dagger said.

"No, he wouldn't. The wife was at her bridge club.
Mitch probably used her as a bargaining chip to get Cohen
to bring the suit to him. And then the bastard killed them
both."

"You didn't find Mitch's prints in the house, though,
right?" Sara asked.

"Nope," Padre replied. "Mitch wouldn't be that stupid to
be seen around the neighborhood."

"I have to hand it to him, though. That was a smart move," Dagger added. "He couldn't chance being seen in the neighborhood. But by falsifying a memo from you to Kiley, he succeeded in incriminating you, Padre."

"So glad you are impressed with him. I'll have to let him know."

They moved to the hallway closet to retrieve their coats, then to the front door. Dagger didn't recall ever seeing such a look of defeat on Padre's face, no matter how positive an attitude he tried to present. What made matters worse was that Padre was sequestered with no way to help himself.

Dagger said, "Nate was an integral part of Guardian. If we assume Mitch killed him, Nate must have really pissed him off."

"It always comes down to money," Padre agreed, slipping into his coat. "If Nate was holding out on him, maybe making a big score on the side, that would be enough of an excuse for Mitch."

"How much do we know about Nate's life the month prior to his death?"

"Obviously, not enough," Sara interjected.

"Add that to our list," Dagger told her.

"Damn that Mitch." Padre jerked the door open with force. "Nice wreath," he mumbled. "Fa-la-la-la-la."

"You better fill Wozniak in soon," Dagger said.

"You fill him in. I would rather the nuttier explanations come from your lips."

24

The next day Dagger was waiting at the back door as Simon's mail truck ambled up the drive. "Just the guy I want to see." Dagger held open the door for Simon.

"Aw, jeez. I don't like the sound of that."

"Coffee? Breakfast?" Dagger pulled out a chair for the mailman.

Simon slipped his jacket over the back of the kitchen chair and sat down. "Already ate and drank. Just hit me with it quick."

And Dagger did, filling him in on the NOCM Project and Padre's suspension. Simon listened in silence then narrowed his eyes and cocked his head. "If you were telling me all this prior to that last weird full moon case you worked on, I would have said you was nuts. Now, it just goes with the Dagger Territory. What do you want me to do?"

"Hang out at bars."

A broad smile spread across Simon's mouth. "You are just too damn good to me."

"Nate Harding was a partier," Dagger explained. "Mitch was the serious one. Find out where he partied, who he partied with, and every tidbit or rumor any bartender heard."

"These kinds of jobs I like." Simon craned his neck to peer around the doorway. "Where's Sara?"

"On a job."

"So, uh, you been doing any birthday or Christmas shopping?"

"I'm working on it. Thought I might buy her a Holiday Barbie."

"Yeah, right. You are only succeeding in keeping her a kid in your own mind. The rest of us see way beyond that. You are probably still giving her those brotherly pecks on the forehead."

Dagger's brows jutted up. He knew where this was going. "So?"

"Hrmpff." Simon stood and struggled into his jacket. "Soon, without even realizing it, those lips are going to slide down to her cheek. Pretty soon it will be a lingering peck to the side of her mouth. Then look out. There will be no lookin' back."

"Shut up and go do your rounds."

Simon threw back his head and laughed. His chuckle carried through the back door and out to the mail truck.

"Padre's a good guy. I don't believe what they are saying about him."

The woman sitting across from Sara at Panera Bread was making fatal stabs at her salad. Jayne's tray was loaded with a salad and bread bowl filled with chicken noodle soup.

"When Padre called this morning and asked me to talk to you, I told him 'anything I could do to help.'" Stab, stab.

Sara sipped her tea and marveled at the woman's ability

to shovel quantities of food fit for a trucker into the body of a petite woman. Jayne wore little if any make-up and had mousy brown hair peppered with gray. Sara was meeting Mitch for lunch at the Rainforest Café so opted for just tea during her interview with Jayne.

"Do you remember anything different about the night before Padre was suspended? Any unauthorized visitors, repairmen, deliverymen, maybe cops who weren't supposed to be in the area?"

Jayne shook her head. "Like I told Chief Wozniak, it was like any other weekday night. Pretty quiet with occasional calls, nothing serious. It's the beat cops that get most of the action. Maybe Christmas week we'll get the suicides, but that night, no." In between stabs, Jayne's fork hovered, then her brown eyes squinted and she sat back slightly. "Now wait a minute..." She shook her head, saying, "Forget it. I'll sound nuts."

"Anything at all. Doesn't matter how nuts it sounds."

"Okay." Jayne set her fork down for the first time and clasped her hands in her lap. She let her gaze sweep the surrounding tables before leaning in and speaking. "The guys play tricks on me sometimes, you know? Sneaking up behind me, setting a plastic skull on a ruler and crawling on their knees so the skull is floating in front of my desk. Well, that night it was really quiet. I actually got an entire *Soap Opera Digest* read without one phone call. But it was eerie."

"How so?"

"I caught the stairway door closing, like someone had just left. Then I heard noises back in the offices. But the building's so old it creaks more than my grandmother's bones. It was just..." She picked up her fork again and whispered, "I felt like someone was watching me. You ever get that feeling? Just couldn't shake it. Then out of the corner of my eye I saw that damn stairway door snapping shut." She shuddered. "But there wasn't anyone there, honest to god, or I would have said something." Stab, stab.

The figure in the wheelchair appeared frail and weak. Brent Langley sat with his head down and shoulders sagging. He was staring out of the window of the hospital room where they had moved him three days earlier.

"I told Sergeant Martinez everything I knew. I'm sure you could read the report."

Dagger stared down at the parking lot. There wasn't much to see from this window other than bare trees, a parking lot filled with cars, and far more pavement than grass.

"People don't know what it's like to have your life altered unexpectedly."

"I don't know. Tell that to Christopher Reeves and Michael J. Fox." *And Sara,* Dagger thought. He guessed Langley had a right to be bitter.

"Fuck you." Langley slowly moved his gaze from the window to Dagger. "So I'm just a self-pitying ass who should be glad he's still alive," he sneered. "I get four weeks of medical leave and then adios." The effort of talking left him coughing and wheezing. He pressed a hand to his chest wound and grimaced.

"You are lucky. According to Padre, the bullet was a jacketed round. If your assailant had used a hollow point, you'd be down to one lung." Dagger glanced around the room and saw an engagement ring sitting on the tray by his bed. The cards gathered next to his suitcase on the bed read *to son, to nephew,* and *to co-worker.* He guessed the ring didn't come with a card, maybe just a verbal sorry or a tip-toe into the room while he was sleeping.

"Have you remembered anything else from that night?" Dagger asked, trying to pull Langley from his doldrums.

"Why isn't Sergeant Martinez on the case?" Langley shrugged. "That's right. He's on suspension."

"Guess there are other people in the world with prob-lems."

"Fuck you." Langley turned back to the window and hunched even lower in the wheelchair.

Padre was so much better with *poor me* cases. Dagger didn't have the patience and was only one more *fuck you* away from pulling the patient out of the wheelchair. He jammed his hands into his pants pockets just to keep them from wrapping around Langley's neck.

"It would have been worse if you were married to her first and then this happened. It's better to know now that she didn't love you for yourself."

Langley opened his mouth to speak, his lips already starting to form the *f* word. Dagger pointed a finger at him. "You say *fuck you* one more time and I'm tossing you right through this window." The look in Dagger's eyes was enough to snap Langley's lips shut. "I need you to tell me what happened that night. Say it quick so I can leave and you can get back to your anger and depression."

"What else is there to say?"

"I'm mainly interested in the part on the tape when you were looking over your shoulder. I need to know why."

"I heard something. Leaves blowing, I guess."

"Don't guess."

Langley ran his fingers along the hospital I.D. bracelet on his wrist. He was either giving consideration to his response or ignoring the question. Dagger wasn't sure. Finally, Langley lifted his face to stare out the window.

"It sounded like…it sounded like footsteps."

25

"Hope you weren't waiting long," Sara said when she located Mitch sitting at the bar.

His eyes were busy running over her body. "Wow. I never knew leather pants could fit so well. Lavender is definitely your color."

Sara hadn't been sure whether to dress like a bike chick, school marm, or pitiful Pauline. Her closet didn't have that many dresses. Her holiday pin was affixed to the top of her sweater.

The waitress showed them to a booth, took their drink orders, and left them with menus. "Your suit looked pretty good on television." Sara snuck a peak over her menu at him.

"Ah, I have been unmasked."

The booth was in a corner against the wall and Sara felt safe and secluded. At almost two o'clock most of the lunch crowd was gone.

"Does it bother you?" Mitch asked.

"Hmmm?" Sara looked up from the menu. "Does what bother me?"

"The notoriety. You are having lunch with an ex-con."

"It all depends on if you did it."

"Of course." He smiled again, but briefly. Even the twinkle faded quickly from his eyes. "I made a lot of money and didn't share everything with Uncle Sam. Politicians are pissing away our money every day of the week. They got as much as I felt they deserved. So I served five years, but you know what? I still have my money and it was a much-needed vacation."

Mitch turned to his menu, the smile frozen on his face. Sara set her menu down and studied him. He was charming and cunning and radiated danger from every pore in his body. Her senses told her he was guilty of more than just tax evasion. But she also remembered Dagger's vault full of money, almost always being paid in cash for jobs, and never claiming the cash income. Then there was Skizzy. She doubted anyone knew how much money Skizzy made or whether he files tax returns. Mitch's mistake was getting caught.

Their waitress returned and took their orders.

"Is she the same lawyer you had the last time?" Sara asked once the waitress left.

"Angela? Yes. She's a great defense attorney."

"Why does this sergeant have it in for you?"

"He's got tunnel vision. Sets his sights on one person, tries to close as many cases as he can so he can get a promotion. There is no righteousness or justice any more. Those are just words." Mitch leaned his elbows on the table and edged forward. Casually he reached over and took a peek under Sara's right sleeve. "No sales ticket?"

"I purchased it when the plastic gods were still talking to me," Sara replied. Truth was, she'd never owned a charge card.

Mitch reached into his suit pocket and pulled out a long thin box which he placed in front of her. "Let's call it an early Christmas present."

Sara stared at the box. Gifts already. He worked fast. "I couldn't," she stammered, flicking her gaze to Mitch, then back to the box.

"Why don't you open it first before you decline."

Sara hesitated, then reached out and slowly tugged at the ribbon. Inside the box was a tennis bracelet made of blue diamonds with the subtlest hint of turquoise color. "It's beautiful."

"They match your eyes. I couldn't pass it up."

Tears welled easily. Sara had a number of her own problems to think of in order to conjure up fake waterworks. "I can't," she sniffed and looked nervously around the room. "I don't know you that well. It wouldn't be right." She placed the lid back on the box and shoved it toward him. But she kept her eyes on the box to give him the indication she could be swayed.

"You don't know me that well, YET." Mitch shoved it back as the waitress appeared with their food. After the waitress left, he said, "Just take it and admire it for a few days before you make up your mind."

"I don't like owing people. That's what my..." She quickly looked away and focused on her shrimp salad. Mitch remained silent but she could feel his eyes on her. She dangled just enough of a bait his way and was making it up as she went along.

"So, this boss of yours has something on you. What? He caught you stealing something?"

Sara stole a quick glance around the room. "Mitch, you

don't want to get involved. He's a dangerous man."

"Danger is my middle name."

Sara tried not to laugh at that cliché. She placed the fork down and waited a few beats. "He helped my grandmother out with something and then he wanted double the amount of money he originally asked for."

"So he's got you working at slave wages to pay it back."

"Something like that." Sara forced a look of embarrassment. Mitch bit.

"He's forcing you to have…"

Sara filled the blanks in quickly. "He has a lot of out-of-town business associates that I have to…" She dropped her gaze to her lap, then decided now was the time to snap out of it. "It's fine. Grandmother's debt will be paid soon. That's what's important." She picked up her fork and continued eating, stealing glances at the white box every so often.

"Who were the expensive gifts for, Sara? The ones you purchased at Beckman's?"

Sara had to think fast or he might have just caught her in one of her lies. "There's a man from England who comes into town often. He has a daughter my age and he just couldn't bring himself…to engage in…" She paused to take a sip of tea before continuing. "He would take me out to dinner and a show instead. He didn't want to anger my boss by refusing his gift of my company for the evening. Instead he would give me money to try to help me out. I used some of it to buy him a gift."

She pushed her plate away even though she was still famished. "I don't want to talk about this any more."

"What's your boss's name, Sara?"

"You don't want to…I have to go." She slid out of the

booth and took two steps. Sara turned back around, swiped the box from the table, kissed Mitch on the cheek, and said, "thank you," before running out.

Mitch watched Sara leave and had a burning desire to cut out her boss's heart. After tossing several bills on the table, he slid out of the booth and grabbed a seat at the bar.

"Hey, sweetie, give me a vodka and tonic," Mitch told the bartender. Out of the corner of his eye he saw a woman sidle up to the bar and say, "Make it two."

Mitch looked over to see an attractive blonde slide onto a stool next to him and slap her handbag on the bar. Her perfume smelled as rich as she looked. Wasting no time, she turned toward him and said, "You look much better in person than on television, Mitch." She stuck a hand with well-manicured fingers at him, saying, "Sheila Monroe, *Daily Herald*."

Mitch was amazed at her firm handshake and equally amazed at how fast she crept up on him. He could usually sense a reporter from a block away. The bartender set their drinks on the bar and lifted a ten-dollar bill from the stack Mitch had pushed toward her.

"I really can't say anything without my lawyer. I'm sure you understand."

"No problem." Sheila took a sip of her drink and scanned the restaurant. The remaining shoppers had drifted out and the staff was busy cleaning tables. "I would like to do an exclusive on you, though, at some future date. Of course, after you have sued the city for millions and gotten Martinez's butt fired or demoted down to patrol officer."

"No love lost between you two, I take it."

driveway. "Padre finally made it."

"You're face is fire engine red, Padre. Take some deep chi breaths."

"That shit may work for you but red is my color." Padre kicked off his shoes and stretched out on the couch. "I can see Chief Loughton's face now. He probably took one large bite out of Chief Wozniak's ass and now he's looking around for mine."

"Aren't they the same rank?" Sara asked.

"Nah. Wozniak is chief of detectives. He reports to Police Chief Harold E. Loughton. That's *H.E.L.L.* for short." He craned his neck toward the aviary. "Where's my buddy? Why is he always sleeping?"

"He's playing with his block toys," Sara replied. "Be thankful for the quiet."

Dagger asked, "What did you find at Mitch's condo?"

"Nada."

"What about at the Cohen house? Anything to connect Mitch?"

"Nothing so far but they are still checking prints."

"But you got his prints off the car, right?" Sara sat on the floor and stretched her legs out on either side. She bent over and grabbed the arch of her left foot and touched her forehead to the left knee.

Padre propped himself up on one elbow. "How the hell can you bend like that? If I did that, they'd need a crane to pry me apart, but, yeah, we I.D.'d Mitch's print off the car and he doesn't have a clue how it got there." He swung his legs around and grabbed the remote. "Let's see if pretty boy made the noon news." The television snapped on to the

"Well, let's just say he's very uncooperative. Reporters don't like to be stonewalled and we especially don't like the silent treatment. The public deserves to know the truth and I aim to give it to them."

Mitch raised his glass in a toast and smiled. "To the truth."

Sheila tapped her glass to his and took a long swallow. "So, tell me. How did you meet Susie Sunshine?"

"Who?"

"Sara, the girl you were having lunch with. She's not an easy face to forget."

"Ah, Sara. Yes, she is very easy on the eyes. I met her at Beckman's." He chased the lime around in his drink with the swizzle stick as he let the silence drag on.

"Beckman's. Why does that name ring a bell?" Sheila finally asked.

"That's one of the places Sergeant Martinez claims I robbed because, number one, I was there hours before the theft. Number two, I had installed the security system years ago. But those topics are off limits. Nice try, Lois Lane."

Sheila flashed him a smile that quickly faded. "That's a men's clothing store. What could Sara be doing there?"

"Christmas shopping for a man, obviously." He blinked slowly, letting his eyes sweep over her exposed thighs. If she dressed for distraction, it might work on someone who was more easily maneuvered.

"So Sara was buying a gift for a man. And what was it you bought for her?"

Mitch admired her abruptness. Not every woman could pull it off. She had apparently been watching them. He also sensed some history between her and Sara.

"Just a little trinket."

"Come now. You said yourself you just met her. Why would you buy her a gift?"

"Why does any man buy a woman a gift?" He let that comment sink in and watched her reaction. She wasn't easy to read. "She deserves nice things. One night when we went to dinner Sara wore a rather expensive dress. I saw the price tag still on the inside of the cuff. She was embarrassed and said she planned to return the dress the next day. Her boss only pays her seven dollars an hour."

Sheila burst out in raucous laughter. "I'm sorry." She placed a hand on his forearm and stifled another laugh. "That's so unladylike but so humorous. Dagger pays her a hell of a lot more than seven dollars an hour."

"Dagger? That's her boss's name?"

"Yes. And he's very free with his money when it comes to Sara. What else did she tell you?"

Mitch didn't like her tone. Was he being baited by a crafty reporter or was she a woman scorned? "She said her grandmother owed him some money and she was being forced to pay it back. That he was forcing her to entertain out-of-town clients."

Sheila covered her mouth with both hands this time as she broke out into another fit of laughter. Mitch's smile was slowly fading as he realized her amusement was genuine. She took another sip of her drink before continuing.

"He taught her well, I can tell you that much."

"What do you mean?"

"For starters, Dagger hardly knew her grandmother. She died almost a year ago. Second, Dagger would cut a man's throat rather than let him touch Sara. Chase Dagger is a private investigator and a close friend of Padre Martinez. Sara not only works with Dagger...catch the word, honey ...works WITH, not FOR..., but they also live together."

Mitch downed the last of his drink and pushed the empty glass to the edge of the bar, signaling to the bartender for a refill. He used those few moments to gain control of the anger building up. How much could he really trust a woman who just sidled up to him like a snake charmer? Sara had no way of knowing who he was when he ran into her at Beckman's. Was it by chance?

"So, she and her boss are lovers. Interesting."

"There isn't anything romantic going on, at least according to Dagger."

"And you believe him?"

"Yes. Dagger feels responsible for her. Made some promise to her grandmother. My god, the girl can barely function out in public she is so naïve. I don't think she left her house more than ten times in her life."

Mitch didn't remember Sara acting that naïve when he was with her. And how could any man live with her and not have sex on the brain?

"You're probably wondering if I'm telling the truth." Sheila pulled out a cigarette and tapped the end on the cigarette case. The bartender appeared with a lit match. "Thanks, hon." She turned her gaze back to Mitch as smoke slowly drifted toward the ceiling fans. "I know Dagger quite well. I was engaged to him."

He stared at her left hand. A large diamond engagement ring was on her finger. "Was?"

She stared at the ring with a wistfulness he recognized. "What can I say? It won't come off."

This brought a loud laugh from Mitch.

"Seriously, watch your step around Sara. She plays the helpless role quite well. I wouldn't put it past Dagger to have her wired for sound. Legally, he can do it. Padre can't." She pushed the glass away and slid off the booth. Leaning in close, she said, "Take it from me, Mitch. Dagger is one man you don't want to mess with."

Mitch watched the reporter leave. She wasn't hard on the eyes, either. But his mind drifted to Sara as he tried to remember exactly what questions she had asked and how much information he had revealed. He wondered if Sara had worn a wire the night they had dinner. Was the holiday pin she wore today actually a pin? Was Sheila right and their conversations had been bugged? Usually, as with Sheila, he could tell when someone was pumping him for information. His guard had been down because he had been the one to run into Sara; he had been the one to pursue her. Mitch Arnosky was a betting man...and he didn't like those odds.

and he should be here any minute. I guess Skizzy jumped at the chance to keep an eye on Mitch's condo last night."

Dagger waited for her lips to stop moving, then pried his eyes back to her face. His eyebrows arched as though to ask, *and your point?*

"If you were suspected of doing something ten times worse than income tax evasion, not to mention murdering your partner..."

"Somehow, about now, I can clearly understand Mitch's desire to murder his partner."

"Don't interrupt." Sara took a sip of coffee, ignoring his murderous reference. "Wouldn't you move out of town? Given his supposed wealth, he could be living in the Florida Keys or San Diego or the Caymen Islands. So why come here?"

"Maybe to aggravate the hell out of Padre."

"Why give Padre a reason to come after you, though? You've got a new lease on life."

Dagger gave up, shoved two pillows behind his back and sat up. "You must have been thinking about this all night. What have you come up with?" He grabbed her cup and took a swig. This was not vintage Sara. The old Sara would never have come into his bedroom and definitely wouldn't have sat on his bed when he was in it. The old Sara would never have gone into his vault and snooped around the BettaTec map.

"I thought you could tell me." She pulled her cup back and checked the contents. It was empty. The alarm on the gate buzzed. "That's probably Simon." She scooted off the bed, leaving Dagger with the thought of buying a padlock for his bedroom.

Dagger brushed his teeth and finger-combed his hair before joining Simon in the kitchen.

"That damn squirrely friend of yours trampled half those woods driving his Humvee up to the top of the hill," said Simon. "Didn't he ever hear of the word inconspicuous? Then he has to reconnoiter, he says, like he's checking for enemy patrols. Damn nutcase." Simon's laughter rolled from deep within his stomach. "Course, he was done before dawn, 'cause he didn't want no one seeing him." The burly mailman let out a laugh that shook his entire body. "We're just lucky we haven't been getting any snow. Raccoons would have found his bony body frozen like a popsicle stick."

Dagger stirred his coffee and tried to coax his eyelids to stay open. "Is it just me or is the sun unusually bright this morning?"

"Were you out drinking?"

"No, were you? How many bars did you hit?"

"I staggered into a few places, nursed one drink at each, and slurred some unintelligible questions about my good friend, Nate, whom I used to drink with. But so far, nobody remembers him. I will keep trying. With glee," he added. Simon lifted his head to listen for sounds above him. Sara had gone upstairs to change. Leaning across the table he whispered, "You planning a birthday party for her?"

"Should I?"

"Maybe we should take her to her favorite restaurant," Simon suggested. "I'll have Eunie and you can get Padre there. I doubt Skizzy will eat restaurant food."

"Padre may not be free to go out in public by then. Maybe I'll just have cake here and whoever wants to show up can show up."

"Mighty fancy planning on your part, *Mr. Good Time Charlie.*"

"I just don't think Sara would appreciate the fuss."

Simon listened for the sound of footsteps from the floor above, then whispered, "She's going to be nineteen." He held up one finger like a metronome and said, "tick tock tick tock."

Dagger pushed away from the table with a long sigh. "I have to take a shower. Why don't you make yourself useful and whip us up a couple of omelets."

Twenty minutes later Dagger followed tempting aromas to the kitchen where Simon stood, dishtowel tucked at his waist to serve as an apron. Sara was already in the middle of her omelet.

"The bear is out of hibernation," Simon announced, flipping an omelet out of the fry pan onto a plate. "Bon appétit." He set the plate in front of Dagger.

He stared at the variety of colors folded into the fluffy eggs. "What's in it?"

"The kitchen sink," Simon replied. "Watch out for the washers and bolts. Anything else I can get you two? Hash browns, pastries, more coffee, a room at the Ritz?"

"Simon," Dagger cautioned.

"Arsenic," Sara said, oblivious to the suggestive innuendo. The two men stared at each other across the table, then slowly turned their attention to the young woman. "Padre thinks Mrs. Cohen might have been poisoned," she said. "So where would someone get arsenic around here?"

The two men shrugged.

"According to the Internet, you need a permit to purchase some poisons." Sara lifted the lid on the box Mitch had given her yesterday. "Maybe there's something on Mitch's computer the cops didn't find that Skizzy could." She held up the bracelet and admired the sparkling gems. "Isn't it beautiful?"

"You don't like to wear jewelry," Dagger reminded her.

Sara sighed as she placed the lid back on the box. "I know, but it is beautiful."

"Fine. I'll buy you three of them. What's a pimp for?"

"Huh?" Simon gawked at Dagger. "Did I miss something?"

Dagger told Simon about Sara's lunch with Mitch and their taped conversation.

"And he buys her a diamond bracelet?" Simon pulled the box over and examined it. "If you aren't going to wear it, it would sure look nice on Eunie's wrist."

Dagger swiped the box back. "Don't go cheap on that woman. You don't deserve her."

"You should go to Mitch's apartment," Sara told Dagger. "You might be able to find something the cops missed."

"Gotta get him outta there first," Simon said.

"That's easy. I'll finagle a dinner date out of him and keep him busy." She grabbed the box and stood. "I'll give him a call and see when he's available."

Simon flicked his dark eyes to Dagger. A worry line etched quickly across his forehead. "Two months ago she was Gidget and now she's Lara Croft."

"I know." Dagger knew exactly what the problem was. He saw it in Langley, who expressed his anger openly toward everyone and everything. Sara was bottling it all up inside and one day she was going to explode. "Addison affected her more than any of us realize."

"You may have to get her some help."

Right, Dagger thought. He could see her now trying to explain to a shrink what it is in her life that is causing her such angst. Maybe the shrink would like to witness her shifting firsthand. Then the wolf will kill him. One hundred and fifty dollars, please.

Simon nudged him. "Want me to find someone for her? I can have Eunie talk to her. Maybe she's having some woman problems."

Dagger shook his head. "I'm the only one who can help her, but thanks, Simon."

Mitch exited the red BMW and headed for the elevator in the underground garage. Dagger waited behind the wheel of his Lincoln Navigator, then circled the floors of the parking garage and drove onto the street. At the next corner Dagger turned and parked in a fire zone with a clear view of the front and side doors. According to the latest reports in the newspaper, Mitch was still the media darling and Padre the scourge of the city. Internal Affairs was delving into previous cases Padre had worked to determine if there had been a pattern developing in the cop's alleged willingness to manufacture evidence just to close a case.

"You placed the tracker on the wrong car, Skizzy. The Beemer belongs to Mitch's attorney. I don't feel good about it being on an attorney's car."

"Since when?"

"Since it might backfire in Padre's face," Dagger said into the speaker phone as he sat behind the wheel of the

Navigator. "Now get your skinny ass over here."

"You're there. It's under the right rear wheel well."

"I can't. Mitch just exited the front doors and he's on foot. I'm going to follow him." He folded the phone and shoved it in his pocket.

Dagger waited for Mitch to cross the street before exiting the Navigator. Mitch wore designer sunglasses and GQ clothing, but no hat or any type of disguise. Dagger's leather coat billowed from the long strides he took to keep Mitch within view. When he passed, the elderly hugged their packages tightly, as if this man dressed all in black, with a five-o'clock shadow that sprouted the moment the blade left his face, was going to rip their possessions from them with a mere look.

Mitch cut through a parking lot and headed toward The Carriage House Diner. The guy was more than cocky. He was baiting the media, probably going against everything his attorney told him. Or maybe it was a planned strategy of showing innocence by remaining in the public eye, not holed up the way Padre was.

Dagger stepped through the doors and scanned the restaurant, his head swiveling like a Cyborg, eyes hidden behind dark sunglasses. Mitch was seated in a booth next to the windows. Dagger strolled past, followed the curved counter, and took a seat where he had an unobstructed view of Mitch's booth.

Mitch studied the menu with the casual ease of a man without a care in the world. The waitress arrived and filled Mitch's cup. As he stirred cream into his coffee he smiled as though he had read something funny between the swirls and steam.

The familiar scent of perfume preceded Mitch's break-fast companion. Not one set of male eyes missed the shapely legs exposed under the short leather skirt.

Dagger flicked his menu up to cover his face. "Shit," he mumbled under his breath. Sheila Monroe slid into the booth across from Mitch. He shouldn't have been surprised that Sheila was able to finagle an interview.

Dagger kept his head forward but the eyes behind the dark glasses studied Mitch and tried to read lips. Sheila was obviously after an exclusive but Mitch's attorney would be stupid to let him speak to the media. Mitch was laughing now, but it was a polite laugh of someone who wasn't at all amused but was play-acting.

Now she'll touch his arm, Dagger thought.

Sheila touched Mitch's arm and left her hand there for several seconds.

"Reel him in now," Dagger mumbled. Somehow he had a feeling Sheila had met her match. Mitch was only going to tell her what he wanted her to know. It was classic Sheila to cut a deal for an exclusive interview now, with the promise that nothing will run in the papers until the inter-viewee gives the go-ahead.

Dagger's phone vibrated. He checked the number and unfolded the phone. "Yeah?"

"Houston, we have a problem," Skizzy said.

"Speak."

"It's gone."

Dagger stirred his coffee, keeping a watchful eye on Mitch's booth. "Gone." He didn't like the sound of that. "You sure you checked the right car?"

"Gee, let me think about that one. There aren't any other

red Beemers with a license plate that says *SideBar*."

"Fuck." Dagger hung up. He lip-read a few comments about out-of-control cops while Sheila's pen moved quickly across the page. No way was he going to make it out of the restaurant without Sheila seeing him, so he might as well let Mitch wonder if he was being tailed.

He approached slowly, paused for several beats, then pressed his palms flat on the table.

"Dagger." Sheila's reaction bordered on pleasant surprise and shock that she had been caught.

Mitch's smiling eyes turned cold as Dagger pulled his sunglasses off and jammed them in his pocket.

"I gather you two haven't met." Sheila made the introductions. Mitch's smile didn't reach his eyes this time. He stuck out a hand, but Dagger just looked at it and turned his gaze to Sheila's notepad.

Mitch's hand dropped as quickly as his smile. "So you are Chase Dagger, close friend of Sergeant Martinez and business associate of Sara Morningsky."

At the mention of Sara's name, Dagger turned his dark eyes to Mitch. Any normal man would have flinched at the intensity of his stare, but Mitch merely did his slow lizard blink. Dagger straightened and slid his hands into the pockets of his black cargo pants.

"How do you ferret out truth from fiction, Sheila?" Dagger asked without turning his face from Mitch.

"Good reporters have a knack for knowing when someone is telling the truth," Mitch responded for her. "Maybe she should interview Padre, too. After all, he's still in town, isn't he?" He blinked slowly and cranked up the smile Padre had described so well. "By the way, Dagger." Mitch set a button on the table in front of him. "You can have this back. You of all people should know trackers are easy to detect if you have the right equipment."

Dagger gave Skizzy's device a passing glance and was grateful he didn't have Skizzy plant the cameras and bugs he wanted in Mitch's condo. "Not mine. Maybe you should check with the IRS." Dagger slipped his sunglasses back on and left the restaurant. He waited until he was back in the Lincoln before calling Padre.

27

"How the hell did he find out where you are staying?" Dagger paced the red brick kitchen floor in the rectory of St. Michael's.

"He didn't say he knew where I was, just that I was in town. Or maybe he was testing you. Were you followed?"

Dagger's glare said, *give me credit.*

"Will you sit down already. You're making me nervous."

"You saw the papers. They are hanging you out to dry. Does Wozniak have a tail on Mitch?"

Padre's eyes followed him. The kitchen was filled with the aromas from last night's pot roast. "Now you know how devious Mitch is. He knew to check for bugs. You should know by now he can also shake a tail."

"You are unusually calm." Finally, because his legs were tired of treading the same path, Dagger took a seat across from Padre. "Mitch knows Sara and I work together, thanks to Sheila, so her cover is blown."

"Did you tell Sara you saw Mitch and Sheila together?"

"Yes. She isn't worried."

"So, you shouldn't be either."

"You don't understand. Sara is in a *bring it on* mode of

self-destruction."

Padre sat back in his chair and studied him. "You're really worried."

Dagger nodded. "I'm used to protecting her. Now I have to protect the world from her."

Padre laughed at that comment, not seeing the genuine concern in Dagger's eyes. "Come on, Dagger. How much damage can one young woman do?"

"How long do you want me to keep him out?" Sara checked the back of her suede skirt for lint.

Dagger cocked his head to study the length of the slit up the side of her skirt. "I wish you had suggested the restaurant in Michigan City."

"Too obvious." She studied the costume jewelry pinned to her lapel, and after reconsidering, unfastened it. "He might be expecting this. You never know what Sheila told him."

"I don't want you out there without a way to communicate." He straightened her collar and swept her hair back from her face.

"I have a way to communicate." She opened her purse to reveal a stun-gun.

Dagger pulled the weapon from her purse. "Where did you get one this small? Wouldn't a can of mace be more appropriate?"

"Skizzy sold it to me. Kind of cute, don't you think?"

Dagger shook his head to rattle out the words he had just heard. "Just keep your phone on you at all times."

"Don't call me when you are done. That would be a signal any fourth-grader could identify."

Dagger stammered and tried to gather his composure. At what point did he become the trainee?

They drove their own cars. Sara was meeting Mitch at the Fire Hearth Restaurant just outside the city limits. Dagger was headed to Mitch's condo to have a look around. The plan was to have Sara press recall on her phone the moment Mitch entered the restaurant, wait several seconds, and hang up.

Mitch was already seated at the bar when Sara walked in. The restaurant was more crowded than she had anticipated, with clusters of people cramming the bar and waiting area. She halted a mere ten steps into the room and started to back out. Mitch caught her arm and steered her to the door.

"You okay?"

She shook her head and fought back tears. "I don't like crowds, that's all. I just need some air." She walked out into the chill while Mitch went back into the bar for his coat.

"How about if I make you dinner?"

Sara laughed nervously. "That would go over real big." The last place she wanted to be was Mitch's condo.

"Just don't tell him." He shoved his arms into his topcoat. "I'll pay more than the going rate," he said with his patented grin.

Anger flashed in her eyes and she could care less if Dagger was in Mitch's condo now or not. She turned and walked to the parking lot, quickening her pace and ignoring his pleas. It was easy for the tears to form.

"Sara, I didn't mean it." Mitch rushed to catch up and put himself between her and the truck door. "Come on.

Aren't I allowed one faux pas?"

"I'm not for hire and I resent the implication. I'm really not all that hungry, Mitch." She stared him down until he moved out of her way.

"Shrimp creole at The Marina Restaurant? They have a few private booths in the birds nest." He stretched out his arm to hold her back while he pulled out his cell phone. He called Information and let the operator dial the restaurant. After speaking to the maître d' in what sounded to Sara like Italian, Mitch hung up and said, "They are holding a booth for us."

Dagger jammed a gun pick into the door locks, and soon had the back door to Mitch's condo open. "This better work," he whispered. He held a remote-sized box in front of him, pressed a button, and a green light flashed. Skizzy's little invention disrupted surveillance cameras. Dagger would reactivate them when he left.

One lamp had been left on in the living room and in the back area, which he presumed was Mitch's bedroom. Dagger went to work, starting first with the computer. While it hummed and clicked, Dagger checked the file drawers, flipping through manila folders marked with names of utilities, but the folders were empty. Next he checked the garbage can by the desk. Not even a paper clip. The desk was just as clean. He ran a penlight over the bookshelves. Not one speck of dust.

Dagger returned to the computer, placed a headset on, and swiveled a mike toward his mouth.

"It's turned on, Skizzy."

"Roger that."

Dagger rolled his eyes.

"I just gotta get the networks to talk to each other."

"Just tell me when you're ready," said Dagger. After several seconds, Skizzy told Dagger what commands to type in order for Skizzy to copy Mitch's hard drive.

While the computer did its thing, Dagger moved through the open-air condo to the back. The floors were glistening black marble, giving Dagger the sensation he was walking through space. The bedroom was more straight lines and nouveau riche décor. A gallery of lights in the headboard behind the bed sprayed ambient light throughout the room. Dagger opened the drawers in the wall unit, but they yielded nothing but loose change, toothpicks still in plastic wrappers, and colored hankies.

"Who the hell uses colored hankies?"

"Someone who wears ascots," Dagger heard in his ear. "This guy a hoity toity?"

"Right, some guy fresh out of prison by three months."

"He probably let his attorney furnish the place," Skizzy suggested.

"It's the same one he had before he went to prison, according to Padre."

"Maybe the prison hasn't shipped back all of his Renoirs yet."

Dagger swung open the door to the walk-in closet. The high beam swept over shelves and racks. "There aren't too many places to hide a NOCM in his condo. And I don't like the looks of this closet," he said.

"Why?"

"There are only two pairs of pants." Dagger turned off the pen light and made his way to the dresser. He started pulling open drawers. "And there are only several sets of underwear. All of the other drawers are empty."

"What about the rest of the house?"

"Other than some toiletries, very little. And I definitely didn't find any arsenic under the sink. Place looks more like a model home."

"Uh oh. I don't like the sounds of that either," Skizzy said.

Dagger moved through the rest of the floor like a Hoover, sweeping the beam into cabinets, corners and crevices. The bar in the corner didn't contain one glass or bottle of alcohol.

"Other than furniture store rent-a-couch, he doesn't have much in the way of furnishings. Even the ficus trees are fake so no one has to water them."

"What pictures did you want him to have? Bubba and Scooby from the joint, maybe a shower photo?"

Dagger finally admitted the obvious. "This is a halfway house, not a residence."

"I think you're right. He's holed up somewhere else and just goes to that condo to give the pretense he lives there."

"You done?"

"Yeah."

Dagger removed the headset, turned off the computer, and left everything where he had found it. He passed the phone on a side table and noticed Mitch didn't have an answering machine. Out of curiosity, he pulled on the phone jack. It wasn't plugged into the wall. Could be he didn't want any calls or maybe he only used a cell phone.

Dagger pulled the controller from his pocket. He opened the back door and peered out. The hall was empty. He stepped into the hall and before closing the door, pressed the disengage key on Skizzy's toy. He moved quickly down the stairs, pulled off the latex gloves, and tossed them into the first garbage can he saw.

28

"Do you really think Sheila will sit on any interview she does, especially once her father catches wind of it?"

"You sound like you know them pretty well, Sara," Mitch said.

"I had the unfortunate experience of attending a party with the Monroes. After Leyton Monroe skewered the rare steaks, he skewered Native Americans and every law that favored their fishing rights. If your interview means he'll sell more papers, you can bet he'll print it without your okay."

Off in the distance a lighthouse flashed its beacon. The restaurant had thinned out, leaving just three couples at the bar. Mitch lifted the lid on the box Sara had returned to him.

"Wish you would keep it. It really doesn't go with any of my suits."

He flashed the first genuine emotion Sara had seen on his face. Mitch actually was hurt. But she willed herself not to be swayed. "Why come back here, Mitch?"

"Why not?"

"Then you wouldn't have to deal with the media and be held under a microscope."

"I was warned before parole that this would happen. Doesn't matter which state I move to, people will find out, so why hide it? Besides, I'm innocent. Sergeant Martinez is the one who should be worried."

"Why not go someplace where no one knows you, a foreign country somewhere and save yourself the grief?"

"It doesn't help to run. Some day you will learn that."

I already did, Sara thought.

He pushed his glass toward the bartender, who refilled it with cognac. Sara was still sipping her Frangelica.

"What did you think of Sheila?" Sara felt Mitch's arm across the back of her stool, then his hand rubbing against her dress. She had to restrain from resisting his touch.

"She's hungry, beautiful, can probably use her feminine wiles to get what she wants, but I'd rather tell you what I think about Sara."

"Don't," Sara said, her eyes smiled but the tightness in her voice made him sit back abruptly.

"He won't like it?" His voice mocked her now. "The employer, co-habitant, but not my boyfriend, business associate?" He tossed back the remains of the cognac and slapped the glass on the bar. Then he leaned in close, wrapped a firm hand around the back of her neck while the other cradled her face. He was close enough for Sara to feel the hot cognac on her face. He whispered in her ear, "How can someone so innocent-looking be so damn deceptive."

Sara parted her lips to respond but that was when he kissed her hard, shoving his tongue into her mouth, that wet lizard tongue, as he locked on tight, sucking the very breath from her body. His grip was anything but tender and his release was just as harsh.

He left her sitting there feeling more violated than if he had stripped off her clothes. What enraged her was that disgusting, self-righteous look on his face when he left, the look that said *you haven't fooled me in the least*.

She ordered a second Frangelica, this time straight up, hoping that the warm liquor would help rid her body of the taste of him. Sheila might be taken in by his charm but Sara felt the underlying current of danger in Mitch and knew beyond a shadow of a doubt that he was capable of murder.

"How long ago did he leave?"

The bartender turned the bolt on the door to re-lock it after Dagger stepped in. "About thirty minutes."

"How many drinks has she had?" Dagger saw the full glass of brown liquid sitting on the bar in front of Sara.

"She's nursing her second drink."

"I appreciate the call." Dagger pulled two Grants from his wallet but Larry held up his hands in protest.

"Hey, that's not necessary."

"You let her stay past closing and I'm sure you have a lot of work to do."

Larry let his gaze slide to the figure seated at the bar. Sara was leaning back in the stool, one leg crossed over the other, revealing a lot of thigh. She was staring at the contents of the glass, her fingers drumming on the purse in her lap.

"I've learned more than I ever wanted to," Larry said. "Like, there is one murder occurring in the world every sixty seconds. I even know how long it takes eggs from blow flies to hatch on a corpse and that high temperatures and a lot of insect activity can reduce a body to skeletal remains within two weeks."

Dagger smiled with a hint of pride. "Sorry about that."

"Hey, no problem." Larry gazed at Sara again with a look of fascination and adoration. "I just love to watch her lips move."

Next to her eyes, Sara's best feature was her mouth. Her lips were full and sensual, which contradicted the conservative way she dressed and the innocence that permeated her body language.

Dagger shoved the money in Larry's shirt pocket and tapped it a little harder than necessary.

Larry grinned. "Let me know when you're ready to leave."

Dagger tossed his leather coat on the back of a chair and slipped behind the bar to pour himself a beer.

Sara's eyes followed his movements. "Is there anyone in town you don't know?"

"Lots of people. I just know all the right ones." Dagger tossed some ice cubes into her drink, then slid onto a stool next to her. After taking a long swallow of beer, he reached over and grabbed her hand. "I'm sorry that happened, Sara. Are you sure you're okay?"

"I'm not as fragile as you think, Dagger."

He smiled at that comment and raised her hand to his lips to kiss her fingertips. "I'm sure you'd like to believe that. I can see it in your eyes. You try hard to stretch that coat of armor to fit. But I know you, Sara."

She pulled her hand from his and took her time to respond, savoring the liquor. Dagger waited her out.

"It's okay, really. It wasn't like it was with Joey. I could sense Joey's intentions, see it in his eyes. But Mitch is play-

ing a game I haven't quite figured out yet. And I certainly
didn't ask him to ram his tongue down my throat." She shivered at the thought and pulled the glass back for another sip
of the liquor to chase the chills away.

He cupped his hand under her chin and turned her face
toward him. "I'll go break one of his legs. Both, if you like."

Sara relinquished a half-smile and shook her head no.
"He's not interested in me. He has his sights set on something else."

Dagger moved toward her. For a moment his lips
seemed to have a mind of their own but at the last moment
they made an abrupt detour and planted themselves on her
forehead.

"I think your fiancée…"

"Ex-fiancée," Dagger corrected her.

"Whatever. Anyway, I think she definitely filled in all
the blanks for him."

"Somehow that doesn't surprise me."

Sara pushed the half-empty glass away and swiveled in
her stool to face him. "Mitch is playing us. He's playing
everyone."

"His condo is a sham, too. Very few clothes, no dust, no
food, and no NOCM. Not even daily garbage."

"That's one thing I don't understand. The police already
searched his condo. He has to be staying at the warehouse."

"Skizzy made a copy of Mitch's hard drive so we can
see what he's been up to."

Sara brought the glass up to her mouth, then hesitated.
"You think he'll suspect someone was in his condo?"

"I hope so." A smile played at the corners of Dagger's
mouth. "It's time he knew he's being watched. He's been in

town for a couple of months. That's more than enough time for him to get reacquainted with the town and put a plan into action."

"All to get back at Padre?"

"We don't know what his plan is yet, but revenge to some people is the ultimate goal." Dagger threw a twenty on the bar and yelled to Larry that they were leaving. He wrapped an arm around Sara as he guided her to the parking lot. "You okay to drive?"

"Sure. I only had a drink and a half."

"That's one-and-a-half too many for my liking, kid. I don't want Larry getting into trouble for serving a minor."

"Don't forget tomorrow is my day off, Father Frank." Rebecca heard a grunt behind the office door as she carried a bag of garbage down the hall. She was hit with a blast of cold air when she opened the door. She had just set the bag outside the door when she felt something rush past her.

"Huh?" Puzzled, Rebecca stared at the doorway and the aisle beyond. She saw Father Frank emerge from his office and lumber to the kitchen. It was time for his pudding and whipped cream. She pushed the door closed and hurried after him.

"Don't you have a heavy hand with that whipped cream now, Father." She pulled the can from his grasp and shook it vigorously. He never knew she made his pudding with skimmed milk or his meatloaf with ground turkey.

Father Frank grabbed a handful of his sweater as if to prove there was a slender body underneath all that bulk. He scrutinized the size of the dollop Rebecca squirted onto the butterscotch pudding. "Don't be so stingy, Rebecca. You'll starve me to death."

She studied the second chin that hid the priest's neck and let her frown tell him she wasn't being fooled. "I'll go see if our guest wants dessert." She left Father Frank hovering over the can of whipped cream and was just several feet from the kitchen when she felt the icy draft. Rebecca turned and stared down the long hallway. She thought for sure she had closed the back door. Her steps faltered as she maneuvered down the dimly lit entryway. She passed Father Frank's office and peered in. Light from the computer monitor glowed on the wall behind the leather chair. The printer churned out pages in a rhythmic tempo. Satisfied everything was in order, she continued to the back door and slowly pushed it closed. Rebecca stood and waited to see if the wind blew it open again. She pulled on the doorknob to make sure the wooden door hadn't shrunk from the cold. Everything was tight. The door remained closed. Splaying the blinds, Rebecca peered out into the back lot. With a shrug, she turned the dead bolt lock.

29

"There must be something you can do, Angela." Mitch studied the display on the monitor, which told him his security camera had been disabled last night. He circled the kitchen, his cell phone pressed to his ear. "It's obvious someone broke into my home. Sergeant Martinez may be off the case but that just gives him time to work on his own. This has his markings all over it."

"Maybe we should bring in a forensics team to dust for fingerprints."

Mitch laughed. "That would be ironic. Have the cops come in to check for prints on one of their own. Like we can trust their findings." He poured a cup of coffee and leaned against the counter to study his furnishings. It was his attorney's idea that he convey a simple lifestyle, free of exorbitant purchases that would draw attention. After all, he was a man who had been found guilty of avoiding paying hundreds of thousands of dollars in taxes. "Just keep the press apprised of the continued harassment. If anything, it will garner some sympathy."

"And remember, no interviews. You don't talk to anyone about this case."

"Gotcha." Mitch didn't tell her about his meeting with Sheila Monroe and his promise to give her an exclusive.

Mitch hung up and carried his cup of coffee to the living room. "Stupid amateurs." The way Sheila had described Dagger, Mitch expected someone smarter than the average yokel. Mitch had kept current on all the latest technology and knew there was a way to disengage security cameras. So now he knew that while he was adequately distracted by the beautiful Miss Morningsky, Chase Dagger or Padre or both had been sifting through his belongings. Pity he couldn't have caught them on tape. A picture of Padre burglarizing his home would have made great headlines.

He pulled a business card from his wallet and dialed a number on his cell phone.

"Miss Monroe, Mitch here." He smiled at her enthusiasm. It actually sounded authentic. "I've thought about your offer and I'd like to do the interview."

"Wonderful," Sheila gushed. "Let me check my schedule and I'll call you with a time."

Sheila enjoyed the solitude of a quiet office. Her editorial on corruption in the Cedar Point Police Department would segue nicely into Mitch Arnosky's case. The editorial would run in tomorrow's paper. It would have made a bigger impact had it been in last Sunday's paper, but then she wouldn't have been able to spend adequate time on it.

Sheila spread out the back issues of the *Daily Herald*. The trial had been covered extensively. Although the investigation was public knowledge, she needed another angle. Did the police department drop the ball after Nate Harding's death? Did they focus their entire case on the lone surviving member of Guardian Security?

According to Sergeant Martinez, it was Mitch who taught Nate everything about the security business. It was Mitch who knew about computers and Nate who was just the dummy who installed them. But according to school records, Nate was a high school genius. He met Mitch when they both attended a computer class at a junior college.

During their breakfast, Mitch stated he and Nate had never discussed their pasts. Neither one had shared childhood stories. All Mitch cared about was Nate's electronic capabilities.

Sheila tapped out a cigarette and lit it with a gold butane lighter. Employees were not allowed to smoke, but Leyton Monroe smoked his cigars on a regular basis. Sheila had plowed through the offensive plumes on more than one occasion. The air purifier sitting on the corner of the desk hummed to life at the flip of a switch.

Kicking off her shoes, Sheila leaned back and studied the police profile. The phone rang and she tossed a threatening glare at it. Who would call her on a weekend? She punched the button on the phone and yelled, "What?" After less than a minute, Sheila slowly straightened and fumbled for her shoes. "You are sure about this?"

Chief Wozniak sat next to Padre in Father Frank's office. Father Frank was conducting mass in the church next door. Wozniak turned the ring over in his hand, fitted it on the tip of his index finger.

"Father Frank is sure it doesn't belong to any of his parishioners?" Wozniak asked.

"Rebecca cleans his office every day. You can call her at

home and…"

"I already did. She doesn't remember seeing anything this flashy."

"It's *The Rafael,* I'm telling you." Padre rubbed his hands across his face and around to the back of his neck. Father Frank had found the ring this morning on the floor by his chair. It was Rebecca's day off and there hadn't been any recent visitors to the Rectory.

"Damn, I need to think about this." Wozniak stood, his eyes riveted on the diamond. He avoided looking Padre in the face as he carefully placed the ring in his inside suit pocket.

"I didn't take it, John. I know how it looks but you can see the tape from Beckman's. I wasn't in the store, never set foot in it. Mr. Beckman can vouch for that."

"I know, I know. I'm just having a hard time wrapping my brain around this one. How do I walk into Beckman's and plop the damn thing on the counter?" He turned to look at Padre, as if he had needed time to gather the courage. "Chief Loughton is going to want to know where I got it. What do I say?" He glanced up at the crucifix on the wall and sighed. "I can't tell him. He'll run to I.A." Wozniak patted his pocket to make sure the bauble was still there. "I'm not saying a thing. Anyone says anything, deny it. I need time to figure something out."

Wozniak paced behind the chairs like a caged lion, more like a burly grizzly bear, glancing every now and then at the crucifix on the wall. "We have to send Father Frank on a little vacation. He hasn't learned to lie yet. Rebecca didn't work today so she can be completely honest when she says she doesn't know a thing." Sweat glistened on his forehead and upper lip.

"I should have gone out of town with the wife and kids. I hate the position this is putting you in," said Padre.

"If you were any other cop, Padre, I'd throw you right on I.A.'s doorstep. But I know you are just too damn honest to do something like this, or the fingerprint, or the note to Kiley." He stopped pacing and gripped the back of his chair. "We're going to need a goddam," he lifted his eyes to the crucifix, "sorry...miracle." He turned an eye toward Padre. "Give me a hand here, Padre. Turn water into wine."

Padre winced. His only idea was not going to sit too well with Chief Wozniak but it was his only hope of helping his boss to understand. "I think you really need to talk to Dagger."

"Oh, god." Wozniak's painful groan echoed in Father Frank's office. "I can't handle him today. Set something up for tomorrow."

30

The next morning Sara found a warm cup of coffee on the kitchen table next to a copy of the *Daily Herald*. A section of the paper lay crumpled next to the cup. She carefully unfolded the wad of paper and pressed it flat. Sheila's by-line on the Op-ed page caught her eye, so she sank onto the chair and read the skewering of Sergeant Padre Martinez and the Cedar Point Police Department.

Sheila was none too complimentary regarding Padre's handling of the case six years before and his botched attempts this week. She all but agreed with Mitch's accusation that Padre had planted the evidence and should be fired from the force, calling for the resignation of the chief of detectives, the chief of police, and a full investigation by the attorney general's office. Somehow, information was leaked to the press about the ring stolen from Beckman's allegedly being found at the Rectory where Padre was staying. Sheila had reported "unknown sources said," but no one at Saint Michael's would verify the *Daily Herald's* charges. All Chief Wozniak and Chief Loughton would repeat was "no comment." Father Frank was conveniently out of town.

"Dagger?" Sara called out. She walked through the living room to the front door. She noticed the garage door was open and an empty spot where the Lincoln Navigator was usually parked.

Turning, she noticed that Dagger had left the television on, still tuned to the local news. Residents were picketing the police station.

"Einstein, where did Dagger go?"

The macaw flew to the grated door and poked his beak through one of the slots.

"Did he tell you where he was going?" The macaw ruffled its feathers. "Did he make a phone call?"

Einstein bobbed his head up and down. "AWK, PLEASE LEAVE A MESSAGE FOR SHEILA MONROE. TELL HER TO MEET MITCH AT FOUR-TWO-SIX CRESCENT VIEW LANE. AWWWKK."

"Why would he tell her to meet Mitch? Oh, no." Sara grabbed her coat and keys and ran out of the house.

Sheila checked the address on the pink message slip, then looked up at the house set back from the curb. She thought Mitch rented a condo. Why would he ask her to meet him at a house with a *For Sale* sign on the front lawn? There weren't any cars at the curb. She thought a realtor would be on hand to do a walk through. Or maybe Mitch already bought the house and needed her decorating expertise.

The long brick drive led to an impressive colonial with white pillars. Trees were bare but she could imagine flowering dogwoods and magnolia trees in the spring.

Burrowing deep in her fur coat, Sheila took the three steps up to the porch. A Christmas wreath on the front door welcomed visitors. Cautiously she turned the knob and was surprised the door was unlocked.

"Hello," she called out. Her voice echoed against the vaulted ceiling. The oak floors glistened under her feet, but her attention was drawn to the large fireplace in the far wall. It was large enough to hold a pig roast. She just assumed the door drifted from her fingers and closed on its own. There was no longer a chill wind biting at her bare legs. But then the door pounded shut with such force she spun around with alarm, almost losing her balance. Her hand clenched a wad of fur against her chest. She could feel her heart slamming under her fist.

The eyes staring back were murderous. That was the only way she could describe them. The brows hunkered so low the eyes were in shadow.

"Dagger," Sheila stammered. "Sweetheart." He stood for the longest time just staring at her while she continued to babble. "Did you find this house for us? I love it. I don't even have to see the rest of it. Don't you just love the fireplace?"

Dagger pushed away from the door and advanced slowly. Sheila retreated, heels clicking on the floor. She didn't like the way he cocked his head, his gaze running the length of one side of her body, then cocked to inspect the other side. There wasn't anything sensual about it. It was more like he was deciding which appendage to remove first.

"Did you want to see the upstairs? We can check out the bedroom." Her laugh sounded forced and she willed her legs to stop but they kept back peddling until she felt the wall. End of the road. She could have sworn both of Dagger's hands were empty but out of nowhere a gun appeared in his right hand. Her eyes widened and she tried to think of alternate approaches. Nice never did work with him. She reached into her purse and pulled out a can of mace. It was knocked out of her hand before she had a chance to raise it.

He stood just a scant few inches from her and pointed the gun at her stomach. Sheila inhaled and felt her breath catch. She wasn't sure how long she stopped breathing. His eyes turned so dark they were like black holes. The sun streaming in through the tall windows didn't add a glimmer of light to his eyes. They were soulless. This was the look she hated—it was the only time he literally put the *fear of Dagger* in her.

The gun traveled, forcing the coat open, up her midriff, pausing between her breasts.

"Then again, we don't have to wait until we get upstairs." Sheila failed to force a laugh to ease the tension, especially when she realized he hadn't paused the gun at two of her best features. He had it aimed over her heart.

Now it was on the move again, between her cleavage and up to the left side of her neck, right over her carotid artery. The pressure from the gun forced her to lift her head slightly until she was staring right into those cold eyes. Killer eyes. The thought sent a chill through her veins. She had interviewed enough Death Row inmates to recognize that look.

Her only defense was to get angry. She thought back to the wedding she had planned with great care. About how Dagger had stood her up, never made it to the rehearsal and then called off the wedding at the last minute. All because he had met Sara. And now Sara was back. He never showed that much concern for Sheila when they were together. Sara had a hold on him that Sheila hadn't quite figured out. She was usually good at pinpointing a man's weakness. Dagger didn't have any, yet somehow Sara got to him.

Sheila gathered up all the loathing she felt, all the residual anger from the wedding that never was, all the pent up jealousy at the young woman who had turned Dagger's head.

"Go ahead," Sheila challenged as she lifted her chin higher. "Pull the trigger." Her green eyes flared. "What's the matter, Dagger," she taunted. "Lost your nerve? Does it only work when you threaten men or just the weak? I'm not as weak as you think, sweetheart."

Dagger unclicked the safety. Sheila flinched and immediately was angry for doing so. He leaned in close. She smelled his aftershave, a subtle woodsy smell that stirred something deep inside. She used to refuse to let her maid wash the pillowcase he had slept on because she wanted to smell that scent every night. Sheila had almost forgotten what it smelled like.

"You want to come after me, fine," Dagger whispered, his breath hot on her face, "but you leave my friends out of it. Padre didn't deserve the skewering you gave him."

"I reported the facts," she said.

"Facts according to Mitch."

"Mitch didn't tell me about the ring. I received an anonymous tip from someone who works at the Rectory. A female." She studied his face. The rejected woman in her wanted to believe he was angry only because he was jealous of Mitch. "I'm going to prove it." Her voice found new strength. The gun pressed harder against her neck, deflating that renewed energy.

Then she noticed something stirring behind his eyes. The pupils were dark but something darker seemed to shift, awaken. Sheila sensed the change and an underlying current of fear rushed through her. Dagger's left hand grabbed a fistful of platinum hair and squeezed. Sheila gasped. That stirring behind his eyes rolled now, like a dark object trying to find a place to settle in for a long stay.

Neither one had heard the front door open or the quick tapping of shoes across the oak floor. Suddenly, Sara appeared at Dagger's side. Sheila was relieved. If anything, at least she would have a witness.

"You promised, Dagger," Sara whispered, placing her hand lightly on top of the one that held the gun. "You said next time I could be the one to hurt her."

Sheila gasped as Sara slowly turned toward the reporter. A certain amusement flickered in Sara's eyes, a look a cat has before it plays with the frightened mouse. Sheila pressed back harder in hopes the wall could absorb her.

"You are both nuts," Sheila whispered.

Dagger eased up slightly on the gun. And something changed in his eyes. Sheila watched that darkness stir and move, recede into a hidden place.

"You think hard the next time you try to come after anyone I care about," Dagger said.

He released his grip and Sheila heard the safety snap on. The gun disappeared as quickly as it had appeared. Dagger turned and was gone just as quickly, his leather coat swirling around his legs, the door snapping shut behind him.

She stood for several seconds in the silence, tears streaming down her face while she waited for her heartbeat to return to normal. Then Sara moved in, getting within inches of the reporter, not letting her move. She crossed her arms and smiled. Sheila hated her youthful face, the shape and color of her eyes, the entire package. "My father practically owns this town," Sheila said. "He's going to hear about this." But her threats sounded as empty as the house.

"Your father loves money more than you. Mitch is playing you. And here I thought you were a smart reporter."

"You wouldn't know a lie if it bit you," Sheila spit back.

"Mitch is guilty and we are going to prove it. Won't look good for your newspaper. Bad reputation means low sales which means no more Jaguars or diamond bracelets." Sara ran her hand across the fur collar on Sheila's coat, fingered the diamond earrings. Sheila recoiled from her touch. "When will you ever learn that you can't get to Dagger through his friends? All that does is drive him further away."

She watched Sara turn and walk out of the house. Slowly, she slid down the length of the wall and sat on the floor. Hot tears fell, blurring her vision. The anger was still there, but it was redirected now. She was angry at herself. After all Dagger had done, after all he had said, she still loved him. And now she understood with such clarity the difference between her and Sara—Sheila brought out the monster behind those dark eyes; but it was Sara who could send it away.

Sara found him sitting on a picnic table set back from the beach. She felt a biting chill to the breeze off the lake as she stepped out of the truck so she pulled a blanket from the back seat. It wasn't difficult to figure out where Dagger would go. This is where he came after he killed Joey, the man who had tried to rape her. There hadn't been one second of hesitation, no moral or legal thought, just action. Sara remembered the look in Dagger's eyes, and it was there again when he was with Sheila in the house. It was by sheer luck that Sara had arrived in time. She didn't know what would have happened if she hadn't.

Dagger didn't move when she climbed onto the picnic table next to him. She flung one end of the wool blanket over his shoulders and sat down. Neither said a word. Dagger grabbed his end and held onto it. Slowly, Sara ran her hand under his arm and slid her hand into his. She held on tight and he squeezed back. She could feel the adrenaline pulsing through his veins.

They stared out at the waters where soft waves lapped onto the shore. Seagulls screamed as they circled, searching for food bits tossed out by an elderly woman strolling the beach. The sun was somewhere behind the clouds. Even the Chicago skyscrapers in the distance were lost in the overcast.

Sara could feel his pulse decrease, the adrenaline dissipating. Moving in closer she leaned her head against his shoulder. They sat like that for a long time, neither one speaking, knowing no words needed to be said, no questions needed to be asked.

After a while, Dagger said, "We need to get back. I have to move Padre to a better location."

"We have time," Sara said. "Besides, I have a plan."

Dagger turned and studied her. For the first time that day, he smiled.

31

Dagger steered the hooded man through the back door of the pawn shop. "You're going down some stairs now and they are steep."

"Is this really necessary?" Padre whispered.

"It was the only way Skizzy would go for it."

"But I know where the hell his shop is."

"You aren't supposed to know you are in the shop," Dagger whispered. "The staircase takes a turn now."

"Smells musty down here. Are you sure we aren't in some Ebola-ridden cave somewhere?"

"You two are going to get along just fine."

"Can't wait."

It had been Sara's suggestion that Padre stay with Skizzy. The press had been alerted that Padre was staying at the Rectory, and it was causing undue disruption of church activities. Sara had reminded Dagger that Skizzy and Padre had worked together on the Addison case and right now Padre was a fugitive, so to speak.

They had been able to sneak Padre out of the Rectory by using a little-known tunnel that connected the Rectory to the Grotto. From there they loaded Padre into a borrowed floral truck and carted him off to the back entrance of Skizzy's Pawn Shop.

"This the subject?" Skizzy stepped out of the shadows wearing fatigues and tapping a baton against his palm. "Don't remove it yet," he said as Dagger reached for the black hood. "Arms out to the side, soldier," Skizzy barked.

The hood turned toward Dagger and an audible sigh escaped. Padre lifted his arms. Skizzy worked the metal detector up one side and down the other, then stepped back with a nod. Dagger lifted the hood and Padre blinked against the bright ceiling lights.

Skizzy stumbled back and grabbed for a gun off the table. "A cop? You said you wanted me to hide out someone running *from* the cops."

"Put the gun down. Padre is running from the cops. Don't you read the papers?"

Padre's eyes blinked into focus. He took in the plywood cases padlocked on two of the walls and shelving with canned food and water on another wall.

"Where the hell do you park the Humvee?" Padre asked.

"This isn't going to work." Skizzy started walking in a circle, eyes bulged, words directed at his feet. "I can't have the enemy here spying on me. He's probably here to plant bugs."

"Come on, Skizzy. You know Padre. He worked with us against Paul Addison." Dagger clamped his hands on a set of bony shoulders and steered Skizzy to a chair. "Padre never said anything about that massive weapon you used against Addison or the Humvee that isn't titled in your name."

"Oh great." Skizzy tried to stand but Dagger pressed

down harder on the man's shoulders. His friend couldn't weigh any more than Sara but he was like a slippery snake, no spine, able to wiggle free from any restraint.

"It's just for a couple of days. He isn't armed. No camera. No bugs. You've already checked." He felt Skizzy relax a little. "You showed us the videotape of the NOCM Project. We believe someone is running around with one of these suits and has planted the evidence on Padre. He even knew where Padre was hiding. This is really the only place he is safe." Dagger let that sink in a little. If there was anything that challenged Skizzy, it was someone having a leg up on new technology. "We need your help."

Skizzy jerked his beady eyes in Padre's direction. Padre tried to look sullen and beaten, while one eye cruised his surroundings for a bed and a bathroom.

"Only a couple days?" Skizzy asked.

"That's it, maybe." Dagger added the last word under his breath. "I need to get the flower truck back before anyone notices it missing," he said as he moved to the stairs. "I'll send Sara by with some clothes and food. You two play nice."

Padre turned a slow circle, avoiding Skizzy's strange eyes, which seemed to work independently. Sometimes they looked in the same direction. Sometimes they didn't. One appeared to bulge out of his head while the other one receded.

What Padre wouldn't give for a window and a breath of fresh air. He felt the squirrely guy's eyes on him as he walked to a long worktable and picked up a strange metal spider. Without warning, its legs started to move.

"Yowww." Padre dropped the spider on the table. "What

26

"Doesn't it seem strange for someone to come back to the scene of a crime?"

Dagger rolled over and peered through his splayed fingers. Morning light christened the doorway to his bedroom where Sara stood, a cup of something steaming in her hand.

"Don't you ever sleep?" He drew the covers close, in a manner resembling a woman afraid of exposing intimates parts of her body.

"Think about it." Sara climbed onto the bed and crossed her legs. Clad in leggings and a long flannel shirt, she seemed completely oblivious to the fact that she had just barged into Dagger's bedroom.

"You're not going to let me sleep, are you?"

"You said you don't need that much." She swept her hair back and twisted it in a coil but it soon untangled itself and drifted down her arms.

Like everything he chose for himself, Dagger's bedroom was monotone—black and gray. But right now a splash of colors far too bright for this early in the morning was sitting comfortably on his bed.

"Besides, you wanted to be up when Simon stopped by

the hell is that?"

"A bug." Skizzy grinned as he reached over and tapped a few keys on the computer. The spider righted itself and crawled across the tabletop. "Audio and visual surveillance. That's what we used to catch the thief from your Evidence Room."

"Really." Padre picked up the spider again. It had beady red eyes and was so life-like he thought he could see hair on its legs. Skizzy pulled the spider from his hand and gently placed it in a box with other spiders and dragonflies. "What the hell else you got in there?" Padre's fingers were a scant few inches from the box before Skizzy reached over and slapped his hand.

"Don't touch. Don't touch anything down here." Skizzy sat back down and trained his beady eyes on him again.

"I feel like I'm in a cage. Would you quit staring at me?" Padre browsed the canned food on the shelves. All of the labels had been ripped off. Leaning close, he saw initials scrawled on the lids. He assumed the *CN* was for chicken noodle and *V* stood for vegetable. He remembered Dagger telling him that Skizzy removed labels from all the canned goods he buys.

"You know, there are expiration dates on the water."

"Who said that? I never heard that." Skizzy picked up one of the bottles to look for a date stamp.

Padre shrugged. "Besides, it's just tap water. Someone is making a killing. Did you know *Evian* is *naïve* spelled backwards?" Skizzy turned what looked like an evil eye on Padre. Padre had a grandmother who gave people the evil eye.

"What do you do down here? I don't see a television.

There's no radio, not even a deck of cards."

"I work." Skizzy pointed at the computer.

"Well, I would work but all my files are back at the office so I don't have access to them."

"Are they in your computer at the office?"

"Yeah."

Skizzy pulled out the chair and sat at the keyboard. "How many of your files do you want?"

Padre's mouth fell open as Skizzy accessed the police Records Department. A crooked smile formed on the face of the funny little man. Skizzy cocked his head toward Padre and asked, "Want to see the report on you from Internal Affairs?"

"You have a sick sense of humor," Wozniak snarled as he folded his tall frame into the passenger seat of Dagger's Lincoln Navigator. "'Meet me at the site of the headless horseman,' you said. Right."

The Navigator was parked on the gravel shoulder of the forest preserve, the precise location where, two months before, the head of a biker had gone in one direction, while the Harley and the body went another.

Wozniak settled back in the comfortable leather and studied a control panel which looked like it belonged in a space shuttle. A close-up grid of the city was displayed in the middle of the dashboard, one white blinking light indicating the Navigator's location. There usually was another blinking light displayed on the monitor. Sara used to wear an earring that would let Dagger know where she was when she shifted. But after she had left two months ago, Dagger had tossed the tracker in the creek out of frustration.

Wozniak stopped studying the menagerie of buttons and switches and shook his head. "Okay, you've got about twenty minutes of my time. The city is coming down fast around Padre's ears, not to mention a sizable chunk which has been taken out of my ass."

"I thought everyone in the Rectory could be trusted?"

"It was Becca's day off. Some rent-a-maid was there and overheard Padre and Father Frank talking after the ring was found. We got Father Frank out of there so he wouldn't be forced to admit anything. The girl was sent packing once my suspicions were confirmed." Wozniak cocked his head and stared at the skeletal branches, as if expecting to see the head of the biker still impaled on a tree limb. "What have you got that you couldn't tell me over the phone or show me in a public place?"

Dagger handed the chief a file folder. "This is what the Alphabet Boys were after at Doctor Cohen's house." While Wozniak read the information Skizzy had gathered on NOCM, Dagger shoved a CD into the player and pushed some buttons. The grid of the city changed to a monitor.

"That's great. I have time to watch a movie?" Wozniak huffed. He studied the report on NOCM and then saw the video from Skizzy showing the tank and military Special Ops.

Dagger switched tapes and *Predator* started to play.

"I saw this one. Wasn't half bad." Wozniak divided his attention between the reports from the Department of Defense and the video. "Fuck," he spit out. "Don't tell me this is how you think Mitch has been doing all this."

"It fits. Mitch installed the security system in Cohen's house. He had ample opportunity to sneak a peek at what

the doctor was working on. It's possible Cohen hadn't per-
fected it yet, or the Alphabet Boys would have picked up
their new toy and Cohen could be basking in Florida with
the rest of the blue hairs. But Mitch had five years to wonder if Cohen finished his project. Knowing how high-tech
security systems can change in five years, he probably figured he could no longer mess with cameras to get away with
crimes, like he did in the past." Dagger tapped the screen,
which showed the alien zapping off a red hot laser blast to
rip off the arm of Billy Dee Williams. "But this would be
perfect."

"Shit," Wozniak muttered. "I should have known if
Padre had you involved it was going to be another weird
case. With you, there probably IS a damn alien involved."
He rubbed a large hand across his face and shook his head.
His eyes scanned their surroundings as dusk settled quickly
in the forest. "Let's get this over with. I don't like being in
the forest after dark. What do you want me to do?"

"You look like you need this." Simon pushed a beer across
the table as Dagger slid into the booth at the Twenties bar.

"Why can't I just have a nice, simple, missing person's
case? I'll even take another missing dead person." Dagger
leaned against the wall and stretched his legs across the
seat. The bar was tucked in the middle of a residential street,
a mom-and-pop business that had withstood the test of time.

Simon nodded toward the bartender, who wore his hair
slicked back and parted in the middle. A ruffled garter was
wrapped around one arm. "The guy still thinks it's the
Roaring Twenties. He might even have a speakeasy in the
back," Simon said. "He remembers Nate Harding. Came in

a few times and started speaking to an old man named Sullivan. Owned Sullivan Imports. Lou, the bartender, said Sullivan got snockered at least three times a week but didn't cause no trouble. Just rambled. Harding used to buy him drinks and would sit off in a corner with him until all hours. Seemed to be buds. Then Harding died and Sullivan was dazed. Would sit in a corner and cry in his beer."

"Harding didn't look that likeable."

"Thing is, Lou says Harding always nursed one drink but would line 'em up for the old guy, like he was trying to get him sloshed."

"How old?"

"Seventies. Mumbled about Berlin when he was tying one on."

Dagger sipped his beer and studied the autographed pictures on the wall of Capone and other notorious faces from the past. The bar lived up to its Twenties name, offering only ragtime tunes from the juke box. By the look of the neighborhood clientele bellying up to the bar, the atmosphere definitely kept out the bikers and X-Generation.

"Think Harding could have been working a scam?" Dagger asked.

"Sullivan died of cardiac arrest a week after Harding's accident. He was an old man. Hard to say but anyone who hung around with Harding and Arnosky seemed to have a shortened life span." Simon pushed a note across the table. "This is the address of Sullivan Imports. The granddaughter owns it now. They are high-end antique dealers."

That caught Dagger's attention.

32

Dagger handed Padre a bag stained with grease spots.

"You are a savior, my son." Padre wrapped his hands around the hot bacon and egg sandwich and inhaled the aromas. "Thought for a moment the nutty guy was going to have me eating MREs." His gaze drifted to the box of donuts Dagger had placed on the table. "Nine o'clock in the morning. It's three hours past my feeding time. The guy never eats, never sleeps. I hear him walking around upstairs almost every hour on the hour. Don't know what the hell he's doing." He plopped into a chair closest to the donuts.

"Probably checking the doors to make sure he locked them." Dagger swiveled a chair around and sat down facing Padre. "Did you talk to Rebecca?"

"Yeah. I think you are right. When she went out to empty the garbage, she thought she heard footsteps and she felt a breeze, like someone ran past her. But she chalked it up to the wind. Then when she left the kitchen to come find me, she saw the back door open yet she could swear she closed it. That had to be Mitch planting the ring in Father Frank's office."

"Don't get them pages out of order," Skizzy barked

from upstairs.

Padre raised an arm toward the printer. "That damn thing was clinking and clunking all night long." Leaning forward, he whispered, "The damn guy can see through walls."

"And hear," Skizzy yelled again.

"Get your skinny butt down here and tell me what these reports say," Dagger yelled back.

They heard a scampering and thumping of tennis shoes on the stairs. Skizzy appeared in his Army fatigues, tee shirt, and a bullet-proof vest.

"And don't get grease on the pages." Skizzy pulled the pages from Dagger's fingers and sat down in one of the other chairs, the wheels squealing as he inched it toward the computer.

"Whatever your boy used this computer for, he hadn't used it in a while, but then he's only been home a few months, right?" Skizzy didn't wait for a response, just fanned out the pages across the table.

"Didn't they confiscate Mitch's computer for his trial six years ago?" Dagger asked Padre.

"IRS took it and copied everything. Then returned it to Mitch's lawyer."

Skizzy fanned through several sheets of printed paper, separating the past from the present. "All this back gobbledegook with his bookkeeping, which, by the way, if he had half a brain he would have hidden because it conveniently proves the company's total receipts and blatant tax evasion…" A crooked smile wriggled across his face. "Not that any of us would evade paying taxes. Anyway, he's got a number of recent Internet searches, mainly eBay and other trading sites."

"Was he selling or searching?" Padre asked. He poked through the donut box, grabbing a glazed Krispy Kreme.

"Searching for cars, classic books, electronic equipment. He also seemed to be doing some house hunting on the Pacific Coast. Pretty pricey homes, too."

"Probably wants to move to a richer area to install surveillance systems so he can steal more high-priced items." Padre spoke with disdain. He fished around the bag and pulled out a fresh cup of coffee.

"I take it he wasn't job hunting," Dagger said. "Any E-mail contacts with, say, a bank in Switzerland?"

Skizzy shook his head. "What's important is his on-line purchase of a certain item. He used a fictitious name of Leonard Miller and had his purchase delivered to a postal box over the border in Illinois." The skinny guy leaned back in his chair and smiled. "Guess what he bought?"

Padre glared at him, balling his hands into fists. "You know, if you already didn't look like you've had the snot beat out of you a couple of times in your life, I would bend you in half like a..." Padre paused, things clicking in his head. "Arsenic? Oh, please, tell me it was arsenic."

Skizzy grinned now, revealing teeth jutting at different angles. "Yep. Had to obtain a permit but he got his little purchase delivered over a month ago."

"But I thought the tox report didn't show positive for arsenic poisoning." Dagger said.

"Luther said the results were negative but he's having them rerun it just to be sure."

"That should be enough for Chief Wozniak to haul him in for questioning on the death of the Cohens," Dagger said.

He looked over at Skizzy, who was still grinning from ear to ear. "Okay, Skizzy. What are you holding back?"

He dangled a piece of paper in front of them. Dagger barely caught the name of Aiden Technologies.

"You got into their company web site?"

"Roger that."

"I'll Roger you." Padre rose from his chair and made a move toward him but Skizzy just laughed.

"The customer number given to the so-called Leonard Miller is in their computer another time." He swayed back and forth in his chair like an antsy grade schooler who knew something the other kids didn't. Padre made another step toward him. "Leonard Miller made a similar purchase six years ago."

Padre halted and turned his gaze to Dagger.

"Nate Harding," Dagger said.

"Mitch would have got rid of any leftover arsenic so as not to be caught with it," Skizzy added. "Then he had to order a new batch for the Cohens."

Dagger asked Padre, "What was the cause of death on Harding?"

"Heart attack at the wheel besides being a little drunk. Had a history of heart problems. It was supposedly heredi-tary, according to medical records."

"And Luther didn't question it?"

"That was the summer of one-hundred-plus-degree days, when fifty-eight senior citizens died from the heat," Padre reminded them. "They had bodies stacked like cordwood. I would bet Luther was so busy with those bodies that an assistant did the autopsy on Harding. Luther wouldn't have missed that."

"Maybe we need to talk to a relative," Dagger suggested.

"Tried that. Couldn't find anyone six years ago and no one came forward," Padre replied. He and Dagger swiveled in unison toward Skizzy.

"I'm on it." Skizzy turned to the keyboard and began his search.

Chief Wozniak sat in his car in the vacant parking lot of Cedar Creek Theater across from the mall. He didn't trust using his office phone so he had grabbed his cell phone and headed for an isolated location.

He studied the name on the business card Dagger had given him. General William J. Lorenz. Alphabet Boys. Wozniak was sure one call to the general should have him contacting all the rest of the gang. The phone was answered on the second ring. A man identifying himself as Sergeant Vaneer answered the phone.

"I'm sorry, but the general is not available," Vaneer said.

Wozniak had to word his message carefully in order to get a quick response. "This is John Wozniak, Chief of Detectives in Cedar Point, Indiana. The general visited our fine city last week following the alleged murder-suicide of an elderly couple." There was silence on the other end. "Are you still there?"

"Yes, sir," Vaneer finally replied. "As I said, the general is not available."

Wozniak plodded on. "I use suicide quite loosely given the latest developments, including some of the work of Doctor Seymour Cohen that has been showing up in our town. Please let General Lorenz know that it is imperative I speak with him today." Wozniak left his cell phone number and hung up. Checking his watch, he gave the male secretary two minutes to contact the general, another ten minutes for the general to drive his golf cart to his car or leave the breakfast table at the Officers Quarters to return the call on a secure line.

He watched as more cars filled the mall parking lot across the street and wondered when he would have time to finish his own shopping. His cell phone rang exactly seven minutes later.

"I trust you were done with the front nine, General."

"I had understood that case was closed, Chief Wozniak."

"Wish it were that simple but we've had some strange occurrences."

"This is a secure line."

Wozniak had been hanging around with Dagger way too much. Even he couldn't trust anything considered secure and he doubted the general was alone. But at this point in the game, he didn't care.

"You may have taken the paperwork, General, but not the toy. Now someone is using it to commit crimes. You may not care because the Alphabet Boys confiscated all they needed at the time. But if the press catches wind of this, your top secret toy won't be so secret any more."

Wozniak watched the shoppers across the street scurry to the entrances. The cell phone felt warm in his hand. He hadn't realized he was gripping it so hard. General Lorenz ended the call with the abruptness of a drill sergeant dismissing the troops. All the general said was that he would get back to him. Wozniak's gut instincts told him not to expect another call from Lorenz. Instead, one of the local Alphabet Boys would probably show up in his office, casually dressed so as not to draw attention. Then maybe a cloistered meeting somewhere with more locals. Of course, there was an off chance they might do something unexpected.

As he watched the shoppers, thoughts of a remote control Humvee popped into his head. It was something Aaron, his twelve-year-old son, wanted. Wozniak left his car parked in the theater parking lot and gave an early Christmas present to his heart by walking to the mall.

Dagger had refused to tell him where Padre was stashed and Dagger was probably right. It was best Wozniak didn't know. Then he wouldn't have to lie to I.A. or Chief Loughton.

As expected, the mall was packed with shoppers. Many of them were lined up at Starbucks and Cinnabons, getting their morning serving of energy for the day. There was also a long line at Sheridan Toys. Wozniak picked up his cell phone. He knew the number by heart, since every new toy out on the market prompted a call from Wozniak to have one put on hold for him. His favorite sales clerk answered and promised to hold one behind the counter for him.

Twenty minutes later he had the Humvee in his hand and was standing in line at Java Joe's for coffee. The line at Starbucks was far too long. He wasn't quite sure exactly how many coffees to get so he settled on three and carried them out in a cardboard tray.

Wozniak had been gone only thirty minutes, maybe a little more. All his nice heart-healthy walking was nullified by the two Krispy Kremes he'd wolfed down at Java Joe's.

He crossed the inner drive and made his way to the theater lot. The suits were getting out of their cars as he approached. Dark sedans with license plate numbers lower than his I.Q. Government plates. Wozniak smiled as he approached and offered the cardboard tray.

"Coffee black?" He had brought three coffees, one for himself. There were two dark sedans, two men. Expect the unexpected.

33

"Nice story." Mitch pulled out the chair for Sheila. "And I do like your choice in restaurants."

"Don't gush too much about the cooking. It was all catered. I don't do cooking or cleaning either, for that matter." Sheila's condo was on the twelfth floor overlooking Lake Michigan. The wall of windows provided a spectacular view of blue sky and white caps slapping the shore. "You must spend all your time at work. The place barely looks lived in."

"Everything is new. I had a great penthouse several blocks away, wonderful view, but my assistant was murdered there a couple months ago and I just couldn't bring myself to live there any more. I mean, how could I? Everything had been white...the carpeting, furniture, drapes. Then she was slaughtered like a piece of meat. It was horrible."

"You're rambling."

"Am I?"

"Obviously not over it yet."

"No. Especially since the victim was supposed to be me."

"Really?" Mitch scooped scrambled eggs onto his plate as he thought about the guard in the lobby. "Didn't the place have security?"

"It did, but somehow he got in. Could have been a delivery guy or someone claiming to visit someone else. Of course, the guard was fired." She layered salmon onto another bagel spread with cream cheese.

"If you have any doubts about this building, I can certainly get some surveillance cameras installed." Mitch smiled at that comment.

"I think you better lie low for a while."

"So I take it they caught the guy."

"He was killed. Probably one of the few things Cedar Point's Finest got right." She lifted the lid on another silver chafing dish. "Don't forget hash browns." Then on a second chafing dish. "Or French toast." She grabbed a silver pitcher and poured two glasses of orange juice. "One memorable part of the horrible ordeal is that Dagger was arrested for the murder."

"Really." Mitch reined in his genuine exhilaration at the thought. "Now why would they think that?"

"Probably because he had a key to the place and there had been a bit of a falling out between us. I denied Dagger's involvement. He would never hurt me." She paused, having a clear memory of the gun at her throat. "I have to tell you though. No matter how much a part of me enjoyed seeing him in handcuffs, it was even more thrilling when Sara was brought in for questioning."

"Sara?"

"Well, I did help in that regard. I had told the detective that a woman could just have easily committed murder as a man. Wouldn't you find that to be true?" Sheila's hand was holding the knife, inadvertently pointed in Mitch's direction.

"Absolutely." He placed his hand on top of hers and lowered the knife to the table. "There is a certain dangerous look that passes over your face when you mention both Dagger's and Sara's names." He kept his hand on hers and added, "I can help you forget him, even if only for an hour."

She stared at his hand, then lifted her gaze to his face. "Sorry. Dessert isn't on the menu today."

He removed his hand abruptly but his smile was forced. "My fault. Guess I assume too much."

"No problem. I don't like to mix business with pleasure. It would be unethical. The only reason I invited you to my place for breakfast is because every other newspaper will have reporters climbing over booths just to overhear our conversation."

"Understood."

They ate in silence. It was a comfortable silence as they passed condiments and dishes across the table. Sheila took a slice of cantelope from the serving dish and started carving it with quick stabbing motions.

"I certainly hope those exuberant wounds you are inflicting on that melon aren't meant for me."

Sheila stared at the knife as though someone else's hand was directing it. She set it down carefully as if fearing she might actually use it unlawfully.

"No, it isn't." The fork followed suit and she sat with her hands clasped in her lap. "Are you leveling with me?"

"Excuse me?"

"About everything? About Nate Harding for example?"

Mitch studied her body language. She had tensed up and her eyes had the look of a lover betrayed.

"What brought all this up? I've been in prison for five years and someone immediately starts to make me look guilty for crimes I haven't committed, all because he is pissed that he couldn't get previous charges to stick. I'm the wronged one here, Sheila. Even the police department has proof Sergeant Martinez planted evidence. Why would you start to side with him now?" Mitch was irritated, but not as defensive or angry as he let his tone indicate. Sheila was doing a one-eighty on him and he wasn't sure why.

"I'm sorry. I had a horrible encounter with Dagger yesterday." She pulled strands of hair back with a shaky hand. "He scared the hell out of me. It was a side of him I had never seen before."

"All because of the Op-Ed piece?"

Sheila nodded. "Dagger has a very small and tight inner circle, and no one, not even me, is allowed to criticize or malign them."

He reached across the table and grabbed her hand. "You're shaking. You really are afraid of him. Did he threaten you?"

Sheila forced a laugh but her bottom lip quivered and she had to fight to control the tears. "If you call having a gun pressed to your throat threatening. Then Sara showed up. She was almost as threatening, but I have to hand it to her. If she hadn't shown up when she did, I don't know if I'd be here today."

The tears fell freely now but she pushed away from the table and stood, her outstretched hands telling him to keep his distance. She used the napkin to swipe at the tears, then pulled a compact from her purse.

"He's not going to bully me. I just have to make sure my facts are accurate, Mitch." She checked her reflection in the mirror and dabbed at the mascara smudges. "It's not so much Dagger I'm worried about. I'll just start carrying a gun and shoot the sonofabitch myself. It's the newspaper. We were scooped on a big story several months ago and my father hasn't let me forget it. If we lose credibility because there is even a hint of impropriety, sales will plummet and stockholders will ask for my father's head on a platter." Satisfied with the repair work, Sheila sniffled back the last of the tears, tossed her mane of platinum hair and straightened her Carlotta Original suit jacket. "So," she said as she returned to the table, "is there anything else you need to add or revise?"

Mitch smiled at her stamina. She wasn't quite the gullible blonde he had first made her out to be. "All the information you have on Sergeant Martinez didn't come from me. Remember that. The fake print, the E-mail, the ring. Martinez didn't even leave town as the department led everyone to believe. And he supposedly isn't at the church rectory anymore. Do you know where he's at?"

Sheila shook her head. "I have informants working on it. But I didn't ask Dagger."

"If Dagger has a tight circle, Martinez is probably staying with one of them."

"Good luck. I don't know everyone in Dagger's circle. I was never with him twenty-four-seven to know. And that was information he never offered."

"Even in the most persuasive of times?"

Sheila frowned, the memories of intimate times too

painful. "Even then."

Skizzy had located a sister of Nate Harding and the three men were clustered around the speaker phone.

"How did you find me?" Linda Cerrara was not thrilled to be talking about her brother.

"It wasn't easy," Padre replied. "You're clearly a woman who didn't want to be found."

"I washed my hands of my brother when he graduated high school. He was nothing but trouble. Why now?"

Padre explained the case against Nate Harding six years earlier. "Had you known Mitch Arnosky?"

"As I said…" Linda enunciated each word slowly as if Padre hadn't understood her the first time. "I haven't been in touch with Nate since he was eighteen. Haven't spoken to him, haven't wanted to. And, no, he never tried to reach me. Couldn't. I changed my name, then remarried."

"But I'm sure you read the accounts in the newspaper."

"Not in Idaho. They don't cover too many towns outside Idaho, let alone east of the Mississippi."

"But you knew." Padre kept pressing. "You must have known he died in a car accident."

The sigh was loud and strung out. The last thing Padre wanted to do was piss her off.

Finally, Linda said, "Our family attorney informed me of his death. He had a phone number for Nate's attorney but I never called him. I wasn't interested in Nate or any of his estate, which was worthless anyway since the IRS was confiscating everything. Nate never did anything ethical or legal in his life."

Padre asked, "Did they tell you how he died?"

"What? The car accident?"

"No. They say it was a massive heart attack. According to medical records, your brother had a family history of heart problems."

"No way. Our father died at the age of eighty-two of natural causes. There wasn't one family member who had heart problems. That's wrong."

Padre promised to keep Linda apprised of his findings before hanging up but she had said not to bother. She wasn't interested. Padre advised her that they might need to reach her again in the future.

Padre and Dagger watched Skizzy's fingers glide flawlessly over the keyboard. "How could all the medical records on Nate Harding be wrong?" Padre said.

"This makes no sense. It contradicts everything in your reports, Padre." Dagger watched Skizzy jump from monitor to monitor as the printer spewed out numerous sheets of paper.

"Someone was pretty good at covering his tracks but didn't go far enough," Skizzy reported. He pounded a few more keys then hit the print key. "Insurance medical records were altered. See here?"

"That's as clear as mud to me," Padre said.

"Face it, Skizzy. We just aren't up to your expertise," Dagger said. "Just break it down for us."

Skizzy beamed. "The records at the hospital and the insurance company all say he had a family history of heart problems. But someone had to have altered them because military records show no such history. None in the high school records or family doctor from Harding's youth. So someone went back as far as he knew."

"Perfect." Padre clapped his hands. "That's grounds for exhuming the body."

"Not by you," Dagger cautioned. "The mayor and chief of police will never go for it. Not after that Op-Ed piece."

"Shit. Forgot about that." Padre sank back in his seat. "If I don't get out of here soon, Skizzy's going to start to sound normal."

Skizzy turned an evil eye on him. He gathered up the reports from the printer and handed them to Padre. "Alphabet Boys," he said, as if those two words solved all his problems. When this elicited blank stares from Padre and Dagger, he added, "Alphabet Boys don't need permission to exhume a body or tell anyone why they are digging up a grave. They do what they damn well please. That's the government for you."

The gray hawk tailed the red BMW from Sheila's condo to the parking garage below Angela's law office. It watched as Mitch climbed out of the BMW and climbed behind the wheel of a silver Lexus. It had no problem seeing through the dark windows that shielded the driver from the naked human eye. Pretty expensive taste for a guy who was supposed to keep a low profile. The Lexus exited the garage and moved at a fast clip through roads bisecting the forest preserves, past the stone quarry, to the prefab warehouses that used to house Guardian Security. The road dead-ended at the warehouse. At two stories high, it resembled an old railway station, all brick with tall windows and large bays you could drive a train through.

The gray hawk lighted on a building across the street and folded its forty-inch wing span. It watched as the Lexus disappeared into one of the bays. Mitch stepped out of the car and walked to the opened bay door. It surveyed the entrance and watched for several seconds, oblivious to the hawk's presence. Perhaps it was out of habit that Mitch checked to make sure he wasn't followed. Or maybe he felt eyes watching him. But people always looked in front of them or behind, never up. Yet up was where the gray hawk waited and watched. Mitch turned back inside and popped the trunk of the Lexus. He retrieved a bag of groceries, climbed onto a freight elevator, yanked the thick cord to close the gate, and pushed the button.

The gray hawk moved swiftly to the warehouse building, noticing a blue Cougar also parked inside the warehouse. The hawk saw Mitch emerge from the freight elevator on the second floor. He pulled a remote from his pocket and aimed it at a wall. A door slid open and Mitch walked through. With quick wing beats the gray hawk climbed one hundred feet above the street, then silently drifted, wings flat, until it was over the rooftop of Guardian Security. From this vantage point it noticed several skylights, which served as the only windows for the back portion of the second floor. Window blinds were being eased open to let in sunlight. Through the skylights the hawk could see an open loft furnished with an eye for extravagance. The blinds had been closed the last time the gray hawk visited. The hawk watched as Mitch rolled out a black case on wheels. He pulled out a one-piece suit and set it aside. The hawk cocked its head.

Interesting.

Dagger almost choked on his coffee. *Sara, where the hell*

are you?
   At Mitch's lair.
   Lair? Dagger laughed aloud.
   "What the hell is so funny?" Padre asked.
   Dagger just shook his head and leaned back in his chair,
hands over his face.

   *Mitch's warehouse appears to be his permanent home.
He has a secret panel that opens to the back half of the
building. That's how he got away that night. That's how he
was able to vanish when I saw him standing in the doorway.
And he has the NOCM.*

   "Interesting."
   "What's interesting?" Padre asked.
   Dagger kept forgetting not to respond to Sara aloud. It
was tough getting back into the swing of things. He straightened in his chair and asked Padre, "What did you find at
Guardian Securities six years ago?"
   "Nothing incriminating," Padre said. "All files were
legit. No stolen items. No stockpiles of cash. Nada. By then
it was the Treasury boys' case."
   "Bait and switch." Skizzy nodded in agreement with
himself. "To throw you guys off the more serious of the
crimes, he left a paper trail of lousy tax returns for the Feds
to follow. Probably figured five years wasn't too long of a
sentence. Still gets to keep whatever loot he hid from selling the stolen goods."
   "Treasury boys also emptied the place to help retrieve
some of their money," Padre said.
   "Hrmpff," Skizzy snorted. "Like they don't overcharge

people now."

"When's the last time YOU filed a tax return?" Padre asked.

Skizzy slid his eyes briefly to Padre, then back to the screen.

Dagger asked, "What about the warehouse? Did they have living quarters there?"

"No," Padre replied. "Store room, lots of inventory. They were wary of competition so you could only access the storeroom from a door at the end of the hall."

"Not from the front office?"

"Not from what we could tell. The entire business complex was up for sale. It was pretty much stripped clean."

Dagger said, "Interesting."

"Wish you'd quit saying that. Makes me think you know more than you're saying."

"And that should surprise you?" Skizzy swiveled in his chair, making dizzying circles, then stopped and swiveled in the opposite direction.

"Did you know he's tooling around town in a Lexus?" Dagger asked.

"Really?" Padre slapped a hand on the table. "Mitch's attorney. Damn he's clever. She must have rented it for him. Lets him use her red BMW, leaves his Cougar at his apartment. And when he doesn't want to be followed, he's driving around in a rental. Now tell me that guy don't have nothing to hide."

"Have you been at the warehouse since Mitch's return?" Dagger asked Padre.

"Didn't think the place was still in his name."

The two men swiveled their heads to Skizzy.

"I'm on it." Skizzy wiped his hands with a wet cloth before touching the keyboard. He grumbled just loud enough for them to hear, "Amazing how everything I do is illegal until they want something."

It took just ten minutes to find the information Skizzy wanted. "The building was only rented while Arnosky and his partner were still doing business. Once the partner died and Arnosky was the guest of Prison Condos Are Us, his attorney bought the building. Ownership was transferred to Mr. Arnosky three months ago."

"I was at the warehouse last week," Dagger said. "Had the strangest feeling I was being watched but there wasn't anyone there. The only doors down the hall were the restroom and break room. I didn't see any entrance into the storage area."

"Maybe I should tell Wozniak to have another look around."

"Not with that restraining order Mitch's lawyer is slapping on the police department." Dagger stood and stretched, then looked around for his coat. "He's got other plans. Don't know what they are yet. Hard to out-plot a guy when you don't know his goal."

What's happening, Sara?

He's drinking a beer and watching television. Want me to stick around and see if he goes out later?

Not necessary. You've confirmed what we suspected. Now all we need is a crystal ball to know his next move.

34

"Let me get this straight." The chair creaked and moaned as General Lorenz leaned back in the captain's chair. The military plane sat in a hangar at the Gary Airport. It was surrounded by mechanics, dressed in mechanic uniforms, performing mechanic-type duties. The hats covered their buzz cuts and the bulky uniforms hid their weapons. They were anything but mechanics.

It wasn't unusual to see National Guard vehicles at the Gary Airport, so the appearance of a military jet in the hangar didn't draw curious stares. Chief Wozniak doubted this plane was used for military purposes. It looked more like the private jets outfitted to fly celebrities around the country. It was furnished with leather high-backed chairs, lots of leg room, wide screen television, fully stocked bar, and laptop computers built into the seat compartments.

On the large screen in front of them was the scene from the assault at the ATM. Lorenz raised a beefy hand toward the screen. "You believe there is someone walking up behind the victim."

"Yes." Wozniak's head bobbed in agreement. "The victim was shot at very close range. Perp had to have pressed the gun right against the victim's back."

The two men seated in adjoining chairs exchanged glances and smiled. Wozniak had won them over with the coffee from the mall, but their looks told him they were beginning to question his mental capacity to run a homicide department. The two men in dark suits hadn't said anything since arriving. Other than "thanks for the coffee" and "come with us," their vocabulary had been limited.

"According to your newspapers," Lorenz said, "the stolen ring showed up in your detective's possession. He swiveled his chair to face Wozniak. "Let me tell you something, Chief. You better be damn sure you've got your ducks in a row. I won't get our department involved in some local dirty cop business."

"He's my best damn detective and I trust him with my life. Jayne, our clerk, felt something strange going on the night before the latex finger showed up in Padre's desk. Same at the Rectory. It all seems weird but it sounds just like something you boys would be working on."

The red phone on the console rang. Lorenz picked it up, listened for a few seconds. "Okay. I understand." He hung up and Wozniak noticed an immediate change in the general's demeanor. "Tell us what you think."

Us? Wozniak had a feeling the general wasn't talking about the two FBI men in the adjacent seats. His eyes roamed the walls of the jet as his brain roamed the words of caution Dagger had spewed. Mainly, he couldn't let on how Dagger's squirrely friend had retrieved the NOCM information. Wozniak could only guess it was by illegal means. And he hoped he hadn't lost his touch at doing the two-step.

"Did you know birds see in infrared? I didn't know it,"

Wozniak started.

The two men in dark suits lifted their eyebrows in unison. Wozniak ignored them but secretly he was mumbling all kinds of obscenities toward Dagger if he ended up digging a hole too deep to crawl out of.

"Saw the perp myself once we realized what the hell the bird was seeing." Wozniak noticed that Lorenz's chair stopped rocking. Now he knew he was in big trouble because Wozniak hadn't actually seen it himself. He was going on Dagger's word. "Body heat. Saw it through thermal imaging goggles. Nothing with a heartbeat can escape those things."

Lorenz sucked in a chunk of cheek and seemed to work his teeth into it.

"Ever see the movie *Predator*?" Wozniak asked. "That Schwarzenegger movie? Happens to be this bird's favorite movie."

Now the two suits were grinning from ear to ear but a piercing glare from the general wiped even the hint of a smile from their faces.

Lorenz's hand made a circular motion. "Back up a bit. What bird are we talking about?"

"A scarlet macaw. Anyway, he happened to see this ATM tape and was seeing a lot more than the human eye. Macaws are chatty as hell."

"You're going on the word of a bird?"

The two FBI agents were close to losing it, fighting the urge to laugh out loud.

"Not just any bird. Pretty smart guy. Would put some of our politicians to shame." *I am going to kill Dagger.*

"Who owns him? That means other people have seen

this tape."

"I've got that covered. The important thing is, Doctor Cohen died before he could solve the problem of the thermal imaging. Or maybe the papers you took prove he solved the problem but he didn't have time to implement the changes. Either way, someone's running around my town with Cohen's little invention and sooner or later someone is going to find out. Hell, maybe he's looking to sell it to some terrorist group. Wouldn't that be a nightmare, especially if someone were running around D.C. with it. Be a matter of time until their scientists solve the body heat problem."

The red phone rang again. Wozniak couldn't help but let his eyes travel the walls for a camera. He knew it had to be somewhere and was probably plugged into the Pentagon.

"Yes, I will." General Lorenz's answers were short, and—as before—he did more listening than talking. He hung up and ejected the tape. "Any more of these lying around?"

Wozniak almost said "no" too quickly. It would sound too lame and now was not the time to play games. He needed the general on his side. "One other set."

"I'll need it." He slid the two tapes into a black satchel. "Now tell me what else you know."

Wozniak told him about Mitch Arnosky, Guardian Security, and Nate Harding, about the tax evasion charges and how they now believed Harding was murdered.

"What do you think Arnosky's primary goal is?" the general asked.

"At first we thought it was just payback for Sergeant Martinez's relentless pursuit of more serious charges against him. Now we aren't so sure. He's up to something.

I've got people on it but we have to keep our distance. I'm sure you've read about the cloud hanging over the department's head. The medical examiner was unable to perform an autopsy on the Cohens but suspects the wife might have been poisoned with arsenic. It wasn't a prolonged poisoning, so initial tests proved negative. We are re-running it."

"Why did the M.E. suspect arsenic?"

"Garlic odor from the body. According to Mrs. Cohen's friends, who were the last to see her, Ruth Cohen didn't like garlic, didn't take any for medical reasons, like to lower blood pressure, and nothing with garlic was served the night she died. Then we checked Arnosky's hard drive and discovered he had purchased arsenic not just recently but also six years ago. So we believe he might have poisoned Harding, too. Somehow, several computer databases show Harding with a family history of heart problems and that his father died at the age of fifty. Actually, his father died at eighty-two and there's no history of family heart problems. Someone falsified the records, possibly a computer-savvy person like Arnosky. But we can't get Harding's body exhumed because the mayor and chief of police don't want my men to even breathe in Arnosky's direction. Our hands are tied."

"Mine aren't." He gave a nod to the two suits and they wrote down notes. "How do you think Mitch Arnosky knew what project Cohen was working on?"

"He installed the security system in Cohen's house. I think he might have rigged it so he could watch what the doctor was doing. Unfortunately, Arnosky was arrested and served a five-year term, enough time to contemplate the potential of Cohen's little invention. Could come in handy for a career thief."

Lorenz's head bobbed in agreement. The phone rang again. He listened for a shorter period of time.

"You have my department's full cooperation," the general said after hanging up. "I can't stress strongly enough the seriousness of this project. All of it is classified and we do not expect to see anything in the press or hear comments from anyone outside of the need-to-know crew. Do I make myself clear?"

"Absolutely." Even as he said the word Wozniak knew the names on the general's need-to-know list were probably a lot less than on his own.

35

Sheila couldn't remember the last time she burned the midnight oil. She should have left the office at six o'clock. Only proved the sorry state of her social life these days. She turned off her computer and pushed away from the desk just as Dagger loomed in the doorway.

"My god, you scared me." Her first impulse was to back away but she stood her ground. "Came back to finish the job?" She grabbed her purse from the bottom drawer.

"Can we talk?"

Sheila pulled a Glock from her purse and set it on the desk. Next to it she placed a letter opener, a pair of scissors, and the new can of Mace she had purchased. She sat down with the ease of someone prepared for anything.

"Talk."

Dagger eyed her arsenal with a half smile. "I don't think you have enough there."

She wanted to smack that smirk to the back side of his head. "You have five minutes."

"I won't need that much time. I just wanted to apologize for the other day and promise that it won't happen again."

"You're lucky I didn't call the cops." She shook out a

cigarette from her pack and lit it. A lazy stream of smoke drifted from her lips as Sheila kicked off her shoes. Dagger was leaning against the doorjamb, hands in his coat pockets. Her eyes drifted to the bulge in his pocket and she wondered if his fingers were wrapped around a gun. "Never thought I'd see the day when you said you were sorry for anything, except maybe standing me up at the altar." She bent down to retrieve her shoes. "Even then that was a half-ass attempt. What was it you said? 'Sorry, but it isn't going to work between us,' or something like that." She jammed her feet back into her shoes and stood. "The least you can do now is take a jilted lady to din…" She looked up but the doorway was empty. Dagger was like a damn shadow sifting in and out of cracks and around corners.

"Damn him," she mumbled, tossing the letter opener and scissors back into the drawer, her gun and Mace back into her purse. At least he had apologized. That was a start. Sheila slipped into her coat and locked the office door.

The elevator sighed to a stop on the executive parking level. Sheila fumbled through her purse for car keys. There was another reason she didn't like working late. Her car was the only one left on this level.

Dark pockets rimmed the outer perimeter. She should have had a guard escort her but Layton Monroe would have scoffed that he wasn't paying the guard to babysit, even if it was for his one and only child. The least Dagger could have done was offered to see her home.

"You are a big girl," she whispered to herself as she contemplated grabbing her gun. The Glock might look threatening, but the truth was she was afraid of the thing.

The new silver Jaguar glistened under ceiling lights. It

was an early Christmas present from her parents. Sheila was used to being pampered. No matter how gruff her father might seem on the outside, she was still his little girl.

Her heels clicked along the concrete. Sheila kept her eyes focused ahead, avoiding the deep shadows and pockets that appeared to move along with her. The stacked parking garage was three levels attached to the *Daily Herald* building. She pressed a button on the remote and immediately heard the Jaguar's engine hum.

When Sheila was twenty-five feet from her car, the first string of ceiling lights went out. It cast the farthest section of the floor in total darkness. She stopped in mid-step and listened. *Just a fuse, that's all,* she tried to convince herself. A faint dripping echoed but there was something else…footsteps. She could swear she heard the soft padding of shoes and rustling, like fabric rubbing together.

A second string was extinguished, closer this time and on the opposite side of the aisle, as if someone were playing a game of light bulb checkers. And the game was advancing.

Sheila couldn't hear the footsteps now. All she heard was her blood pulsing through her veins, quickening its pace. "Who's there?" she called out. One section of lights she could understand. But two within a matter of minutes?

When the third section went out, Sheila screamed. It was the area directly behind her. And because this time she heard someone whisper her name.

"Who's there?" she yelled, this time mustering the courage to pull the gun from her purse. *It couldn't be,* she thought. "Dagger, is that you? I have the gun." What she really wanted was her phone to call the police. In her heart she knew she couldn't shoot Dagger.

There was a chuckle this time, soft, almost playful. "Sheeeiillaaa." A man's voice whispered too softly to distinguish the voice. It wasn't like Dagger to play childish pranks. But then it wasn't like Dagger to press a gun to her throat either.

She clenched the Glock tightly, not even sure how to turn the safety off. Then Sheila turned and ran. She didn't look back. Even when she heard the footsteps quicken to a run. Even when the fourth section of lights went out. She put the car in reverse and thanked her lucky stars that she had a remote starter on the car.

There was a loud bang on the trunk, as if someone had pounded a fist against it. Sheila screamed and pressed her foot down harder on the accelerator. She checked the rearview mirror but saw nothing other than concrete pillars. The Jag careened around the corner and sped down the ramp to the first floor. Tires skidded as Sheila almost lost control of the car. With the turns and speed she was doing, it was impossible for anyone to be hanging onto her trunk.

As the car leaped onto the deserted street, Sheila finally found her cell phone and dialed the police.

"We'll see this time, Dagger. I'm tired of playing games with you." An uneasy feeling settled over her. Words from a previous conversation nagged at the back of her brain.

"Cedar Point P.D," the voice on the other end said.

Sheila checked the rearview mirror as she brought the Jag to a stop at the light. There weren't any headlights in her rearview mirror, nor anyone emerging from the garage on foot.

"Cedar Point P.D." The previously calm voice sounded

impatient now.

Sheila's thoughts raced, but now that her heartbeat had slowed to normal and she was out of the garage and on a public street, the urgency passed. She folded her phone and tossed it on the passenger seat.

36

Sullivan Imports occupied a prehistoric structure burrowed between two modern three-story buildings in the town square. Specialty shops selling everything from toys and collectibles to antiques and clothing, lined the square. Sullivan Imports hung onto its antiquated appearance like a great aunt stuck in the Nineteenth Century. The shop opened at nine o'clock during the holiday shopping season, and Dagger made sure he and Sara arrived first thing the next morning before the crowds.

"You brought the pictures?" Sara asked. A bell above the door tinkled as they stepped inside.

"Yes, for the third time."

"Just checking."

Dagger stared up at the irritating bell for a few beats too long.

"Don't even think about it," Sara said as she nudged him along. "You aren't going to endear yourself to the owner if you yank the bell off the wall."

"You know, having you for a partner is like having…"

"A conscience?" She smiled her incredible smile.

Dagger just shook his head and charged ahead.

"Can you believe all this stuff?" Sara was standing in front of an ornate glass bowl with feet. It glistened in a rainbow of colors.

Dagger studied the groups of paintings on the wall, then moved his attention to the furniture from the Queen Anne or Louis era, he wasn't sure. A salesman was moving furniture to roll up a tapestry rug for a customer. Dagger almost knocked over a floor lamp, which he fought quickly to straighten. Crystal beads hung in tiers on the lampshade and jangled with as much irritation as the bell above the door.

"I think the word *garish* was invented after the first one of these rolled off the assembly line." Dagger let loose of the lamp but held his hands close to make sure the beads stopped dancing.

"Will you quit touching things?" Sara whispered. Two elderly shoppers glared at Dagger. He jammed his hands into his pants pockets.

They browsed the aisles while waiting for a salesperson to become available. A woman whose hair was coiled in back like a hairy cinnamon roll approached them, her fingers locked as though ready to belt out an aria.

"May I help you find something?"

"The owner," Dagger replied, breaking out in his best *pleased to meet 'ya* smile.

She took a dainty step back as if assessing his diamond stud earring, ponytail, and all-black clothing.

"Oh, that would be Pru Sullivan." She pulled her locked fingers higher toward her neck. "You must be Xavier, the Parisian designer here to select the furnishings for La Maisson Castle."

"Not even close," Dagger replied. He handed her his

business card. She unlocked her fingers and took the card from him.

"A private investigator." She furrowed what was left of her eyebrows and ran her gaze down his frame again. "I see. So you aren't from Paris."

"Not even Paris, Illinois."

She looked genuinely disappointed and sighed heavily as she turned to walk to the back of the store.

Dagger asked Sara, "Do I look French?"

"Not a chance." She lifted a music box and turned the key on the bottom. The Swiss village on the lid came to life, villagers twirling around a chalet. She set the box down when the prim and proper saleswoman returned, fingertips reunited in locked formation.

"Please follow me." Miss Prim and Proper waltzed her way between claw-footed furniture, life-sized sculptures, and Tiffany floor lamps. Dagger kept his hands in his pockets. She led them through a doorway and into a back room.

"Someone to see you, Pru." She placed Dagger's card on the desk and left.

The woman looked up from a piece of pottery sitting under a magnifying lamp clamped to the desk. Her lips were pursed in a bitter-lemon look. With a little makeup and a smile, she would have been attractive.

Dagger glanced at the name plate. He would be in a continuous foul mood, too, if his parents had named him Prucilla.

"What can I do for you, Mr. Dagger?" She bent over the magnifying glass as she examined the pottery.

"Did you know a Nate Harding?"

"What auction firm is he with?" She turned the pottery

over, moved the lamp aside, and used a hand-held magnifying glass.

"This would have been about five, six years ago."

"Mr. Dagger…"

"Just Dagger is fine."

She looked up and pursed her lips even more, reminding Dagger of Lily Tomlin's Ernestine. Pru made a quick assessment of Sara, who stood just inside the doorway dressed in plum-colored corduroys and a yellow cropped velour sweater. "Dagger, I have met a lot of people over the past six years. How could I possibly remember one name?"

Dagger pulled a photo from his pocket and held it up. "Actually, it's probably someone your grandfather might have known. His name was Charles, right?"

Pru inched her chin up slightly as one eyebrow made a hair's breadth of a twitch. "Doesn't look familiar." She concentrated on the pottery again, moving the magnifying glass back and forth. "You are welcome to leave the photo with me. Maybe a bolt of genius will strike me in the middle of the night."

Dagger stole a glance over his shoulder at Sara. She stepped back and turned away. "Mind if I sit down?" He pulled out a chair before she could respond. "Maybe if I tell you a little bit about him, it might ring a bell."

Sara wandered down a short hall away from the hustle and bustle of the showroom. One door said *Employees Only*. Pushing the door open, she saw a couple of tables and chairs, refrigerator, sink, and counter with a coffee machine. She continued to the end of the hall to another door on her left. After checking to make sure no one was around, Sara opened the door to find a stairway leading down to what looked like a storeroom. She closed the door behind her and descended the stairs.

The basement wasn't damp and musty the way most basements are. Heat vents and a dehumidifier gave the downstairs the comfort of home and guaranteed the safe-keeping of the antique valuables stored there.

Sara wove her way around the furniture and grandfather clocks, past storage crates and unopened boxes. Everything was in some type of order and plainly labeled. Turning, she saw an antique roll top desk in the corner. Pictures lined the top of the desk, mostly of a man in a military uniform. The pictures looked aged, the uniforms from an era gone by. Sara picked up one frame and turned it over. Slipping the back off she checked for writing. It was dated 1944 with *Charles/Berlin* written in a flowery handwriting. Several other pictures of the same man had been taken in uniform, some with fellow soldiers, some with civilians, a few with an attractive woman with dark hair. The woman looked a little like Pru. Another photo with the woman and Charles wearing a suit were taken with another man standing in front of a store with a sign across the window which said A&R Ball.

Sara glanced toward the stairs before checking the desk drawers. Inside she found five-cent stamps, a stapler, and a stack of envelopes yellowed with age. Someone at some time had used it as a desk, but maybe not Pru. Charles? Sara checked the bottom drawer and found several manila folders containing newspaper clippings and a stack of photo-copies of artwork. Some were paintings by Monet and one list was labeled Baron Guy de Rothschild.

Somewhere upstairs a door slammed. Sara closed the drawers and crept back upstairs. She edged the door open and peered out. The coast was clear. Sara hurried down the hall and into the showroom, where Dagger was still talking to Pru. She figured Dagger must have worked his charm because Pru was finally smiling and her face hadn't broken.

Pru's face fell back into lemon twist mode as she peered around Sara as if to ask, *Where did you go?*

"Sorry, I had to use the bathroom."

Pru turned back to Dagger and handed him her business card. "If you have any other questions, please feel free to call."

"What did you promise Pru to put her in such a good mood?"

Dagger jammed his sunglasses on the bridge of his nose and smiled. "Drinks, dinner, a weekend in Paris on my Lear jet."

"Yeah, right."

"Don't talk until we get into the Navigator. I have a feeling the witch can read lips."

After the Navigator pulled away from the curb and was several blocks away, Sara said, "She's lying."

"Yep." Dagger turned the corner and checked his rear view mirror out of force of habit. "She definitely knew Nate Harding or at least knew of him. The pictures of Nate and Mitch didn't get much of a response until I started asking questions about her grandfather imbibing with Nate in a local bar. She admitted to having seen Mitch but claimed it could have been from all the recent publicity." He turned down a back street between the Dairy Queen and a bank.

"How about a latte or whatever the hell passes for coffee these days?"

"Okay."

The main lot for Panera's was packed. Dagger had to pull into a back lot before finding a parking space. The moment they stepped into the restaurant, Sara froze. It was only eleven o'clock in the morning but the line for soup and sandwiches was ten deep. Dagger grabbed her elbow and steered her toward two forgotten small tables by the front windows. He parked her in a chair with her back to the crowd.

"Deep chi breaths," he told her with a squeeze of her shoulders. "The line at the bakery is shorter so I'll get our order there."

He watched Sara slip out of her jacket and hang it on the back of her chair. Her eyes were darting back and forth as though trying to see behind her. The noise level was loud as voices and laughter carried.

Dagger returned with a cappuccino for her and a regular coffee for himself, as well as two cinnamon rolls. "Tell me what you found in the basement." He figured if he kept her talking it would keep her mind off the packed restaurant.

Sara told him about the photographs and the papers in the roll-top desk. "Who was Baron Guy de Rothschild?"

"He was a French Jew who had an extensive art collection Hitler stole. There were vast fortunes in artwork stolen by Hitler during World War II. Some people in Belgium claimed that it legally belonged to their government. Then there was a guy by the name of Alexander Ball, a New York art dealer, who assisted Nazi art dealers in France locate the paintings for the express purpose of stealing them."

"Wait," Sara said. "Did you say Ball?" Sara told him about the photo of two men and a woman standing in front of a building with the name of A&R Ball.

"Interesting." They ate in silence while ideas and scenarios played in their heads.

"This is good," Sara said as she stirred her coffee with the straw. "Hate to think how many fat grams we are consuming."

"Don't think about it. That's my motto."

"The man in the photo was probably Pru's grandfather. The woman in the photo resembled Pru so it was probably her grandmother."

"If the photos are as old as you describe, then Charles was in Europe during World War II."

"And maybe he smuggled home some souvenirs he shouldn't have."

Dagger watched her stab the pieces of the cinnamon roll with her fork. She had taken the time to cut it into dainty pieces. He, on the other hand, had devoured his in about eight bites. Night and day. He was dressed like a Ninja warrior and she was a flawless Renoir in a splash of vibrant yellow and plum.

"So, how much do you think those paintings are worth?" She finished the roll and tossed the plastic glass on the tray.

"The Monet alone, about ten million."

Three teens gathered at the table next to them, all aglitter with boy talk and comparing their body piercings. Dagger moved his chair closer to Sara's.

"Do you think Nate bought the paintings from Pru's grandfather?" Sara whispered.

"I don't think *bought* is the operative word. More like *stole*. That would explain why Sullivan was crying in his beer. He probably spilled too much to Nate and Nate stole them."

"Are there a lot of paintings still missing?"

"There was a book published in the 1990s, *The Rape of Europa*, which detailed the art looting. I believe some guy by the name of Habermen or Haber-something was Hitler's official art procurer."

"Can we make a stop on the way home?" Sara asked.

"The library?"

Sara smiled, then a strange cloud passed over her.

"What's wrong?" Dagger asked.

"He's here. Mitch is here. I feel like someone just walked across my grave."

Dagger slipped his sunglasses on and stole a glance over her shoulder at the tables and booths. Mitch was seated four tables away, his back to them, reading a newspaper.

Dagger closed the distance with several long strides and stopped at Mitch's table.

"That's funny," Mitch said without looking up from the newspaper. "According to Sheila, you don't cast a shadow."

Dagger pulled out a chair and sat down. "You have a pretty good sense of humor for a guy whose freedom is hanging by a thread." He pulled off his sunglasses and set them on the table.

Mitch snapped open the paper and folded it to the editorial page. "In the five years since I've been gone, the tobacco companies have been raped of billions of dollars, no one is responsible for choosing to smoke or spilling hot coffee in their lap or eating like gluttonous pigs. What is this world coming to?"

"Before you know it," Dagger replied, "irresponsibility will be a disability." Mitch was not a man easily rattled, but that was how Dagger wanted him to feel. "How much did you pay him?"

"Who?"

"The tech at the precinct. How much did you pay him to claim to receive an E-mail from Padre?"

"E-mails don't lie. They've got the copy to prove it."

"He could have typed it himself and made it look like Padre sent it. I'm sure you have enough money stashed away to make it worth his while."

Mitch folded the paper and set it aside, smiling broadly and turning his serpent eyes on Dagger. "You should know me pretty well by now. I'm too greedy to share any money I might have. Unless it's with a beautiful woman."

37

Sheila was waiting in her Jag outside the front gate when they returned. Dagger waved at her to enter behind them.

"I know I should have called first. I know the house rules so don't start," she said as she followed them through the front door.

"I already apologized, Sheila." Dagger tossed his jacket on the couch. Sara picked it up and carried it to the hallway closet.

"You have her so well trained."

Dagger shot her a look.

Sheila winced and shook her head. "I don't know why I said that. That's not why I'm here." She paused to take in her surroundings. "You've redecorated." She ran her hand across the couch fabric. "Tacky, but nice."

"AWK, WICKED WITCH, WICKED WITCH." Einstein hissed from behind the safety of the grated door.

"Make it quick, Sheila." Dagger sat down on the couch.

Sara hovered nearby, hugging the library books to her chest, finally taking a seat at Dagger's desk to sift through one of the books.

Sheila took off her fur coat and placed it on the loveseat

before sitting down. "I'm going to trust that you will be completely honest with me." Dagger draped one arm across the top of the couch and listened as Sheila told him about the event in the parking garage. His arm slowly slid from the couch when Sheila got to the part about the lights going out and hearing footsteps but no one was there. "This was right after you visited me in the office. That wasn't you in the garage, was it?"

"No, it wasn't."

"I got this really strange feeling." She waved a hand in the air, gold bangle bracelets clanging against each other. "Forget it. It would sound like I'm being paranoid."

Dagger could tell something had really spooked her. Had he frightened her that much? "Just spit it out, Sheila."

She rose and slipped on her coat while telling him about her breakfast with Mitch. "It just seemed strange, that's all. He seemed entirely too interested in how you were a suspect in my assistant's murder. Just like that," she said with a snap of her fingers, "it is made to appear as if I'm being stalked. It just followed too closely after our conversation. Maybe your suspicions about him are rubbing off on me."

"Do yourself a favor, Sheila." Dagger rose to walk her to the door. "Stay away from Mitch. He's dangerous. Work on an editorial to exonerate Padre because that is what's going to happen. If you don't, the *Daily Herald* will be scooped again."

Sara watched the monitor and pushed the button to close the gate after Sheila's Jaguar drove through. "She's really scared. Do you think it was Mitch?"

"Sheila has pissed off a number of people, but Mitch is the only one I know of who is invisible."

Sara carried the library book to the couch and rambled on about her findings while Dagger worked on the computer. "You won't believe the number of art pieces that were involved. There were even some instances where museums were unaware that the paintings hanging on their walls had been reported stolen."

Dagger didn't know who was chattier…Einstein or Sara. Neither one had stopped talking since Sheila left. Sara was practically reading the book to him verbatim. She kept finding more startling information.

"It is believed that more than one-point-five-million objects were stolen by the end of World War II and around one hundred thousand are still missing. They now have a searchable database linking sixty-six museums. It's the Nazi-Era Provenance Internet Portal or www.nepip.org."

Dagger half listened while he built a biography on Charles Sullivan.

"Think you can take time out to inhale for a second?" Dagger pulled the pages from the printer. "Let's say Sullivan got his hands on some paintings confiscated from Hitler or his minions. He pops them in the mail to himself or maybe has someone ship them to him. Somehow he gets them back to the States and hangs onto them."

"Why?" Sara abandoned her book and walked over to the desk. Einstein was craning his neck to see around the door. "The wicked witch is gone, Einstein."

"Don't know. Maybe he needed to find a buyer."

"Maybe he didn't know they were real."

"Oh, he knew. Why else would he smuggle them out of Europe?"

"Could have thought they were great replicas. Would

look good hanging on his wall. Then he heard about the thefts and started to wonder if he had the legitimate ones. But he couldn't have them appraised here in the States. People would know he had them and ask where he got them. Worth that kind of money, people would steal for them. Kill for them."

Dagger just stared at her. His mouth must have been gaping because Sara said, "What?"

He just shook his head. "You surprise me sometimes."

"What about Pru? How do you think she fits into the puzzle? Do you think she was dating Nate? Maybe she's the one who helped Nate steal them from her grandfather."

"Maybe. Nate gets a tipsy Charles to talk about the war. Charles lets it slip about the paintings. Nate gets friendly with the granddaughter and they devise a scheme to get the paintings."

"And cut Mitch out of it entirely. That would make Mitch angry enough to kill Nate." Sara opened the desk drawer for a Brazil nut. "How did her grandfather die?"

"Heart attack."

"Maybe he felt guilty." Sara held up the nut to Einstein, who jammed two toes between the grating to retrieve the treat.

Dagger punched a few buttons on the computer to dial Skizzy's place. Once connected, he told Padre about the unseen visitor in the parking garage at the *Daily Herald,* about Sullivan Imports, and Dagger's theory on Mitch's motive for killing Nate.

"Did it look like Sullivan Imports used Guardian Security?" Padre asked.

"No. I checked the system when I was in Pru's office."

"That all makes sense," Padre said. "Mitch finds out about the artwork and is not a happy partner. He kills Nate so as not to share the wealth."

Dagger asked, "What about Nate's body?"

"I spoke to Wozniak earlier. General Lorenz made good on his promise to get the body exhumed. Luther's handling it on a hush-hush basis. The fewer people know, the better the chances of keeping it off the headlines."

"How soon?"

"Tomorrow," Padre replied.

"If Mitch got his hands on the artwork and sold them for a pretty penny," Dagger reasoned, "that would explain how he can drive around in a Lexus."

"Nah, he would have bought the damn thing, not rented it," Padre said. "But it certainly might explain why Mitch is still in town. Pru may know where the paintings are and she could be his primary target. You need to talk to her again."

Dagger watched the store from across the street. There was very little traffic in front of Sullivan Imports. The square was buttoned down for the night. Shoppers were home. That reminded him that he still had shopping to do.

The lights in the main showroom of Sullivan Imports snapped off, followed by the lights outside of the building. Dagger made his way across the street and down the alley. He saw a shadow in one of the offices as he made his way to the back door. He slipped the gun pick into the lock and thanked the pick gods for the most useful tool in his arsenal.

Classical music filtered down the hallway and the smell of coffee oozed from the employee breakroom. Dagger gripped the Kimber as he crept down the hall. Last thing he wanted was for Pru to scream her head off.

He didn't say anything, just stepped into the room aiming his Kimber at her.

Pru looked up from the magnifying lamp. "What...?!"

"Shhhhh." Dagger put a finger to his lips. "Hands where I can see them."

The color drained from Pru's face. "I knew it when I laid eyes on you that you were a thief." There wasn't fear in her voice, just anger and disgust.

Dagger holstered the gun and sat down. "I'm not here to rob you. I'm here for answers." He saw her eyes flick to the phone on the corner of the desk. "Don't think about it. Of course, if you'd rather explain to the police about artwork your grandfather stole from Germany, then by all means, pick up the phone."

"He didn't steal them," she spat out. "He wouldn't steal anything."

"But you would. Did Nate romance you and convince you to steal the...?"

"No."

"What did he promise you? Get you out of this dreary life? You must have been shocked to find those paintings rolled up in a corner. Here they were right under your nose when you could have been sitting pretty with forty million dollars. Did it anger you that your grandfather sat on them all this time?"

"Are you about done?" Angry tears welled. Dagger was having that type of effect on women lately. Pru leveled an icy glare at him. "They are worth a hundred and sixty million and the price keeps going up."

One hundred and sixty? Dagger started contemplating

how good at least one of the paintings would look hanging on his bedroom wall.

"And grandfather didn't steal them, exactly." Pru pulled a tissue from her pocket and dabbed at her eyes. "He saw all the artwork Hitler was stealing for his own collection. It appalled my grandfather. He started sending pieces home, a few at a time. Then the war was over and countries were fighting over who the paintings belonged to and grandfather didn't know what to do. He thought he was doing a good deed but to come forward would incriminate himself. So he just hung onto them."

"Why should I believe any of this?"

Pru pulled a bottle from her bottom drawer and poured a shot into her coffee cup. She held it up to Dagger but he shook his head. "You don't have to believe any of it. But I have letters my grandfather wrote to my grandmother. He lists every painting. My god, he had a Degas, Matisse. It was unreal the treasures Hitler stole. My grandmother would scour the newspapers for information in hopes of identifying the rightful owners. So many people died. There was no way to tell who was still alive and where they went after the war."

"How did he get the paintings home?" Dagger grabbed a water glass from the tray on the credenza and filled it half full with the scotch.

She snapped off the magnifying lamp and leaned back, cradling her cup in her hands. "He used zinc tubes. He'd put two or three pictures at a time inside the tubes, solder the ends so they were safe from the elements, and ship them home inside the caskets headed for his military base. He was able to save twenty-three of the paintings. Grandmother lived on the base and had a job in receiving."

"How did Nate get involved?"

"It's not what you think. He didn't wine and dine me and get me to steal the paintings. I never met Nate. Grandfather realized the years had crept up on him and it was too late to do anything, so he was drowning his sorrows just about every night. I guess Nate overheard him mumbling to himself, kept plying him with liquor. Before he knew it, grandfather let himself be convinced that Nate could find the rightful owners. By the time he sobered up and straightened up, the paintings were gone. Grandfather was heartbroken."

The tears sliding down her face looked genuine. She poured another shot into her coffee cup. "It killed him. Then Nate died and I didn't have a clue where the paintings were and couldn't go to the cops. Everything had just spun out of control. I figured if the police found the paintings among Nate's possessions, it would have been reported in the news. All I could think was that Nate found a buyer before he died."

"Hmmmm." Dagger knew if Nate had that kind of money on him, Mitch would have found it. And if Mitch had that kind of money, he'd be long gone. Mitch was still in town because he didn't know what Nate did with the paintings. "Maybe you can help your grandfather rest in peace."

"How?"

Twenty minutes later Dagger was sitting with Skizzy and Padre in the back room of Skizzy's Pawn Shop. Dagger had called Sara from his car to give her an update.

"Sara is E-mailing Sheila to tell her the Sullivan/

Harding angle. I don't know why. All it will do is encourage Sheila, make her think I'm the one sending her E-mails from *A Little Bird*."

"For a smart guy," Padre said, "you know nothing about women. Sheila aces this story, she'll be on Cloud Nine, stock will climb, subscriptions will increase, and she'll think she's too good for you. I agree with Sara on this."

"Of course you would. She'd tell you to hole up for a week with a guy who's expecting an alien invasion any minute and you'd jump."

"Did you know aerial rods brought down Flight Four Hundred over Long Island several years ago?" Padre deadpanned. "Do you have any idea how many animal parts are in our canned foods? Think about it. All them little feet and antlers."

"Antennae," Skizzy corrected him, setting three Miller Lites on the table. The back room served as Skizzy's living area and was the size of two large holding cells. He pulled folding chairs from a closet and dusted them off by batting them with a dishtowel.

Dagger held the bottle of beer up to the light. "You've probably never checked for insect parts in your beer."

"Pickled and preserved," Skizzy and Padre said in unison. They each made a fist and rapped knuckles in a closed high-five.

Dagger's bottle hovered near his lips. *Skizzy and a cop high-fiving?* "What about the exhumation?" Dagger asked.

"Still on for tomorrow," Padre said.

"The paintings are probably hidden somewhere in the loft at Guardian. That's why Mitch made it his main residence. He's probably taking the place apart board by board." Dagger grabbed the videotapes from the box on the couch. "There is something you can do, Skizzy. Close your ears, Padre." To Skizzy he said, "You have copies from the ATM and Beckman's. These are from news program so you have a composite picture of Mitch. I'll just need Wozniak to provide a tape from the entrance at the precinct."

"What am I supposed to do with them?" Skizzy asked.

"Fairly simple. I just need you to make his invisible image visible on all these tapes."

Padre removed his hands from his ears. "If it comes from CPPD, his crafty lawyer will smell a fake a mile away."

"Skizzy's good," Dagger replied. "Besides, CPPD won't be the one turning them in. The Alphabet Boys will. After all, they work stolen art cases, right?" Dagger wiggled his eyebrows.

Padre thought about that briefly. "Oooooh. I like it."

38

At eleven o'clock the next morning Dagger and Padre entered a suite on the fifth floor of the Ritz Carlton Hotel. Padre sported sunglasses and a baseball cap pulled down low over his eyes. Behind him was Pru Sullivan, a large manila envelope bulging with pictures and correspondence.

Wozniak stood and introduced Pru to two men in dark suits and starched shirts. "McCallister and Bruen of the FBI." The men nodded in unison and escorted Pru and her folder to a room down the hall. Once the door clicked shut, General Lorenz emerged from another room.

Lorenz was out of uniform and looked like a banker. He placed a folder on the coffee table. Dagger caught his last name on the label. He dragged his eyes to the general who was giving off an *I know everything about you* aura. Dagger smiled secretly, knowing whatever Lorenz had was invented in the basement of Skizzy's Pawn Shop.

"You have an interesting background, Mr. Dagger," Lorenz said.

Dagger just shrugged. According to Skizzy's handi-work, Dagger never finished college, or the Marines, or the police academy. The less colorful of a past, the better.

"Get yourself some coffee," Lorenz said, motioning toward the buffet against the wall. "Then tell me how you think these paintings tie in to the NOCM Project."

Wozniak and Padre followed orders like good little soldiers, then sat down in the two barrel chairs across from the general. Dagger stripped out of his coat and tossed it across the back of the couch. He grabbed a bottled water and perched on the arm of the couch.

Dagger filled them in on Charles Sullivan and his involvement with Nate Harding. "Nate somehow got Sullivan to show him the paintings. According to Pru, Sullivan believed Nate's claim that he could locate the rightful owners. Once the paintings were given to Harding, Sullivan knew he made a mistake. But he couldn't go to the police because he was in possession of stolen property."

"How do you know Harding didn't find a buyer?" Lorenz asked.

"We would have heard about it," said Padre. "Something worth that kind of money missing that many years, someone would have squealed." He tossed the baseball cap on the floor, dropped the glasses next to it, and rubbed his fingers through his hair.

"And how does Arnosky and the NOCM fit in?" Lorenz asked.

Dagger explained, "We believe Nate hid the paintings to keep them for himself, Mitch found out about it, Nate refused to share the wealth, and was killed. Mitch spends five years in prison thinking about Doc Cohen's little invention and how it might come in handy."

Lorenz made a circle with his hand. "Back it up there. How would Mitch know where to look for the paintings?

Nate could have given them to anyone to hold onto."

Padre chuckled. "You think someone is going to sit on that many valuable paintings out of the goodness of his heart, knowing damn well that what Mitch did to his partner he would do to anyone?"

Wozniak's phone rang. He pulled it from his jacket pocket and unfolded it. "Yeah?" He listened for several seconds. "You are sure about that? Uh huh...yeah. Well, run another test just to be sure. And run another one on Cohen." He folded up the phone and set it on the table.

"That about the tox report on Harding?" Padre asked.

"Preliminary tests came back negative for arsenic."

Lorenz leaned back and crossed his arms. "This was going to nail Arnosky? These tox reports were your ace in the hole?"

"Now wait." Wozniak held up two beefy hands, fingers splayed, as if Lorenz's words were bullets. "Luther's going to re-run it. He used only a hair sample. Next is bone and fingernail."

Dagger stood and paced the room slowly, half-listening as Lorenz questioned why Mitch would need the NOCM if all he wanted to do was search the warehouse for the paintings.

"He needed it to frame me," Padre countered. "How else could he plant the latex print, the ring, or get into my computer after office hours to send CSI an E-mail?"

"Awful lot to go through," Lorenz said with a shake of his head. "Why bother with payback if you are going to be wrapped in close to two hundred million dollars."

"Diversion," said Padre. "Keep the press and police focused on me and no one sees what he's doing."

Dagger tried to wrap his feeble brain around Mitch's way of thinking. Then it hit him. "Oh, god." He clasped his hands behind his head and stared at the ceiling. "It couldn't possibly be that simple."

"What?" the three men said in unison.

Dagger returned to the couch arm. "You said it before, Padre—Mitch was always leading you. What is his goal? Mrs. Cohen wasn't poisoned but we were led to believe it because her body had the garlic odor. That's easy enough to duplicate. Now the tests rule out poisoning but not before we start to get suspicious about Harding. So we exhume the body. After all, Mitch has cleverly hidden his supposed purchases of arsenic knowing full well we would suspect murder. But the tox report on Harding also comes up negative. I bet if we check with Aiden Technologies we will find the computer records for the arsenic purchases were all bogus. Follow the dots, Padre."

"Wait." Padre leaned back in deep thought for several minutes while Lorenz refilled his coffee cup. "First Mitch uses the prototype in a darkened parking lot. After all, he couldn't trust that it really worked and he needed the cloak of nightfall. Next, he tried it in a store with the lights blazing and a surveillance camera rolling. Then the precinct, an empty office with just a night clerk as a witness. And finally, the Rectory. Mitch was testing the damn thing. All for what?"

Three sets of eyes blinked simultaneously. Then one by one, they got it.

39

"What a surprise." Mitch held open the door for Sheila. "Let me take your coat."

"I can't stay long." Sheila tossed her coat on the couch and inspected Mitch's furnishings. "Nice. I like the marble floor. You must have a cleaning lady in here daily."

"I'm not that messy."

"Man after my own heart." Sheila pulled a notepad from her purse and took a seat in a side chair.

"Coffee? Have you had lunch?"

"Nothing, thanks. Just wanted you to know they exhumed Nate Harding's body early this morning, before sunrise and away from the watchful eyes of the public."

"Really." Mitch sank onto the couch. "Who authorized it and for what purpose?"

"Thought you could tell me. My sources tell me that Nate might have gotten his hands on some paintings stolen from Hitler's private collection, originally stolen from the Jews."

Mitch remained silent for several seconds while Sheila doodled on her notepad. "Believe me, Nate didn't have the brains to get his hands on anything priceless."

"What if you didn't know him that well? What if he had his own lucrative side job? What if he placed cameras in places you were unaware of and happened to see the stolen artwork? That other partner might have been the one who killed him."

He stared at the notepad but couldn't see any decipherable notes. "Who said Nate was murdered?"

"Why else would they exhume the body? My guess is he was in partnership with Prucilla Sullivan. My sources tell me her grandfather served in Germany in the Second World War. What if he got his hands on some of those paintings? What if..."

"Lot of what ifs." Mitch stood and walked to the kitchen. "Sure I can't get you something?" he called out. Sheila declined. Mitch returned with a bottled water. "My guess is they are trying to prove he was murdered just to nail me on a bogus charge." He returned to the couch and took a pull off the water bottle. "Your ex-fiancee is probably behind it."

"Why would you think Dagger would have anything to do with it? He can't authorize an exhumation."

Mitch gave a shrug. "The police department can't do anything. Their hands are tied. My lawyer saw to that. Dagger seems the type to go to any means to help a friend." He set the bottle on the table and stood again, mouth set in a grimace. "Guess it won't end until I leave town." He walked to the window and stared at the traffic below. "I think I need to call my attorney."

"She should at least find out who authorized the body to be exhumed. It would be a stupid move on the part of the police chief to get his department involved."

"You're right." Mitch turned to find Sheila slipping into her coat.

"Anyway, I had promised to keep you updated," Sheila said.

"And I appreciate that."

"I'm sorry you couldn't fill in the blanks on Nate."

"Me, too." After saying their goodbyes, Mitch closed the door and smiled broadly. Everything was going as planned.

Mitch exited the elevator on the garage level and headed toward his car. When he rounded one of the pillars he saw a woman leaning against his car. He slowed his pace to give himself a chance to figure out if he knew her from somewhere in his past. Or was she just another nosy reporter.

"Sorry, I don't give interviews." He pressed the remote and a beep-beep echoed off the walls.

"I'm here for answers, not questions."

Mitch regarded her with as much interest as he gave the doorman. "Talk to my lawyer." He climbed in on the driver's side. She opened the door and climbed in on the passenger side.

Her hand was in her coat pocket and it was pointing in his direction. "Start driving."

His eyes blinked slowly as they ran from the coat pocket to her face. "Not until you tell me what you want. You aren't going to shoot me in a parking garage where people can walk out at any minute."

"Try me."

There was a hatred seething in her eyes. He doubted she was there to rob him. She had dark hair that brushed her col-

lar and a certain collegiate look, like a librarian or professor. Was she related to the Cohens?

He smiled an accommodating smile that meant to
unnerve her. Mitch shoved the key in the ignition. Once out
of the garage, he headed north with no specific route in
mind.

"Where did you want to go eat?" he asked in a light-
hearted way. She wasn't smiling. "Maybe we should start
with introductions. I'm Mitch Arnosky, but I have a feeling
you know that." He stole another glance at the bulge in her
pocket. "How do I know that isn't just a finger gun?" His
question was answered with a clicking sound as she cocked
the gun.

They rode in silence. This was putting a wrench in
Mitch's plans for the evening. Dusk was rolling in from the
east. Mitch turned on his lights and tried to keep quiet, but
it wasn't his style.

"I've never had a stalker before. Did get letters in prison,
though. Marriage proposals even." He made casual conversation, even propped his elbow on the armrest and stifled a
yawn.

Once they were away from the busy streets, she pulled
the gun from her pocket as if to prove she had one. "I want
the paintings back."

"Ahhh, the paintings." He smiled broadly and slid his
lizard eyes her way. That explained a lot. She was related to
Charles Sullivan. Too young to be a daughter. Has to be a
granddaughter. "Why didn't you say so?" The forced smile
quickly fell away. He decelerated and made a U-turn.

"What are you doing?"

"I've been looking for those myself." He dropped his

gaze to the gun. "Now with another set of eyes, it might go a lot quicker."

Sara listened again to the message on Dagger's answering machine from Pru Sullivan. All she said was that she was going to confront Mitch and get the paintings back.

"Wonderful." She dialed Dagger's cell phone and was greeted with a recording. She left a message and ran upstairs to change. "I thought you were smarter than that, Pru." Sara checked the time on the alarm clock by her bedside. It was six-thirty. Definitely dark and definitely cold. Dagger was still with Padre and Chief Wozniak.

"WHERE ARE YOU GOING. WHERE ARE YOU GOING. AWK." Einstein stared at the keys dangling from Sara's fingers as he poked his beak between the gratings.

"I'll be back."

"I'LL BE BACK," Einstein repeated in his best Schwarzenegger impersonation.

Sara pushed the truck past the speed limit with headlights on high beam. She kept glancing at the phone on the dashboard. She knew what Dagger would say. He would tell her to stay home, stay out of harm's way and let the police handle it. Chief Wozniak could probably send a car over to check things out. Exactly where would Pru be? She tried to remember Mitch's cell phone number. Recall wasn't her weak suit and she guessed his number on the first try.

"Toss the phone over here," Pru demanded. Mitch tossed it in her lap. "Hello?"

"Pru, it's Sara. I take it Mitch is with you."

"Right."

"Are you in his apartment?"

"No."

"Can you give me a hint where you are?"

"Not a clue."

"That's a cryptic phone call," Mitch said.

"Shut up." She turned her attention back to the caller.

"Let Dagger handle this, Pru," Sara said.

"He's got the paintings and I'm going to get them back."

Sara heard a dial tone. Pru had disconnected the call. Sara steered the truck toward the warehouse. That was the only logical place they could be headed.

Mitch had a fifteen-minute head start on her. She just hoped Pru didn't kill him. Mitch was the only proof they had that Padre was framed. If Mitch died, Padre would never be able to clear himself.

A mile from the warehouse she turned off the truck's headlights. In the distance, Sara could see lights streaming from the warehouse skylights. Her enhanced vision didn't detect movement outside of the building. Her visual acuity would be able to see Mitch if he were camouflaged. Sara parked the truck a block away. She was dressed in black from neck to toe but still moved cautiously, preferring to stay close to the buildings.

Mitch's Cougar was parked outside the bay door. Peering through the car window, she saw a set of keys dangling from the ignition. She opened the door and grabbed the set.

Inside the bay was Mitch's Lexus. She checked inside for keys but there weren't any. Her eyes scanned the lower floor as she listened for sounds. There weren't any.

The freight elevator door was open. A little too inviting. Instead, Sara chose the darkened stairwell, agility propelling her up two stairs at a time. Hawks see much better in low light. The tapetum lucidem, the layer at the back of the eye, acts like a mirror and produces eyeshine. This is why the eyes of nocturnal animals, even cats, seem to glow at night.

When she reached the second floor she hesitated in the doorway of Guardian Security. The tiny hairs on her arms shot to attention. It was too quiet. She studied the wall and tried to remember where the panel was that opened to Mitch's apartment. Pressing a hand to the wall, she felt for vibration, movement. Then she leaned closer to listen for sounds, talking, moans, cries. What she heard was a heart beating, slow and rhythmic, either in sleep, or maybe unconscious.

Sara detected an odor...chloroform. She felt the presence behind her seconds before he struck. Assuming the chloroform was for her, she took a deep breath well before the soaked hankie covered her mouth and nose. She struggled against the arm that trapped her against his body to give the impression that the chloroform was working. She struggled gallantly at first, then weakened her fight and let her legs buckle.

She felt strong arms lift her, then heard the sound of a door sliding open. Sara kept her eyes closed but could feel the warmth from lights. She was set on a chair and held in place while each arm was tied to an armrest and each leg to a chair leg. The rope was cinched tight sending stabs of pain through her appendages.

As her head lolled, she opened her eyes the slightest amount to study her immediate surroundings. Expensive carpeting. Even the chair arms had been hand-carved. To her left she saw what looked like a couch upholstered in an elaborate brocade fabric. A body was lying on the couch.

She closed her eyes as she sensed the air moving. Mitch breezed past her and she lifted her head in time to see him walk into another room and close the door. Sara lifted her head again and turned to Pru. Her chest was rising and falling. There was a trickle of blood drying at Pru's hairline but she was alive.

She didn't have much time. Sara focused briefly on her arms. Instantly her hands and wrists faded into talons, slipping from the ropes with ease. Just as quickly, she shifted back. She did the same with her feet, but this time changing them into a slight blur of fur as she shifted just that portion of her body into the wolf and back to human. Sara stepped out of the ropes and ran over to the door. Mitch was calling Dagger. She could easily hear both sides of the conversation.

"Listen carefully, Dagger. You have an important decision to make."

"Crawling out from under your rock, Mitch?"

"I have two beautiful women with me."

"Really. How much did you have to pay them?"

"That's good. You should have been a comedian." Mitch rolled the suitcase from the closet and unsnapped the locks. "I'm having a hard time deciding which one."

"Haven't you killed enough people, Mitch?"

"I didn't say I was going to kill them."

Mitch listened to the silence and smiled. It wouldn't be long now. All these millions of dollars was worth a five-year stint in prison. All he had to do was drive to Seattle, hop over the border to Canada where the buyer would meet him, then off to the Cayman Islands to vacation with his money for the rest of eternity.

"I want to talk to Sara."

"That would have been my pick, too."

"NOW," Dagger demanded.

Mitch chuckled. Amazing what love did to a man. "Both ladies are a little...uh, tied up at the moment."

"You left Sara alone?"

"Really, Dagger. How much trouble could a one-hundred-and-twenty-pound woman get into?" Mitch wasn't prepared for Dagger's reaction. He was laughing. It wasn't just a chuckle. It was a full-throated *you sucker*-type laugh. And then there was a dial tone. Dagger had hung up on him.

"Son of a..." Mitch pushed open the door to the main room. His eyes took in both the empty couch and chair at a single glance. He touched the ropes on the chair. They were still knotted.

The door to the outer office was open. He pulled a gun from the desk drawer, then crept to the doorway. As he crossed the threshold, a leg jutted out and kicked him in the chest, knocking him back against the door jamb. The gun flew from his hand and Mitch landed face down on the floor. Dagger's laughter pealed through his head. He was certain he tied those ropes tight. How the hell did she get out?

Mitch shook the cobwebs from his head and sprang to his feet. He felt along the wall for a light switch. "Here chickie, chickie."

"What's the matter, Mitch? Afraid of a little girl?"

He heard her voice but couldn't see a damn thing. His fingers found the switch and flipped it on just as a shoe connected with his jaw.

"You bitch," he screamed. He touched his lip and came away with blood on his fingers.

Sara calmly circled him, watching his hands and feet. "Gee, Mitch, I wonder if that's a Sig Sauer you have there?"

Mitch just smiled. A Sig Sauer had been the gun used on the assault against Brent Langley.

"What happened to my houseguest?" Mitch asked.

"I gave Pru the keys to your Cougar and sent her on her way," Sara replied. "So it's just me and you, Mitch."

"I like those odds." Mitch flicked his wrist. Suddenly, a stiletto appeared in his hand.

Sara dropped her gaze briefly to the knife. "You picked up a new trick in prison, I see."

"Oh, you ain't seen nothing yet." He cocked his arm and sent the knife flying. She spun out of the way and the knife penetrated the wall behind her. "Good spin. You are just full of surprises." Mitch's eyes searched for the gun and located it near the stairwell. Now he had her. To get out of the building, Sara would have to get past him. "Nowhere to go, Chickie."

"Gee, I'm so distraught." Sara flashed a Mitch-type smile that barely reached her eyes and faded immediately.

"I like that. Even in the face of death you can still crack jokes." He moved closer to the door, then made a dash for the gun, lifted it and turned. Sara's reactions were quick. She turned and dove toward the window just as he fired off several shots. He wasn't sure if it was the bullets or the force of her body that caused the window to shatter. Sara dove head first through the window and into darkness.

"Oops. Sorry about that. Nice knowing you." Mitch walked up to the window, following droplets of fresh blood. "If the bullets didn't kill you, the fall definitely did." He stood at the window and looked down. The pavement was empty. There wasn't a body.

40

"You guys are sure about this?" Lorenz stomped his feet and huddled inside of the quilted coat, which looked warm enough to tackle a climb up Mount Everest.

"We're pretty certain," Chief Wozniak said. "We have had two cops guarding the entrance to the cemetery since we exhumed the body. No one gets in or out without them noticing."

They were sequestered in a shed one hundred yards from the hole in the ground that used to house Nate Harding's body. The casket lay open next to the hole. Lorenz settled the thermal vision goggles on his head and stared through the grimy window. He jockeyed with Wozniak and Padre for position.

"I have to get closer," Dagger said. "This is too far away." He exited the shed and wove his way between monuments. This was the oldest cemetery in Cedar Point, with tombstones and crypts dating back to the eighteen hundreds. Two FBI agents were hidden inside one of the crypts and Skizzy was inside another. Everyone was wired for sound and Skizzy was in charge of videotaping.

Sara had called five minutes ago. She had been trailing

Mitch from a distance, leaving the truck lights off and rely-
ing on her night vision so her presence was undetected. On
one hand he wished she had shifted so he could communicate with her. Once Mitch arrived at the cemetery, Dagger
couldn't rely on his cell phone. Lorenz had ordered everyone to shut off their phones at that point. It was amazing
how much weight the guy pulled. The general had even
obtained keys to open the cemetery's garage so their cars
could be hidden.

"Do you have any idea how many toxins are seeping
into the ground from decomposing bodies? Then the shit
gets into the water tables and into our drinking water."
Skizzy's voice came through Dagger's ear piece. "Course,
who's to say the bodies are in the coffins. Government probably sells the organs and then sells the bodies for research,
probably sending them down to that Body Farm in
Tennessee," Skizzy continued. His voice was low and soft,
like a play-by-play golf tournament announcer's.

"Who the hell is talking?" Lorenz's voice wailed.

"Who the hell are YOU?" Skizzy countered.

"Silence," Dagger said, "we have company." He knelt
behind a large marble monolith with a pair of angels
perched on each side. He scanned the entrance road with the
thermal vision binoculars. A Lexus by-passed the entrance
and turned down a service road. Dagger fanned the binoculars in a wide arc but didn't see the truck Sara was driving.
She had called him the moment she left the warehouse
mumbling about her jacket being ruined. He no longer had
any reaction whenever she was injured. Mitch had shot her
in the shoulder and she had healed immediately. It was then
that Dagger told her they suspected the paintings were in the

coffin with Harding's body. Now that the body had been exhumed, it would be the perfect time for Mitch to retrieve the paintings before the coffin was put back into the ground.

"We may need some backup. I should have had a couple of squads here," Wozniak said.

"No witnesses, chief," Lorenz said. "We do this my way. You keep your two guys at the entrance and that's it. That was our agreement."

"Making deals with the devil," Skizzy mumbled.

"Who the hell IS that?" Lorenz hadn't been told about Skizzy. All Wozniak had said was that they needed to catch Mitch on tape. Lorenz wouldn't let him use cops and he didn't want to bring in any more of his own men. So Wozniak said he'd take care of it, then left the task to Dagger.

"He's on his way." Dagger followed Mitch's movements with the thermal vision binoculars. Camouflaged in the NOCM, Mitch moved swiftly, walking past the guards, and dodging tombstones. Wozniak had checked the coffin when they arrived and felt metal tubes inside the lining. To prevent the paintings from being damaged by a decomposing body, Mitch would have had to store them in something protective, the same way Sullivan had when he smuggled the paintings into the country. For legal purposes, they had to leave everything as is and let Mitch lead them to the stolen artwork.

"Damn suit glows like a lighthouse beacon." Skizzy didn't know when to shut up. "What did that little mistake cost us taxpayers? Eight million?"

"Will someone shut this…"

"Skizzy, zip it," Dagger ordered. "We're almost there." Mitch was closing in fast. According to Sara, Mitch was packed and ready for a road trip, probably taking off as soon as he retrieved the paintings.

"Don't do anything stupid, Dagger," Wozniak said.

"Dagger operates on instinct," Padre said. "Just let him do it his way."

Mitch wasted no time ripping at the side lining of the casket. He extracted two metal cylinder tubes, each about five inches in diameter and three feet long. What happened next couldn't have been scripted better. Sara found the switch for the floodlights forensics had set up around the dig. The lights snapped on. Mitch stepped back, his head swiveling from side to side.

"Pretty clever, Mitch." Sara had no problem seeing Mitch. He froze at the sound of her voice, as though staying still would keep him camouflaged. "You should have made sure the good doctor didn't give you a defective suit before you killed him." To anyone without thermal vision goggles, all that could be seen were two tubes floating several feet from the ground. Sara smiled. "What's the matter, Mitch. No snappy comeback?"

"Who the hell is she?" Lorenz whispered.

"Shhhhhh," three voices said in unison.

Mitch placed the tubes on the ground and pulled the one-piece head cover back. His serpent eyes stared at the wet stains on her dark quilted jacket. He unfastened the front snaps and pulled off the suit, kicking his shoes free. "I know I shot you."

She rotated her shoulders as if to prove she wasn't injured. "What's a little flesh wound between friends."

"I think I just might have met my match," Mitch said. "How would you like to go to Canada with me, Sara?" He nodded at the tubes on the ground. "I've got a hundred sixty million bucks here and I can't spend it all by myself. What do you say?" He smiled that slick smile that didn't reach his eyes.

Dagger set the binoculars down and slowly pulled the Kimber from his belt clip. Wozniak had stressed that he wanted Mitch alive. He needed him to clear Padre of the false charges. That was the only thing keeping Dagger from putting a bullet in Mitch's head. Other than that, he didn't need to hear any more distractions, so he pulled out the ear piece and dropped it on the ground. Sara maneuvered Mitch to where his back was to Dagger. She was getting too close to him, Dagger thought, in her effort to make sure Mitch had no escape.

Mitch suspected as much because he made a step to one side, grabbed a handful of Sara's hair, and pulled her to his chest. A knife appeared in his right hand as if sprung from his shirtsleeve.

"I know you're out there somewhere," Mitch yelled. "I learned a lot in prison and I can cut her carotid before the bullet does fatal damage to my brain. Now toss the gun over here."

Dagger stepped from behind the tombstone. He kept his eyes on the knife as he pointed the Kimber at the sky and popped out the clip. He didn't want to avert his eyes to the crypt where Wozniak and Company were hiding. For all he knew they had emerged from the crypt and were headed his way. It was just too dark beyond the bright lights to see.

"Now toss the gun away."

Dagger hefted it to the side and winced at the possible scratches that would result. He still had the gun in his ankle holster and had a feeling he would need it.

"How much did you say the paintings were worth, Mitch?" Sara asked, suddenly feigning interest.

"Sorry, sweetheart. Missed your chance. If you for one second looked at me the way you look at Dagger, I might believe you. You two deserve each other." With that Mitch shoved Sara at Dagger and grabbed the metal tubes.

Dagger had his gun out and aimed before Mitch took his second step. Rustling could be heard in the distance, feet running and thundering across the ground. Dagger was just ready to squeeze off a shot when the knife whizzed through the air with such speed he barely had time to lean out of the way. For a brief moment everything seemed to move in slow-motion. Dagger's momentum propelled his feet out from under him. He could see the steel tip closing in on his chest.

Out of nowhere Sara appeared, reached up with her right hand to grab the stiletto by the handle just a scant inch from Dagger's neck. At the same time her left hand unsheathed Dagger's knife from his belt. She seemed to spin in mid-air away from Dagger as he landed flat on his back. He had never witnessed such a look of vengeance in Sara's eyes before. He saw the two knives in her hands, arms whipped overhead, then the wrists cocked.

"SARA, NO." Dagger's words cut through the silence just as the two knives sliced through the air at an unbeliev- able speed. When Dagger had asked her, "Would you kill for me," he hadn't meant in cold blood. All he meant was could he depend on her to watch his back.

Mitch had no place to go. Sara seemed to anticipate his moves and the knives hit their target. They penetrated each side of his shirt collar and impaled him to a tree.

One by one faces appeared from the shadows, each staring at Sara. Dagger wasn't sure if it was shock, awe, or disbelief on their faces. In unison they turned to stare at Mitch, his face distorted and crushed against the trunk, eyes glued to his stiletto still quivering from the impact. Both knives were buried in the wood up to their hilts.

Wozniak broke the silence. "Not bad. You didn't wet your pants, did you, Mitch?"

During the commotion, somehow the NOCM suit was removed from the premises. Dagger figured one of Lorenz's minions secreted the evidence away. But the FBI was there to quickly confiscate the paintings and Mitch.

Two of the men struggled to remove the knives from the tree. They were in too deep, so the fabric was cut from around the knives. Once Mitch was freed from the tree and handcuffed, he turned and stared at Sara, taking a shaky step backwards.

"What the hell are you?" Mitch asked.

41

"What the hell are you?" Arnold Schwarzenegger's character was asking the alien as it spewed green blood from its mouth. The alien echoed Arnold's comment as it laughed, rows of teeth clicking against clawed lips. Then a long talon flipped open a control panel on its wrist. It took a few seconds for Arnold to realize the alien was setting off a bomb, and then only scant seconds for him to escape.

Einstein tap-danced on the perch, his eyes riveted on the large screen TV. As the credits rolled, Dagger pressed the rewind button. "Okay, Einstein. I don't want to see that movie for at least another year. Pick another one."

"I'LL BE BACK, AWK."

"Not that one either."

"Anyone want more cake and coffee?" Eunie asked as she raised the carafe. Dagger held up his cup for a refill.

"Shouldn't Simon be back by now?" Sara was sitting on the floor surrounded by empty boxes, ribbon, and tissue paper. As long as everyone was together for her birthday, they also exchanged Christmas presents.

The alarm at the gate sounded. Dagger checked the monitor, pressed the button, and watched Simon's car lumber through the gate followed close behind by Padre's car.

"Skizzy thanks you for the cake and ice cream," Simon said as he kicked off his shoes at the front door. "And this is for you, from Skizzy." Simon handed Sara a cigar box. Skizzy's idea of birthday wrapping was to tie a string around the box and write Sara's name on the lid.

"Did you want a sandwich or something, Padre?" Eunie had made herself at home in Sara's kitchen.

"Nah. I can't stay long."

"That was a nice editorial on you and the Police Department," Eunie said.

"Miz Monroe is going to be hell to live with," Simon chuckled, "seeing how she scooped everyone on the stolen art story."

Sheila had already called to thank Dagger for the heads up on Sullivan even though Dagger denied he was the one to send her the information.

Padre handed Sara an envelope. "Happy birthday. Sorry I didn't have much time to shop. The wife picked up a gift certificate for the Rainforest Café."

"Thank you, Padre. That really wasn't necessary." She wrestled herself free from the discarded boxes to give him a hug. Skizzy's gift box rattled and thumped as she shook it.

"If it's coming from Skizzy, you don't want to shake it much," Simon cautioned.

It had been three days since Mitch's arrest, and Padre looked beaten and haggard. He should be leaping for joy now that he was back at work and his reputation restored, but there was a look in his eyes Dagger didn't like. Dagger caught his friend's eye and held his gaze.

Sara untied the string and lifted the lid on the cigar box.

Inside was a gun made of a dark blue metal. "It's so small."
Sara felt the weight. It was almost immeasurable.

Dagger picked up the gun and studied it. "A Kel-Tec P
Thirty-Two. Just six-and-a-half ounces with a two point six-
eight barrel length. Not bad." He glanced at Padre but the
cop wasn't making his usual comments like, "I don't see
this happening, tell me it's registered."

"I don't like guns," Sara admitted.

"You don't like knives either but you could have fooled
me. Oh, by the way." Padre dug around his shirt pocket and
held up several business cards. "The Alphabet Boys want
you to give them a call when you hit twenty-one. They all
want you for CIA, FBI, Navy Seals, you name it. FBI will
even pay your college." He slid the cards across the coffee
table. "You guys should have seen her out there. She was
like an avenging angel, swooping down to save Dagger
from losing one of his nine lives."

Dagger gathered up the cards and flung them over his
shoulder. "She doesn't take orders very well." A swatch of
white bandage could be seen at the neckline of his Henley.
The blade tip of Mitch's knife had nicked him. A comment
Sara had made once popped into his head—"Did you ever
stop to think, Dagger, that maybe Grandmother meant for
me to protect you?" He settled his gaze on the young
woman, remembering the bullet hole in her quilted jacket,
the two story fall from Guardian Security with barely a
bruise, and Mitch's astonished "What the hell are you?" If
only they all knew.

"The Alphabet Boys were also curious how you could
see Mitch without the goggles on," Padre said.

Sara looked up from the gun and quickly said,

"Footprints. His feet made indentations in the grass."

"That's what I thought."

"Heh," Simon chuckled, "military can't use their toys in the snow either. Can't camouflage those footprints."

"So," said Padre, "I didn't see a Jeep or Beetle convertible outside, Sara. What did Dagger buy you?"

Sara grabbed an envelope from the table and handed it to Padre. "It's wonderful."

"She left enough hints lying around the house," Dagger said. In the envelope was a picture of the outdoor waterfall and pond Sara had been admiring in the landscaping magazines. Dagger was going to build it for her.

"A hot tub," Padre said.

"No," Sara laughed. "It's a pond." She pulled a wrapped box from under a stack of opened boxes and handed it to Padre. "Your turn."

"For me?" Padre checked the tag on the box. The gift was from Dagger, Sara, Simon, and Eunie. "I haven't finished my shopping yet."

"You've been busy," Eunie said.

Padre ripped through the wrapping and lifted the lid on the box. "Man, and I was just starting to break in my old one." They had given him a leather briefcase. "Thanks. That was nice of you."

"Come on, Padre," said Simon. "Now that everything's shaken out, what happened with that Mitch character?"

Padre's smile was forced, another hint to Dagger that something wasn't right. "It was priceless. He thought he would cut a deal with the DOD. He'd keep their little secret about NOCM if they would get CPPD to drop all charges, even murder charges, against him. Course, everyone plays dumb. NOCM? What the hell is that? Imagine the look on his face when we show him the tapes. Skizzy did a fabulous job, by the way." He paused to look toward the bar. "You got a beer or something?"

"Sure." Dagger eyed the cop while he retrieved a cold beer. Twisting off the cap he noticed Padre had delayed the story until he could get the proverbial courage in the bottle.

"Thanks." Padre took a long pull and set the bottle on a coaster. "Anyway, Pru got some good press. The letters her grandfather wrote his wife prove he was trying to do a good deed." He took another long pull from the bottle. "So, we have tapes showing Mitch at each of the crime scenes including accessing my office. Naturally Mitch is scream-ing that the tapes were doctored but we've got him over a barrel now. His lawyer is telling him to plead guilty. I'm completely exonerated, which just pisses the hell out of Mitch. We've got him on three counts of murder, the attempted murder of Brent Langley, and the coup de grace? The multi-million dollars in stolen art. Damn…what a country, hey?" Padre finished to the applause of his audi-ence. But Dagger noticed a deep furrow in Padre's forehead as he slugged back the rest of the beer.

Thirty minutes later, Einstein was tucked away for the night and the boxes and wrappings removed. Sara was see-ing the last of the guests to the door. Padre was outside on the patio drinking another beer and staring up at the sky. Dagger eased into a jacket, grabbed a beer, and joined him. Through the window he saw Sara straightening up the kitchen and loading the dishwasher.

"Okay, what gives?" Dagger asked. "You've been cleared of all charges, you're back at work, Mitch is going to prison, but you look like someone just kicked your dog."

"He struck a deal."

Dagger stared back. He knew this wasn't something Padre would joke about. "How?"

"He's got a second NOCM. Would give it up only if the Alphabet Boys agreed to clear him of all charges and put him in a witness protection program, give him a new identity, and send the bastard on his way."

"And they agreed."

"Yep." Padre took a swallow of beer and winced as though the beer was going down as poorly as his news. "Mitch was so confident, he even confessed to killing Nate by fiddling with the car's cruise control. Anyway, Lorenz couldn't chance Mitch going to the press or selling his toy to the highest bidder. As far as the FBI is concerned, they've got their paintings. General Lorenz will have his NOCMs. The Cohen's will be written off as a murder/suicide. The assault on Brent Langley was an unfortunate incident. And Beckman has his ring back."

"What about all the evidence Mitch planted on you?"

"All charges still stick as far as the press and public will know. Court documents say Mitch agreed to plead guilty, and the press will be notified he is being given life without parole and transferred to an undisclosed prison site. Only the Alphabet Boys will know he isn't going to make it to that prison. They will meet him at a predetermined site and trade the NOCM for the new lease on life." He raised his bottle in a salute. "What a country."

"Padre leave?" Sara asked.

Dagger slipped a small box from the Christmas tree. It

had been tied with a ribbon and hung like an ornament. "I have one more gift for you." Sara's face lit up. It was a velvet jewelry box. Dagger untied the ribbon and pulled back the lid. Inside was one diamond earring.

"A tracker?"

"I thought I better replace the one I tossed in the creek."

Sara had never owned a real diamond before. Colors danced off the facets in a brilliant rainbow display.

"There is a string attached," Dagger said. "We have to make a deal." He held the box out to her. "Nobody leaves." Dagger needed assurances. He didn't want to go through the waiting and not-knowing that he had before.

Sara pulled back her hand. "I need to make an amendment to that."

"Okay," Dagger said slowly. He wasn't sure what kind of an amendment she could want. Maybe thirty days' notice?

"We tell each other everything," Sara said.

Dagger stared at her and frowned. He studied the earring again and after a while said, "I would need to make an Addendum B. And that is *someday* I'll tell you everything." He watched disappointment etch across her face. "It's the best I can do, Sara." He held the box out to her. This time she nodded and pulled the earring from the box.

She took her time examining it. It wasn't flashy or bulky. Just the right size. Then her eyebrows furrowed and she looked up sharply. "This isn't Mr. Van Pelletier, is it?"

Dagger laughed, and gathered her in his arms. "No, it isn't Mr. Van Pelletier. I wouldn't do that to you." He kissed her forehead and said, "Happy birthday, Sara."

42

Two dark sedans ambled in single file down a lonely stretch of road west of DeKalb, Illinois. Cornfields stretched for miles on either side, now flat and plowed under for the season. A cluster of trees stood sentry a half mile away. There wasn't anything special about this part of the state, which is why it made a great meeting point. Snow sifted in front of the headlights and was starting to stick to the ground, just in time for Christmas.

A third car trailed behind, a black Cadillac with tinted windows and a moonroof. Mitch had expensive taste. Besides the new wheels he had also requested that the satellite tracking system be removed. He had plenty of cash on him and still had his bank account in the Caymen Islands.

The cars assembled in a rest area and the men piled out. Mitch popped open the trunk of the Cadillac and smiled. "It is so nice doing business with you government boys." Mitch was traveling light. Other than one suitcase and a laptop, he had no other belongings than the clothes hanging on the pole in the back seat.

Lorenz just glared at him, gave a nod to one of his underlings, and waited for the suitcase to be opened. "Make sure it's intact," the general grumbled.

"It's fine, Sir," came the reply. Another nod instructed the officer to remove the suitcase.

Lorenz handed Mitch a folder. "It would do best for you to dye your hair, get some glasses. Your face is too recognizable at the moment."

Mitch snatched the folder from the general's hands. "Not in Tahiti." He climbed back into the Cadillac.

The cordovan leather seats, compliments of the taxpayers, was turning Lorenz's stomach. He spun away from Mitch without so much as a "have a nice trip." It took the driver five minutes to get Lorenz back to his helicopter. The general had no idea where Mitch was headed and could care less. What he needed was a hot shower to wash away the filth of his job.

The helicopter was just banking over DeKalb when an explosion on the ground lit up the night sky. "What the hell was that?" the pilot yelled.

Lorenz leaned over the pilot's shoulder. A second ball of fire erupted sending a shock wave that vibrated through the cockpit. "Maybe a propane tank," he suggested. Lorenz stared down at the ground and tried to get his bearings. That was the approximate location where Mitch had driven. "Damn Bureau," he mumbled. "Always have to be flashy."

Several miles away the FBI agents also saw the ball of light in the distance. Bruen turned to McCallister and shook his head. "Military never does things on a small scale."

43

Dagger returned home after two in the morning. He hung up his coat and wandered through the darkened living room. "You didn't have to wait up for me," he said to the shadow silhouetted by the front windows. Sara was leaning against the jamb staring at the night sky. She turned from the window. He saw all kinds of questions in that look.

"Why isn't life fair, Dagger?" Her face was a mask of confusion. "Why don't people get what they deserve?"

He had thought he was careful when talking to Padre and Skizzy. Damn her heightened senses. Skizzy was able to break into Lorenz's E-mail and discover the meeting point. Then he did his relaying and spoofing magic, but this time using Mitch's IP address. Skizzy again broke through BettaTec's firewall but as far as BettaTec knew it was coming from Mitch's laptop in the trunk of the black Cadillac, a beauty of a car that had been incinerated over three hours ago. Dagger had gone to the meeting point just to make sure things went as planned. He had stayed a safe distance away hidden in the cluster of trees.

"Justice doesn't always prevail in the outside world, Sara."

"So you try to make things right."

He ran his hand through her damp hair, exposing her left ear. "I give justice to people like Seymour and Ruth Cohen, Brent Langley, Charles Sullivan, Padre." His finger traced the spot where her earring should be. She had removed it so he wouldn't know she had followed him. But he had known, had felt her watching him.

"I wanted to make sure you were okay," Sara said.

"It's agonizing not knowing, isn't it?"

Sara nodded and he knew she now understood the torment he had gone through those two months.

"But don't do it again, okay? I need you to always wear the tracker."

She nodded in agreement. "Do you think Padre suspected what you were going to do?"

"He'll never hear it from me. If the license plates survived the explosion, they will be in a bogus name. Mitch's prints and DNA had been removed from all databases so forensics won't be able to I.D. any remains. As far as the public knows, Mitch is incarcerated. As far as authorities know, Mitch is on a beach somewhere. As far as we know, and probably Lorenz and the FBI, Mitch won't ever be heard from again."

"And I suppose Mitch's Cayman Island account has been emptied."

Dagger answered with a smile. "Possibly. Father Frank will receive an anonymous donation to help build another home for boys. Simon's and Skizzy's mattresses will be a little fuller."

"Nothing for Padre?"

Dagger shook his head. "He'd be too suspicious. I've

been squirreling away money for him. Skizzy invented a long lost uncle who will leave Padre a log cabin in upper Minnesota and a hefty bank account around the time Padre is due to retire and his kids are ready for college."

His muscles ached as he blinked away the fatigue. "I'm exhausted. It takes longer to drive than fly," he added with a smile.

When he turned to leave she asked, "Do you feel obligated to help justice prevail because you couldn't when you worked for BettaTec?"

Dagger turned back slowly and studied her. His fingertips touched the side of her face. "You used up your five questions, young lady."

"That was for this year."

He smiled and leaned close. His lips barely brushed her forehead before slowly moving down to press against her cheek. "Goodnight, Sara."

After showering, Dagger pulled on drawstring pants and shook the water from his hair. He glanced at the mirrored wall, and after checking that his bedroom door was closed, walked up to the thermostat, lifted the cover, and punched in a code. The wall popped open.

Lights flickered on in the vault. He pressed a button and a wall above the table slid across, exposing the world map. Two small lights pulsated across the screen. He pulled out the chair and sat down, hands clasped under his chin, elbows on the table. Dagger had doubted they would be back up and operating so soon, if at all. He had underestimated their influence, their power, and couldn't afford miscalculations in the future.

Dagger hadn't lied to Sara when he said BettaTec didn't work for the government. Skizzy hadn't been totally wrong when he said it was some covert company. Truth was, BettaTec didn't take orders from anyone—they gave them. The satellites were operational again, floating one hundred and fifty-five miles above the earth. Intercept stations were fully functional. The two BettaTec satellites looked like any of the communication satellites orbiting the earth. The only difference was the BettaTec satellites were on a mission. They were constantly searching...searching for him.

Lee Driver is the pseudonym for S.D. Tooley, the author of the award-winning Sam Casey Mysteries—*When the Dead Speak* (Readers Choice Award 2000), *Nothing Else Matters* (*ForeWord* magazine's Book of the Year Award 2001), and *Restless Spirit* (*ForeWord* magazine's Book of the Year Award 2003 and 2003 IPPY Award Finalist). Her Chase Dagger series is available in unabridged audiobook from Books in Motion.

She is a native of the Chicago south suburbs.

Web site: *www.sdtooley.com*